W9-CFK-853

IN DISTANT WATERS

Mariner's Library Fiction Classics

STERLING HAYDEN
Voyage: A Novel of 1896

BJORN LARSSON
The Celtic Ring

SAM LLEWELLYN
The Shadow in the Sands

RICHARD WOODMAN
The Darkening Sea
Endangered Species
Wager

The Nathaniel Drinkwater Novels:

The Bomb Vessel
The Corvette
1805
Baltic Mission
In Distant Waters
A Private Revenge
Under False Colours
The Flying Squadron
Beneath the Aurora
The Shadow of the Eagle
Ebb Tide

IN DISTANT WATERS

Richard Woodman

SHERIDAN HOUSE

First U.S. edition published 2000
by Sheridan House Inc.
145 Palisade Street
Dobbs Ferry, New York 10522

Copyright © 1988 by Richard Woodman

First published in Great Britain 1988
by John Murray (Publishers) Ltd

All rights reserved. No part of this publication may be
reproduced, stored in a retrieval system or transmitted in any
form or by any means, electronic, mechanical, photocopying,
recording or otherwise, without the prior permission in writing
of Sheridan House.

Library of Congress Cataloging-in-Publication Data

Woodman, Richard, 1944-
    In distant waters : a Nathaniel Drinkwater novel / Richard Woodman.
    —1st U.S. ed.
        p. cm.
    ISBN 1-57409-098-4 (alk. paper)
        1. Drinkwater, Nathaniel (Fictitious character)—Fiction.
        2.Great Britain—History, Naval—19th century—Fiction. I. Title.

PR6073.O618 I5 2000
823'.914—dc21

                                                                00-021003

Printed in the United States of America

ISBN 1-57409-098-4

Contents

For my brother, Oliver

NORTH AMERICA
PACIFIC COAST
1808

Alaska
• Mount Elias
Sitka

Pacific

Vancouver Island

Nootka Sound

Columbia River

Bodega Bay
Drake's Bay
San Francisco

P.ta de los Reyes

Ocean

California

R.M.W.

PART ONE

Low Water

'It is very difficult for history to get at the real facts. Luckily they are more often objects of curiosity than truly important. There are so many facts!'

Napoleon

 The Deserter

Although he had been waiting for it, the knock at his cabin door made him start. An unnaturally expectant silence had fallen upon the ship following the noisy tumult of reaction to the pipes and calls for 'all hands'. Beyond the cabin windows the spring ebb-tide and the westerly gale churned the yeasty water of the Great Nore and tore its surface into long streaks of dirty spume. *Patrician* snubbed her cable in the tideway, her fabric creaking and groaning to the interplay of the elements.

Somehow these noises, the working of the rudder stock in its trunking below him, the rattle of the window sashes, the whine of the wind seeking gaps in the closed gun-ports and the thrum of it aloft acting upon the great sounding box of the stilled hull, exploited the strange silence of her company and permeated the very air he breathed with a sinister foreboding.

Beyond the vibrating windows the shapes of the ships in company faded and reappeared in his field of view as squalls swept dismal curtains of rain across the anchorage. At least the weather prevented a close mustering of the squadron's boats about *Patrician*; she could do her dirty work in a measure of privacy.

The knock, simultaneously nervous and stridently impatient, came again.

Captain Drinkwater stood and picked up the paper at which he had been staring. He felt the hilt of his sword tap his hip as he reached with his other hand for the cockaded hat. His chair scraped on the decking with a jarring squeal.

'Come in!'

Midshipman Frey appeared in the opened doorway. He too

was in full dress, the white collar patches bright on the dark blue cloth of a new uniform to fit his suddenly grown frame. Above the collar his face was pale with apprehension.

'First lieutenant's compliments, sir, and the ship's company's mustered to witness . . . punishment.' Frey choked on the last word, registering its inadequacy.

Drinkwater sighed. He could delay the matter no longer.

'Very well, Mr Frey. Thank you.'

The boy bobbed out and Drinkwater followed, ducking under the deck beams. Out on the gun deck he raised two fingers to the forecock of his firmly seated hat as the marine sentry saluted, and emerged a few seconds later onto the quarterdeck. The wind tore at him from a lowering sky that seemed scarcely a fathom above the mastheads. In his right hand the piece of paper suddenly fluttered, drawing attention to itself.

'Ship's company mustered to witness punishment, sir.' Lieutenant Fraser, his Scots burr muted by the solemnity of the occasion, made his formal report as first lieutenant. Looking round the deck Drinkwater sensed the awe with which this moment was touched. It was one thing to kill a man in the equal heat of battle, but quite another to cut short his life with this cold and ruthless act that ended the judicial process. Like Fraser, Drinkwater sought refuge in the euphemistic naval formulae under which personal feelings could be hidden, and hated himself for his cowardice.

He met Fraser's eyes. 'Very well.'

He walked forward to stand beside the binnacle and looked steadily around the ship. She was much larger than his last command, but the same faces stared back at him, an old company that was growing tired of war, augmented by a draft from the Nore guardship to bring his crew up to complement. Well, almost . . .

They spilled across the upper deck, perched up on the larboard hammock nettings and across the launch and long-boat hoisted on the booms to accommodate them. Only the starboard gangway was uncluttered, occupied by a detail of a dozen men, the ship's most persistent petty offenders against

4

cleanliness and propriety. They stood with downcast eyes in contemplation of their melancholy duty, for the rope they held ran up to the starboard fore-yardarm and back on deck to terminate in a noose.

Beyond the people massed amidships, Drinkwater could see the anxious face of Midshipman Wickham supervising the men closed up round the heavy carronade on the fo'c's'le. He stared alertly aft, awaiting the signal. Behind Drinkwater, dominating the men in the waist with their muskets and fixed bayonets, the scarlet ranks of the *Patrician*'s forty marines stood rigid, bright against the monotone of the morning. In front of them, still wearing the bandages of his recent wound and with his hanger drawn, Lieutenant Mount stood at his post. His gorget was the only glint of brilliance on the quarterdeck. Alongside Mount, tense with expectancy, his drum a-cock and twin sticks held down the seams of his breeches, was the diminutive figure of the marine drummer.

Close about the captain in a ragged semi-circle were the commissioned and warrant officers, wearing their swords and the full-dress uniform prescribed for their ranks. Above them all the white ensign snapped out, jerking the slender larch staff as the gale moaned through the recently tautened rigging.

'Bring up the prisoner!'

A ripple of expectancy ran through the assembly amidships. Led by the new and lugubrious figure of the chaplain and escorted by Sergeant Blixoe of the marines, the wretched man was brought on deck. As he emerged, Midshipman Frey hoisted the yellow flag to the masthead, Drinkwater nodded, and Wickham fired the fo'c's'le carronade. The short, shocking bark of the 42-pounder thudded out. A brief, acrid stench of powder-smoke whipped aft and Drinkwater saw the prisoner blench at the gun's report. Despite the liberal dose of rum he had been given, the poor fellow was shaking, though his tied hands drew back his shoulders and conferred upon him a spurious dignity.

Clearing his throat, Drinkwater raised the crackling paper and began to read.

'To Nathaniel Drinkwater, Esquire, Captain in the Royal Navy, commanding His Britannic Majesty's frigate Patrician *at the Great Nore . . .*

5

Whereas, Thomas Stanham, Able Seaman, late of His Majesty's Ship Antigone, *hath been examined by a Court-Martial on charges of desertion . . .'*

Stanham had drawn himself up, perhaps, in his extremity, feeling some cold comfort from the tacit sympathies of his old messmates around him. Drinkwater knew enough of the man's history not to feel grave misgivings as to the natural justice of the present proceedings together with a profound sense of regret that Stanham had been tried and sentenced with no one to plead for him. His crime was that of having deserted Drinkwater's last command, HMS *Antigone*, just prior to her departure to the Baltic in the spring. A topman of no more than twenty-one or twenty-two years of age, Stanham had been driven to this desperate course of action by lack of shore-leave and a well-meant letter from a neighbour living near his home in Norwich. According to this informant, Stanham's wife had been 'carrying-on' in her husband's prolonged absence. In company with another Norfolk man Stanham had deserted, slipping ashore from a bum-boat when a marine sentry was distracted. Had he shortly thereafter returned to his duty, Drinkwater would have taken a lenient view of the matter and treated Stanham as a mere 'straggler'. Such things were best dealt with within the ship and the cat o' nine tails was a swift justiciar and powerful deterrent. But the enforced and hurried transfer of his entire company from the shattered *Antigone* to the *Patrician*, had necessitated the submission of all her books to the Admiralty and the Navy Office.

Drinkwater was sick at heart at the circumstances that had conspired to set Stanham before his shipmates in these last few moments of his life. *Antigone* had returned from the Baltic with the most momentous secret of the entire war. In order to preserve the source of this news, no one connected with the ship was allowed leave, a proscription that included Drinkwater himself. But the *Antigone* had suffered mortal damage to her hull when the Dutch cruiser *Zaandam* had exploded alongside her. As a result she had been condemned and her remaining company transferred to the razée *Patrician*, just then commissioning as a heavy frigate at Sheerness. The tedious and often protracted business of closing a ship's books had been specially expedited on the express instructions of John Barrow, the all-powerful Second Secretary of the Admiralty. Behind this obfuscation, Drinkwater knew, loomed the figures of George Canning, the Foreign Secretary, and Lord Castlereagh, the Secretary for War. Even Lord Dungarth, the Director of the Admiralty's Secret Department, had apparently condoned Barrow's severity and expedition. It only added to Drinkwater's present mortification to consider his own personal interest in this cloak of secrecy.*

But there were other agencies at work conniving against the unfortunate Stanham. Even as the Admiralty clerks examined *Antigone's* books and discovered the rubric *R* against the name of Thomas Stanham, a letter arrived at Whitehall appraising Their Lordships that acting upon information laid before them, the Norwich magistrates had apprehended Thomas Stanham, a deserter from His Majesty's Service. There was not the slightest doubt to contest the information, affidavits had been sworn accordingly by reliable persons and, to compound the matter, the said Stanham had caused an affray in resisting arrest in which he had maliciously caused one of the constables to be gravely wounded. The magistrates desired to know Their Lordships' pleasure.

Drinkwater knew the scuttlebutt well enough: Stanham had been betrayed by the man who had made him a cuckold. He read on, pitching his voice against the gale.

'Whereas it has been enacted under the several laws relating to the sea-service . . .'

Quite apart from the necessity to get the former *Antigone*s to sea, the Admiralty were increasingly worried about desertions from the ships of the Royal Navy. The long war with the French Empire was dragging on. Russia was no longer an ally, the Prussian military machine perfected by Frederick the Great had been smashed in a single day by Napoleon at Jena and Davout at Auerstadt, while Austrian defiance seemed likely to be the next object of Napoleon's indefatigable attention. It suited Their Lordships to visit the utmost extremity of the Articles of

* See *Baltic Mission*

War upon the wronged Stanham, and no plea in mitigation had been allowed.

'. . . *Every person in or belonging to the Fleet, who shall desert, or entice others to desert, shall suffer Death . . .*'

Drinkwater paused to look up again. That phrase 'in or belonging to the Fleet' bound Stanham like an iron shackle. It ran contrary to the common, canting notions of liberty so cherished by rubicund Englishmen up and down the shires. His eyes met those of the prisoner. Stanham stopped shaking at that terrible final word and his gaze held something else, something unnerving. Drinkwater hurried on.

'*And the court hath adjudged the said Thomas Stanham to suffer death by being hanged by the neck at the yardarm. You are hereby required and directed to see the said sentence of death carried into execution upon the body of the said Thomas Stanham.*'

There followed the languid flourish of the presiding admiral's signature. Drinkwater lowered the paper and crushed it in his fist.

'Do you wish to say anything Stanham?'

Again their eyes met, the gulf between them immense. Stanham nodded and coughed to clear his throat.

'Good luck to me shipmates, sir, and God save the King!'

The sudden upward modulation of Stanham's homely Norfolk voice struck Drinkwater as having been the accent of the late, lamented Lord Nelson. He nodded at Stanham as a low rumbling came from the hands.

'Silence there!' Fraser's voice cut nervously through the wind.

'Master-at-Arms! Do your duty!'

Behind Drinkwater there was a snicker of accoutrements at a low order from Mount. The marines' muskets came to the port, forty thumbs resting upon forty firelock hammers. The drummer hitched his snare-drum, brought his sticks up to the chin and then down, to beat the long roll as the master-at-arms led Stanham to the starboard gangway. With a lugubrious expression that Drinkwater found revolting the chaplain brought up the rear. The shamefaced hanging party moved aside to let the grim procession pass.

A short ladder had been set against the rail and the hammock

8

nettings removed just abaft the forechains. Stanham was halted at the foot of the ladder and the chaplain moved closer. While the master-at-arms drew the noose down over Stanham's head and settled the knot beneath his left ear, Drinkwater watched the chaplain bend forward, his lips moving above the open prayer-book, a thin strand of hair streaming out from his almost bald head. Even at a distance Drinkwater felt the inappropriateness of another stilted formula being deployed. He saw Stanham shake his head vigorously. The chaplain stepped back and nodded, an expression of exasperation on his gaunt face. Drinkwater found his revulsion increase at this untimely meanness.

A dark cotton bag was pulled down over the prisoner's head. Stanham's face was extinguished like a candle and a gasp ran though the ship. There was a muffled thump as a small midshipman fainted. No one moved to his assistance; it was Mr Belchambers's third day in the Royal Navy.

Stanham was guided up onto the rail. Beyond the lonely figure Drinkwater could see the rigging of the neighbouring ships dark with their men, piped to witness the example of Their Lordships' remorseless justice being carried out on board *Patrician*.

Drinkwater nodded his head and Wickham saw the signal. The report of the carronade rolled across the water, the brief white puff of smoke alerting the other ships of the solemnity of the moment. Again the sharp stench of powder-smoke stung their nostrils and Drinkwater caught a glimpse of the flaming wadding as it disintegrated in the wind. Beside him the marine drummer stopped his ruffle.

'Prisoner made ready, sir.'

With the gale blowing aft the master-at-arms's voice carried with unnatural loudness. He had done his duty; it extended thus far. To launch Stanham into eternity waited for Drinkwater's own command.

'Mr Comley!' Drinkwater's voice rasped with a sudden, unbidden harshness.

'Sir?' The boatswain stood with his rattan beside the hanging party.

9

Drinkwater could no longer take refuge in formulae, his honest nature revolted against it. To instruct Comley's party to 'carry out the sentence' would have smacked of cowardice to his puritan soul. The awful implications of power were for his shoulders alone, it was to him that the death warrant had been addressed. In this was some small atonement for his own part in this grisly necessity.

'Hang the prisoner!'

The hanging party moved as though spurred by the vehemence in Drinkwater's voice. There was no time for thought, no cause for apprehension to the watching Mount, ready to coerce the party with his muskets.

Comley's men leaned to Stanham's sudden weight as his body rose jerking to the starboard fore-yardarm.

Amidships another man fainted as all watched in terrible fascination. Stanham kicked with his legs, tightening the noose with every desperate movement in his muscles, arching his back as he fought vainly for air. He was a strong man with a powerful neck that resisted the snapping of the spinal cord and the separation of the vertebrae that would bring a quick, merciful end.

Drinkwater found himself willing the man to stop, to submit to the Admiralty's omnipotent will and die quietly as an example to others, but Stanham was not going to oblige. The dark tangle of his blood-choked brain was roaring with the anger of betrayal, of treachery and injustice. The dark shape of his body set against the rolling scud, seemed possessed of a protest from beyond the grave. Drinkwater cursed the Norwich informer, cursed John Barrow and his lack of compassion and cursed himself for bringing back such a secret from Russia that men still died for it.

Gradually asphyxia subdued the spasms. Stanham had given up the ghost. It seemed that a collective sigh, audible above the wind and the responding hiss of the sea, came from the *Patrician*'s assembled company.

'Eight bells, sir.'

'Make it so and pipe the hands to dinner.'

The yellow flag fluttered down from the masthead as the four double rings of the bell tolled the hour of noon. Pipes twittered amidships and the men began to move below. Faintly similar noises could be heard from other ships. The rumble of voices grew as the men glanced upwards in passing forward.

'Another good man bin stabbed by the Bridport dagger, 'en . . .'

'No good 'll come of it . . . 'tis bad luck . . .'

The mutter was drowned by the crash of the marines' boots as Mount dismissed his guard and reposted his sentries. Frey was bending over the swooning midshipman. Mr Belchambers was not yet thirteen years of age and his name was sonorously inappropriate for so small and insubstantial a figure. It was odd, Drinkwater thought, that men like Stanham had to be hanged while there seemed no lack of foolish boys to come and play at being men.

'We shall get under weigh the instant the wind eases, Mr Fraser,' Drinkwater growled as he turned below. 'I received my orders by the same despatch-boat as brought this . . .'

He held up the crumpled piece of paper.

'Very well, sir . . . and him sir?' Fraser's eyes jerked aloft.

'Leave him for an hour . . . but no more, Mr Fraser, no more, I pray you.'

Above their heads Stanham's body turned slowly in the wind. Dark stains spread across his clothing and it was subject to the most humiliating ignominy of all; his cuckolded member was engorged with his stilled blood.

Cape Horn

Drinkwater lay soaked in sweat, aware that it was neither the jerking of his cot, nor the violent motion of *Patrician* that had woken him, but something fading beyond his recall, the substance of his nightmare. Wiping his forehead and at the same time shivering in the pre-dawn chill, he lay back and tugged the shed blankets back over his aching body. The quinsy that had presaged his fever was worse this morning, but the terrors of the nightmare far exceeded the disturbances of illness. He stared into the darkness, trying to remember what had so upset him, driven by some instinct to revive the images of the nightmare.

And then with the unpredictability of imagination, they flooded back. It was an old dream, a haunting from bad times when, as a frightened midshipman, he had learned the real meaning of fear and loneliness. The figure of the white lady had loomed over him as he sunk helplessly beneath her, her power to overwhelm him sharpened by the crescendo of clanking chains that always accompanied her manifestation. As he recollected the dream he strove to hear the reassuring grind of *Patrician*'s own pumps; but he could hear nothing beyond the thrum of wind in the rigging transmitted down to the timbers of her labouring hull. The big frigate creaked and groaned in response to the mighty forces acting upon her as she fought her way to windward of Cape Horn.

Then Drinkwater recognised the face. The white lady had had many forms in her various visitations. Though he thought of her as female, she possessed the trans-sexual ability of phantoms to appear in any guise. This morning she had worn a most horrible mask: that of the hanged man, Stanham. Drink-water recognised it at once, for after the dead man had been cut down he and Lallo, the surgeon, had inspected the cadaver. It had been no mere idly morbid curiosity that had spurred him to do so, that day at the Nore ten weeks earlier. He had felt himself driven to see what he had done, as if to do so might avert some haunting of the ship by the man's spirit.

Drinkwater had seen again in his nightmare the savage furrow the noose had cut in Stanham's neck. The face above was darkly cyanotic with wild, protuberant eyes. In the flesh Stanham's body had been pale below the furrowed neck, gradu-ally darkening with blotchy suggillations where the blood had settled into its dependent parts. This morning, beneath the horrors of the face, Stanham's ghost had worn the white veils which marked his apparition as a disguise of the white lady.

Full recollection brought Drinkwater out of himself. Un-pleasant though the memory was, he was no stranger to death, or the 'blue-devils', that misanthropic preoccupation of naval officers forced to the lonely exile of distant commands. With an oath he swung his legs over the edge of the swaying cot and deftly hoisted himself to his feet as *Patrician* hesitated on a wave crest, before driving down into a huge trough. He half ran, half skidded across the cabin, fetching up against the forward bulk-head as the ship smashed her bluff bows into the advancing wall of the next sea and reared her bowsprit skywards. Drinkwater swore again, barking his shins on the leg of an overturned chair and bellowed through the thin bulkhead at the marine sentry.

'Pass word for my coxswain!'

As he rubbed his bruised knee and swallowed with difficulty he finally remembered the true disturbance of the nightmare. It was not its recurrence, nor the ghastly transmogrification of poor Stanham, but the fact that the dream was always presentient.

He fought his way aft, across the dark cabin, and slumped in a chair until Tregembo arrived with a light and hot water and he could shave, passing the moments in reaction to the knowledge that came with this realisation. God knew that a great deal could go wrong in this forsaken corner of the world where there seemed no possible justification for sending him, even given the anxieties of the most pusillanimous jack-in-office. In the extremity of his sickness and depression he felt acutely the apparent abandonment of the only man in power with whom he felt he had both earned and enjoyed an intimacy. Lord Dungarth, once first lieutenant of Midshipman Drinkwater's original ship, had treated him with uncharacteristic coolness since he had brought the momentous news of the secret accord between Tsar Alexander and Napoleon out of Russia. It was not the only service Drinkwater had rendered his Lordship's Secret Department and Dungarth's inexplicable change of attitude had greatly pained him, combined as it was with the proscription against shore-leave and the enforced estrangement from his wife and family.

But these were self-pitying considerations. As the *Patrician* fought her way from the Atlantic to the Pacific Ocean, he had gloomier thoughts pressing him. Presentiments of disaster were to be expected and, as he shuddered from his ague, he felt inadequate to the task the Admiralty had set him, not for its complexity, but for its apparent simplicity. It seemed, in essence, to be a mere exercise upon which almost any interpretation might be put by persons anxious to discredit him. So hazy were his orders, so vague in their intent, that he was at a loss as to how to pursue them.

To carry His Majesty's flag upon the Pacific coast of North America on a Particular Service, was all very high faluting; *to make war upon Spanish Trade upon the said coast*, was all very encouraging if one took as one's example the exploits of Anson fifty years earlier. But this was the modern world, and he was not allowed a free hand, being ordered to concentrate his efforts upon the *North* American coast, far from the rich Spanish trade routed to the Vice-royalties of Peru and the *entrepôt* of Panama. Besides, to any British commander, the Pacific was haunted by the ghosts of a murdered Cook and the piratically seized *Bounty*.

As for what he took to be the core of his orders, the instruction *to discourage Russian incursions into that sea and upon the coasts of New Albion*, they seemed to Drinkwater to be the most nonsensical of them all, harking back to the dubious claims of Francis Drake

14

and serving to remind him that his Russian connections had landed him in this desperate plight, thousands of miles from home or support. Mulling such thoughts as he fought his quinsy and waited for Tregembo, shaking with the mild fever of an infection, he was in a foul and savage mood. His coxwain's unannounced appearance stung him to an uncharacteristic rebuke.

'Knock before you enter, damn you!'

Sourly he watched Tregembo fuss over the hot water and the glim, whose light was transferred to a lantern and the lashed candelabra, illuminating the cabin with a cheerlessness that revealed the tumbled state of its contents.

'You'll catch your death, zur, sitting like that . . .'

'Don't fuss, Tregembo,' replied Drinkwater mellowing and seeing in the seams and scars of the old man's highlit face the harrowing of age and service. He opened his mouth to apologise but Tregembo forestalled him.

'The fever's no better, zur, if I'm a judge o' temper.'

Drinkwater stood with the sweat dry on him and drew his nightshirt over his head. He grunted and took the soap from Tregembo's outstretched hand.

'I'll get Mr Lallo to make up some James's Powders, zur . . .'

'You'll do no such damned thing, Tregembo . . .'

'Dover's Powders then, zur, they be a powerful sudorific . . .'

'Damn James and Dover . . . fresh air will cure me, fresh air and hot coffee, be off and find me some hot coffee instead of standing over me like a poxed nursemaid . . .'

'There be fresh air a plenty this morning, zur,' muttered Tregembo as he left the cabin and the remark brought the ghost of a smile to Drinkwater's haggard face, even as it reminded him of his greatest problem, his crew.

Over four years earlier, in the spring of 1803 and the brief period of peace, he had taken command of the sloop *Melusine*. She had been manned by picked volunteers, men who chose to stay at sea in the Royal Navy, rather than chance their luck in the uncertain world ashore. Many of them had been aboard ship for long before that. The resumption of war had carried them to the Arctic aboard *Melusine*, and to the Atlantic and

15

Baltic in the frigate *Antigone*, into which ship they had been turned over when Drinkwater reached post-rank. Now the process of transfer had been repeated and that core of volunteers still lingered at the heart of *Patrician*'s company.

But men volunteer for perceived goals and these resented being taken advantage of even more than the pressed men. The latter were made up of the victims of the Impress Service, the Quota-men and the Lord Mayor's men, the dregs of Debtor's prisons and the hedge-sleeping vagrants that armed parties of officers and seamen had discovered in sweeps made along the ague-plagued coast of Essex, whence Drinkwater had sent his boats. In successive waves these men had made up the deficiencies in number that death and an increase in tonnage had made necessary to man the enlarged complements of Drinkwater's successive ships. What to those eager volunteers had been thought of as a single commission, an arctic voyage with a bounty at its conclusion, had not yet ended.

The people were divided, the one-time volunteers forming a slowly contracting minority, apt to regard itself as an élite, and suffering from the poor conditions of a Royal Navy on a wartime footing. Earlier that year in the Baltic their mood had become ugly. Lieutenant Quilhampton had suppressed an incipient mutiny by the force of his personality alone, but the news of it had made all the officers wary, heightening the tensions in the ship and drawing again those sharp social distinctions that blurred easily in a happy ship. Inconsequential things assumed new importance. The rivalry between seamen and marines coalesced into something less friendly, more suspicious; and the twinkle of the marines' bayonets lost its ceremonial glitter, fencing the vulnerable minority of the officers from the murmurs of the berth-deck.

For his own part Drinkwater had, that summer, been driven to supplementing the men's pay by a bounty of his own, a circumstance which had imperilled his domestic finances, leaving his wife and dependants at a disadvantage and a prey to the fiscal inroads of inflation and income tax.

Drinkwater scraped his face, nicking his cheek as *Patrician* staggered into another heavy sea. He swore, rinsed his razor

16

and bent unsteadily to his task. The face that stared back at him was drawn with anxiety. The receding hair exposed his high forehead and the streaks of grey at his temples were prominent, even in the half-light of the candle-lit cabin. He still wore a queue, an unfashionable defiance behind, for what nature deprived him of in front. But though his eyes were tired and their lids dotted with powder burns like random ink-spots, though the scar that puckered down one side of his face joined the distortion of his features necessary to the task of shaving, and though he was gaunt from the effects of ague and quinsy, there was about the line of the mouth a determination that marked him for one of the most experienced frigate commanders in the Royal Navy.

Ungraced by much political interest, only his long-standing friendship with Lord Dungarth could be said to have aided his career; but even that had not been without effort on his own part. Dungarth had ensured that all Drinkwater's skills had been fully exploited by his Secret Department, that great coup from beneath the raft at Tilsit, when the two Emperors' conversation had been overheard verbatim, had repaid any debt of advancement his lordship might conceive to be owing.

Drinkwater wiped his chin and called for Tregembo, indicating he had finished with bowl and razor. He tied his stock and drew on soft leather hessian boots. Winding a muffler around his neck he put on his undress uniform coat and a heavy boat cloak. Tregembo fussed about the cabin, moving quietly in respect of the captain's ominous silence. Picking up his hat Drinkwater jammed it on his head and went on deck.

In the high southern latitude dawn was early. The eastern horizon was suffused with a light still too weak to penetrate the cloud rolling to leeward from the west. On the starboard bow an inky darkness blurred the meeting of sea and sky, and the perceptible horizon was reduced to the crest of the great waves that loomed out of the gloom and roared down upon them, driven by the interminable winds of the Southern Ocean.

As *Patrician* dipped her reefed jib-boom, one such wall of water rose on her bow, its vast face gaining in brightness as it approached the vertical and reflected the growing light from the east. *Patrician* rolled away from it, her topsails, hard reefed though they were, suddenly flapping from want of wind and a hush falling eerily upon her decks. Her hull seemed suddenly inert as the advancing sea sped towards them, its slope streaked with spindrift, debris of a million million successive disintegrations of its toppling crest.

'Hold on there!'

Drinkwater grabbed the nearest hammock stanchion and braced himself as Lieutenant Quilhampton called the warning to his watch. It seemed as if they all held their breath.

And then the frigate began to lift her bow as the trough that preceded the wave passed beneath her and she felt the breasting rise of that mountainous wave. From a sluggish tremor the angle rapidly increased and then she canted and the bow reared skywards. Aft, the waterlevel rose almost to the rail, so that the sea squirted in round the gun-ports and from below came the crash and curse of men and loose gear tumbling about. Drinkwater prayed that the double-lashed breechings of the guns had not worked slack during the night and the dual crash that ended this strange hiatus momentarily persuaded him that he was mistaken. But instinct made him look upwards to where the wind had reached the topsails. The maintopsail was already in shreds, pulling at its bolt ropes like wool caught on a fence, and the foretopsail was bending its yard like a bow. An explosion of white reared up all along the starboard rail as they reached the breaking crest and it flung all its fury at the ship. She rolled to leeward and lay down under the violent onslaught of the wind. The air, a moment earlier almost motionless before the advancing mass of water, was now suddenly filled with the terrible noise of the gale, solid with the particles of water it had ripped from the surface of the ocean and drove downwind with the velocity of buckshot.

But the leeward roll saved *Patrician*'s deck from the worst of the breaking sea, though there was not a man upon it who was not instantly soaked to the skin. The ship toppled as the wave passed beyond her tipping-centre and she plunged downwards, into the welter of lesser waves that scarred the back of the great sea.

'Foretopmast's sprung above the lower cap, Mr Q . . . up helm! Get the ship before the wind and we'll take that tops'l off her!'

'Aye, aye, sir!' Quilhampton dashed the water from his face with his one good hand, and swung round, staggering as *Patrician* lurched; but the huge sea had been the culmination of many, an ocean-bred monster in whose trail, for a while at least, midgets would follow. 'Up helm, there!'

The ship's bow paid off to the southward and then to the east of south. Drinkwater anxiously stared aloft, trying to gauge the extent of the damage in the growing daylight and irritated at losing distance to windward. He had brought the frigate well south of Cape Horn, in a great tack to the south and west in order to double the tip of America as speedily as possible in an area where days of low scud made obtaining meridian altitudes difficult and only a fool would feel confident of his latitude.

'Stand by to take in the foretopsail!'

Quilhampton was bawling at his watch. Their response was slow, they seemed dazed, as if the great wave had some strange effect on them. But that was impossible, a figment of Drinkwater's fevered imagination. He held his peace for a moment longer.

'Man the clewlines and buntlines!'

The men were mustered about the pinrails and Drinkwater was reminded of something he had tried hard to forget; the dilatory action they had fought with a Danish privateer, caught off Duncansby Head, and which had escaped by superior sailing through the rocks off the Orkneys. *By superior sailing* . . . how that phrase haunted him, that sudden failure in performance that had endangered the ship now as it had done before. His patience snapped.

'Call all hands damn it! All hands, d'you hear there!'

The squealing pipes made little impact on the gale, but the thin noise roused the ship as Quilhampton continued to shout at his men.

'Clewlines and buntlines! Haul taut!'

Drinkwater caught sight of the rise and fall of starters, of a scuffle forward of the boats and a man thrust out of the huddle round the mast.

19

'Leggo top bowline, there! Lively there! Leggo halliards! Clew down! Clew down, God damn you, clew down!'

'I think we have trouble forrard, Mr Q . . .'

'Aye, sir . . . no, there goes the yard . . . lay aloft and furl . . aloft and furl!'

Men from the watches below were coming on deck and filling the waist with a worse confusion as another crack from aloft met the violence of a heavy leeward roll. Above the shouting and the orders, the wind screamed with renewed venom and the heeling deck bucked and canted beneath their slithering feet. Green water poured aboard and sluiced aft, streaming over the men at the pinrails and knocking several off their feet.

'Aloft and furl! Mr Comley, damn you, forrard, sir, and hustle the men!'

Perhaps it was the disgruntled look which the boatswain Comley threw at Quilhampton, perhaps the passing of an ague-fit which stimulated Drinkwater to intervene, but he could stand chaos no better than inefficiency and such chaos and in-efficiency threatened them all in that wild sea. He began to move forward, along the starboard gangway towards the forechains.

What he found forward of the boats appalled him. The sharp perceptions of a feverish brain, the madness of the morning and the lingering suspicions and doubts about his crew coalesced into an instant comprehension. The few men who had begun to climb into the weather shrouds were half-hearted in their efforts and though no one actively prevented them, there were shouted discouragements thick in the howling air.

'Don't risk yer life for the bastards, Jimmy . . .'

'Let the fucking mast go by the board . . . we'll be home the sooner . . .

'Oi'll fockin' kill you if you so much as lay that rope on me again, so I will . . .'

A man rolled against Drinkwater, one of the boatswain's mates, his face pale in the cruel, horizontal light of dawn, his eye already dark with bruising.

'Aloft and furl, damn you all!' Drinkwater roared and hoisted himself up into the starboard foremast shrouds. He caught sight of the small, white face of Midshipman Belchambers. 'Take my hat and cloak . . .' The wind tore the heavy cloak from his grasp and thrust it at the boy, who escaped thankfully aft.

'God's bones, d'you want to rot in hell, you damned lubbers? Aloft and furl!' He was aware of sullen faces, the spray stinging them as they looked up at him. The wind tore at his own body and already the cold had found his hands. There was no time to delay. Above them the foretopsail flogged and the mast shook and groaned while something was working loose, its destructive oscillations increasing with every roll of the ship.

He began to climb.

The force of the wind tore at him. *Patrician* was running before it now, throwing away the hard-won windward yards, rolling with an unrestrained ferocity that threatened to tear loose the sprung topmast and send the resulting wrack down on deck. For the preservation of the ship, speed was essential. He did not look down, but the vibration of the thick hemp shrouds told him that men were following him aloft. He fought his way upwards, the thin ratlines twisting beneath his feet and the wind tearing at the bulk of his body, so that his clothing bellied and pulled him forward to where the sea hissed and roared alongside the running frigate. Some active topman drew alongside him.

'That's it, my lad, up you go, up you go!'

He caught a glimpse of a sheepish grin that was instantly lost as more men caught him up, swinging outwards, into the futtock shrouds with the agility of monkeys. Captains aloft were such a rare event that even the most discontented topman would be put on his mettle to outdo the intrusion.

Midshipman Frey struggled up.

'Good morning, Mr Frey.' Frey's eyes widened and Drinkwater nodded upwards. 'Have the goodness to pass ahead of me.'

The boy gulped and swung himself outboard, his back hanging downwards as *Patrician*'s hull rolled them out over the sea, then his kicking heels disappeared and Drinkwater took advantage of the return roll and followed him into the top.

Pausing for breath, Drinkwater took stock of the situation. The foretopsail yard, loosed by its halliards, lay roughly over

21

the top of the foreyard, the huge flapping bunt of sail thundered in wild billows only partially restrained by the weight of the yard and the buntlines and clewlines. Drinkwater waved the topmen aloft and out along the yard. He could see Frey already at the extremity of the windward yardarm, his pea-jacket blown over his back and his sparse shirt-tail flapping madly.

'Come on lads, lay out and furl that tops'l!'

He clung to the topgallant mast heel-rope downhaul and looked aloft. The fore-topgallantmast had been struck, sent down and lashed parallel to its corresponding topmast to reduce the windage of unneeded tophamper. Now, as he stared up-wards, his eyes watering and the wind tugging at him, he saw that the housed topgallantmast was acting like a splint to the frac-tured mast. The latter had sprung badly, the split starting from a shake in the timber. Drinkwater cursed and wondered how long that spar had been pickling in the mast-pond at Chatham. The topmast was almost split in two; whatever he decided to do, it would have to be quick, before both spars were lost. He peered on deck. Morning had broken now, though the sun had risen in-to a cloud bank and daylight was dimmed. Its arrival somehow surprised him, such had been his preoccupation.

Quilhampton looked upwards anxiously, clearly considering that Drinkwater's action in going aloft was unseemly. Beside him Fraser stood staring up, one hand clapped over his tricorne hat.

The men were laying in from the yard, having passed the reef-points and Drinkwater called to them to begin to clear the gear away ready to send the topmast down on deck. It would be a long, complex and difficult job in the sea that was running, but he sensed in their changed expressions that the surly disinterest had been replaced by a sudden realisation of the danger they were in. Besides, he had no intention of making life too easy for them; those lost miles to leeward nagged him as he made his way down on deck.

After the clamour of the foretop, the quarterdeck seemed a sanctuary. Fraser began to remonstrate.

'Sir, you shouldn't ha' . . .'

'Be damned to you, Fraser, the men are disaffected . . . in

22

your absence it was necessary I set 'em an example . . . now have the kindness to order the spanker and foretopmast stays'l set . . . just the clew of the spanker, mind you, I want this ship on the wind and then we'll sort out the mess of the foremast . . .'

Fraser nodded his understanding and Drinkwater regretted the jibe at the first lieutenant. It was mean, but he was in a damnably mean mood and meant to ride down this discontent, even if it first meant riding his officers.

'We'll set a goose-winged maintops'l when we've finished, and see if we can't claw back some of the leeway we've made . . .'

Hill, the elderly sailing master summoned on deck at the cry for all hands, nodded his agreement and put the traverse board back by the binnacle.

'It's a damn . . .'

'Deck! Deck there!'

The scream was high pitched and uttered with such urgency that it carried above the gale. The officers looked up at Midshipman Frey. He was leaning against the barricade of the foretop, pointing ahead.

'Sir! There's a ship, sir . . . a ship! Right ahead!'

'Impossible!'

That first reaction was gone in an instant. As he scrambled into the mizen rigging Drinkwater's active mind considered the odds of another ship being under their feet in this remote spot. And then he saw her, an irregular, spiky outline flung up against the eastern sky as she breasted a crest. His practised eye saw her hull and her straining sails and then she was gone, separated from them by a wave. She was perhaps three quarters of a mile away.

When she reappeared she was fine to starboard, under close-reefed topsails and beating to windward as *Patrician* had been doing an hour earlier. A curious idleness had filled the hands as they waited for the officers to get over their astonishment. Drinkwater rounded on the latter.

'Gentlemen! You have your orders, kindly attend to them!'

They scattered, like chastened schoolboys. Only Hill, his white hair streaming in the wind, stood close to Drinkwater, trying to catch the stranger in the watch-glass.

23

Fishing in his pocket Drinkwater pulled out his Dollond glass and raised it to his eye, swearing with the difficulty of focusing it on the other ship.

'She's a ship of force, sir,' Hill muttered beside him.

Drinkwater grunted agreement. Her dark hull seemed pierced by two rows of gun-ports and, like themselves, she wore no colours. She beat to windward bravely, passing his own lamed ship as she licked her wound and escaped the worst fury of the storm by running before it. Once again that phrase *by superior sailing* was recalled to his mind.

Although not superstitious, Drinkwater was, like most philosophical sailors, aware of the influence of providence and the caprice of fortune. Nothing had yet happened aboard *Patrician* that persuaded him he was in command of anything but an unlucky ship. Among his ill-educated crew he knew that feeling had developed to a conviction since the execution.

'What d'you make of her, Mr Hill?'

'With that black hull and making for the Pacific, I'd stake my hat and wig on her being a Don, sir . . .'

'Your shore-going wig, Mr Hill?' Drinkwater joked grimly and neither man took his glass from his eye.

'For a certainty, sir . . .'

Drinkwater grunted. He had seen the Spaniards' lugubriously popish fancy for black ships in Cadiz shortly before Trafalgar, but he was recalling the nightmare and its ominous warning. He stared at the ship for other clues, but found none. A minute later she was gone, lost in the bleak and heaving wastes of the Southern Ocean. Captain and master lowered their glasses at the same moment.

'A Don you say, Mr Hill?'

'My life upon it, sir.'

Drinkwater shook his head. 'Rash, Mr Hill, rash . . .'

'You don't agree, sir?' Drinkwater managed a grin at the obviously discomfited Hill.

'I've a hunch, Mr Hill, a hunch . . . nothing more and not worth the trouble of a wager . . . come now, let's get a new foretopmast off the booms . . .'

24

 The Radoub

Drinkwater swallowed painfully and stared balefully at the first lieutenant. There were moments, and this was one of them, when he would have wished for the return of Samuel Rogers, for all his drunkenness and bullying temperament. Rogers would have understood what was to be done, but Rogers had been blown to the devil with six score others when the *Zandaam* exploded alongside the *Antigone* off Orfordness, and poor Fraser had inherited the first luff's uneasy berth. A quiet, competent Scot, Fraser was an obsessively worrying type, a man who let anxiety get the better of his spirit which was thereby damped and warped. Drinkwater had once overheard Mount referring to him in conversation with James Quilhampton.

'If yon Scot,' Mount mimicked in false North British dialect, 'ever occasioned to fall in the sea, he'd drown.' Then, seeing Quilhampton's puzzled look, he added plainly, 'He possesses no *buoyancy.*'

Drinkwater regarded Fraser, his expression softening. He was a prey to anxiety himself; he was being unjustly hard on a conscientious officer.

'It's high summer hereabouts, Mr Fraser, though it has a damned uncivil way of showing it, but I want the men worked . . . d'ye hear? Worked, sir, and damned hard. Not a single task that ain't necessary . . . I'll have no gratuitous hazing, but I want every man-jack of 'em to know that they don't refuse to go aloft on *my* ship!'

Drinkwater drew breath, his anger at his predicament concentrated on the helpless Fraser.

'Aye, aye, sir.' But the first lieutenant hesitated.

'Well, Mr Fraser? What's the trouble?'

'Well, sir . . . such tasks . . . we've sent down the fore-topmast . . .'

'Tasks? Are you suggesting your imagination cannot supply *tasks*? Good God man, was there ever a want of tasks on a man-o'-war?'

It was clear that Fraser's imagination fell somewhat short of Drinkwater's expectation. The captain sighed resignedly as the frigate lurched and trembled. A sea smashed against her weather bow and the spray whipped aft, stinging their faces.

'Turn up all watches, Mr Fraser. I want the people worked until they drop. I don't care that it blows a gale, nor that the ship's doing a dido, or that every man-jack of 'em hates my lights by sunset, but we had one brush with an enemy off the Orkneys that I don't want repeated . . . and that ship we sighted this morning, be he Don or Devil, bore *two* decks of guns. If we have to fight her in our present condition, Mr Fraser, I'll not answer for the consequences . . . d'you comprehend my meaning? And I mean the officers to turn-out too . . .'

'The officers, sir?' Fraser's jaw dropped a little further. Anxiety about the unstable state of the crew and the captain's reaction to their behaviour this morning was worming his belly. Drinkwater pressed relentlessly on.

'Now, as to tasks, Mr Fraser, you may rattle down the lower shrouds, slush the new topmast and reeve a new heel-rope. I don't doubt an inspection of the gun-deck will reveal a few of the gun-lashings working and the same goes for the boat gripes. Let's have the well sounded hourly and kept dry as a parson's throat. Have the gunner detail a party to make up more cartridges, the quarter-gunners to reknap the flints in the upper deck gun-locks and overhaul the shot lockers. Turn a party to on scaling the worst-corroded balls and send some men to change all the shot in the garlands. Get an officer aloft with a midshipman and a pencil to carry out an examination of all the spars for further shakes and let me have their findings in writing . . .'

Fraser caught the reproach in Drinkwater's eyes and coloured at his own negligence. He had taken so much of *Patrician*'s gear

26

from the dockyard on trust, since she had been so recently refitted after being cut down to a razée.

'Yes, sir.'

'Very well. You can carry out an inventory of the tradesmen's stores and have a party assist the cooper to stum some casks ready for watering and if that ain't enough, Mr Fraser, do not neglect the fact that we lost two good topsails this morning . . . in short, sir, I want you to *radoub* the ship!'

'Aye, sir . . .'

'And the officers are to take an active part, Mr Fraser . . . no driving the men, I want 'em *led*, sir, *led* by officers so that, when the time comes, they'll follow without hesitation . . .'

'The time, sir . . . ?' Fraser essayed curiously catching a moment of mellowing by the captain.

'Aye, Mr Fraser . . . the time . . . which may catch a ship at a disadvantage and deliver her to the devil in an instant.'

'Or a Don, sir?'

'You comprehend my meaning . . . very well, see to it at once. Pipe all hands . . . Mr Hill and I will tend the deck.'

Drinkwater remained on deck the whole of that day. They set more sail and began to claw back the lost miles to windward. At apparent noon both he and Hill were gratified by twenty minutes of sunshine during which they obtained a perfect meridian altitude and fixed their latitude.

'Fifty-six degrees, fifty-seven minutes south, Mr Hill?'

'Fifty-five minutes, sir . . .'

'Close enough then . . . let us split the difference and lay that off on the chart . . .'

Both men reboxed their instruments, Hill's old quadrant in its triangular box, Drinkwater's Hadley sextant in a rectangular case fitted out with green baize and a selection of telescopes, shades and adjusting tools which gave it the appearance of a surgeon's knife-box. Drinkwater caught the look of satisfaction in Hill's eyes as he handed over the closed case to Midshipman Belchambers.

'I never claimed Hadley's sextant a better instrument than my old quadrant, Mr Hill . . .'

Hill smiled back. 'No sir, but they say the best tunes are played on old fiddles.'

They made their way below, pocketing their tablets and pencils to allow them to grasp the ropes of the companionways. They leaned over the chart and Hill manipulated the parallel rules, striking the pencil line from west to east on the parallel of fifty-six degrees, fifty-six minutes southerly latitude.

'Well clear of the Horn and the Diego Ramirez Islands.' Drinkwater indicated a group of islands some sixty miles southwest of Cape Horn. They fell silent, both pondering the unspoken question: their longitude?

Were they yet west of the Horn, able to lay the ship's head to the north of west and pass up into the Pacific? Or were they still east of the meridian of the Cape, or Diego Ramirez? That longitude of sixty-eight thirty-seven west?

'Perhaps we will be able to obtain a lunar observation later,' observed Hill. 'The sky shows signs of clearing.'

'Yes,' agreed Drinkwater, 'we might also obtain our longitude by chronometer, though I know your general prejudice against the contrivance.'

Hill looked sidelong at the gimballed clock-face in its lashed box. Cook had proved its usefulness thirty years ago, but Hill preferred the complex computations of a lunar observation to the simpler solution of the hour-angle problem which, he thought, smacked too much of necromancy. Drinkwater smiled wryly and changed the subject as he rolled up the chart.

'I hope to water at Juan Fernandez by mid-January, Mr Hill.'

'Aye, aye, sir . . . we'll have enough casks by then.' Hill referred to the stumming then in progress in the orlop deck where sulphurous smoke emanated from the primitive cleaning process. 'And the labour'll do the men no harm.'

'Quite so.' Drinkwater put the chart and rules away, preparing to return to the deck but Hill stopped him, taking advantage of the intimacy permitted a sailing master and the long familiarity the two men had known.

'Sir . . . that ship, the one we sighted this morning . . . it has been worrying me that you thought my opinion in error . . .'

'I have the advantage of you, Mr Hill,' Drinkwater smiled

28

again, so that Hill was reminded of the eager young acting lieutenant he had long ago known on the cutter *Kestrel*.

'I'm sorry, sir, I didn't intend to pry . . .'

'Oh, the content of my orders are such that their secrecy applies principally to their comprehension. The truth is that I don't believe that ship was a Don.' He looked up at the old master. Hill was massaging his arm, a wound acquired at Camperdown; his expression was rueful.

'The truth is, I think she was Russian.'

Captain Drinkwater stood at the weather hance regarding the long deck of the *Patrician*. Wrapped in his boat-cloak he ignored the frequent patterings of spray. There was some abatement in the gale and the wind backed a touch, enabling them to claw more westing against wind and the Cape Horn current that set against them at a couple of knots. Midshipman Belchambers hovered near, ready to dash below for sextant and chronometer should the sun appear again. To windward, patches of blue sky punctuated the low, rolling cumulus and it was hard to comprehend the fact that this was the season of high-summer in the southern hemisphere. There was little in the leaden aspect of the clouds, nor the grey streaked and heaving mass of the ocean to suggest it.

Along the deck and aloft men worked in groups and singly. Lieutenant Quilhampton swung about the mainmast with Midshipman Frey and Comley, the boatswain, was overhauling gear on the fo'c's'le and keeping a lively eye on a party of men in each set of weather shrouds who were rattling down. The grim, motionless presence of Captain Drinkwater intimidated them all, for it had slowly permeated the collective consciousness of the hands that their peevish unwillingness to obey orders had not only been let off lightly, but had endangered the ship. To a degree Drinkwater sensed this contrition, partly because he also shared much of the men's embittered feelings. For, notwithstanding their task and the problems which beset it, the voyage had not been a happy one.

From the moment they had run Stanham to the fore-yardarm, it seemed, providence had ceased to smile on them.

29

Ordered north with a convoy to Leith Roads from the London River, *Patrician* had dragged her anchor in an easterly gale in the Firth of Forth. Drinkwater had been dining aboard another ship at the time, in the company of an old friend and messmate from his days as a midshipman.

Sir Richard White had got into Leith Roads three days earlier after his seventy-four gun *Titan* had been badly mauled in a gale off the Naze of Norway where Sir Richard had been engaged in a successful operation extirpating nests of Danish privateers hiding in the fiords. He had also enjoyed a considerable profit from the destruction of Danish and Norwegian trade, having a broad pendant hoisted as commodore and two sloops and a cutter under his direction for prosecuting this lucrative little campaign.

Sitting in his comfortably furnished cabin, Drinkwater was reminded that there was another Royal Navy to that which he himself belonged, a service dedicated to the self-advancement of its privileged members. He did not blame Sir Richard for taking advantage of his position, any more than he blamed him for inheriting a baronetcy. It was now that the recollection of his old friend's circumstances rankled, as he wrestled with a disaffected crew, a contrary gale and the remotest ocean in the world. But he had enjoyed the conviviality of the distant evening. Sir Richard's officers were pleasant and made much of Drinkwater. He could imagine White's briefing prior to his arrival; his guest was a friend, a seaman of the old school, a tarpaulin of considerable experience, and so on and so forth, all designed to provoke good-natured but superior attitudes. Drinkwater was too old to worry much, though when he thought about such things, they still angered him. At the time he had enjoyed White's company. They had grumbled over the income tax, and agreed on the excellence of the port. They had deplored the standard of young officers and disagreed over the propriety of the new regulation that made masters and pursers equal in status to the commissioned officers. And then the news had come that *Patrician* was making signals of distress and Drinkwater had had a rough and wet return to his ship in his gig, to find chaos in place of an ordered anchor watch and the ship dragging from sheer neglect

30

of the cable at the turn of the tide. The contrast with the well-ordered state of affairs aboard *Titan* was inescapable.

In a fury he had ordered the ship under way, only to recall that he had given Lieutenant Quilhampton shore-leave, and been compelled to fetch a second anchor. Poor Quilhampton. Drinkwater looked up at him in the maintop dictating some memorandum to Frey. They were as close to friendship as a commander and his second lieutenant could be, for Drink-water's wife and Quilhampton's mother enjoyed an intimacy and Quilhampton had been Drinkwater's earliest protégé. He felt a surge of anger against the Admiralty, the war and the whole bloody predicament of his ship at the thought of poor Quilhampton. The young man was wasting the best years of his life, crossed in love by the implacable exigencies of the naval service. Drinkwater wished it was he, and not Fraser, who was first lieutenant.

'Your steward enquires if you wish for some coffee, Captain?'

'Eh? Oh, thank you Derrick . . .'

Drinkwater roused himself from his reverie and nodded to his clerk. Derrick's face had lost neither its sadness, nor its pallor in the months since his impressment by Mr Mylchrist and the cutter's crew. Taken from the banks of the River Colne as he walked from Colchester to Wivenhoe, Derrick had protested his refusal to take part in belligerent operations with such force and eloquence that the matter had eventually been brought to Drinkwater's attention. So too had the strange offender. Drinkwater remembered the man's first appearance in his cabin on that last forenoon at anchor at the Nore, some five days after they had hanged Stanham.

'Take off your hat!' an outraged Lieutenant Mylchrist had ordered, but the man had merely shaken his head and addressed Drinkwater in a manner that brought further fury to the third lieutenant's suffused face.

'Friend, I cannot serve on thy ship, for I abhor all war . . .'

'Be silent, damn you! And call the captain "sir" when you address him . . .'

'Thank you, Mr Mylchrist, that will do . . . I think I know the temper of this man.' Drinkwater turned to the solemn yet

31

somehow dignified figure. 'You are of the Quaker persuasion, are you not?'

'I am . . .'

'Very well . . . I cannot return you to the shore, you are part of the ship's company . . .'

'But I . . .'

'But I shall respect your convictions. Can you read and write? Good, then you may be entered as my clerk . . . attend to the matter, Mr Mylchrist . . .'

And so Drinkwater had increased his personal staff by a clerk, adding Derrick to Mullender, his steward, and Tregembo, his coxswain, and finding the quiet, resigned Quaker an asset to the day-to-day running of the ship. If he had entertained any doubts as to the man infecting the ship's company with his peculiar brand of dissenting cant, he need not have worried. The hands regarded Derrick with a good-natured contempt, the kind of attitude they reserved for the moon-struck and the shambling, half-idiotic luetic that kept the heads clean.

'Thank you Derrick. Tell Mullender I shall come below . . .'

'Very well, Captain, and I have the purser's accounts fair-copied and ready for your signature.'

Drinkwater took another look round the deck and, as Derrick stood aside, he went below for a warming mug of coffee.

'Deuced if I understand the man,' Lieutenant Mylchrist tossed off the pot of shrub and stared with distaste at the suet pudding the wardroom steward laid before him. His eyes met those of his messmates, staring from faces that were tired from unaccustomed exertion. 'He's a damned slave-driver, though why he had to drive *us* . . .'

'Stuff your gape with that pudding, Johnnie, there's a good fellow,' said Mount, with a note of asperity in his voice. 'Ah, Fraser, here, sit down . . . Steward! Bring the first lieutenant a bottle!'

'Thank you Mount.'

'Well, there's one consolation . . .'

'And what might that be?' enquired the chastened Mylchrist.

'We'll all sleep like logs tonight.'

32

'Except those of us with a watch to keep,' muttered Mylchrist.

'You make sure you keep it, cully, not like that episode in Leith Road where you neglected the basic . . .'

'All right, all right, there's no need to go over that again . . .'

'Maybe not, you see yourself as a victim today, but the plain facts are that you'll be a worse victim if you don't take the captain's point.'

Mount stared round the table. He was, with the exception of Hill, the oldest officer in *Patrician*'s wardroom, something of a Dutch-uncle to the lieutenants.

'Well what exactly is the captain's point?' asked Mylchrist sourly.

'That this ship is a bloody shambles and has no right to be.'

'She's no different from the other ships I've served aboard . . .'

'Bloody Channel Fleet two days from home and a couple of cruises in the Med. For God's sake Johnnie don't show how wet you are. Goddamn it man, Midshipman Wickham was in the Arctic freezing his balls off before you'd heard a shot in anger . . .'

'Now look here, Mount, don't you dare patronise me . . .'

'Gentlemen, gentlemen, be silent!' Fraser snapped, and an uneasy truce settled on the table. 'Mount's right . . . so is the captain . . . it's no your place to strut so branky, Johnnie . . . the men say she's a donsie ship . . .'

'Poppycock, Fraser . . . the ship's not unlucky, for that I take to be your meaning. The trouble is we're out of sorts, frayed like worn ropes . . .' Mount smiled reassuringly at Fraser, 'and that business off the Orkney upset us all.'

'Captain Drinkwater most of all,' said Quilhampton, speaking for the first time. 'I think he feels the shame of that more keenly than the rest of us.'

Quilhampton rose and reached for his hat and greygoe. 'I must relieve Hill . . .' He left the wardroom and a contemplative silence in which they each relived the shame of the action with the Danish privateer. They had chased her for four hours, sighting her at dawn, hull down to leeward ten miles to the east of the Pentland Skerries. The Dane had run, but once it was clear the heavy frigate could outsail her in the strong westerly wind, she

33

had tacked and stood boldly towards the *Patrician*. Unbeknown to the captain on the quarterdeck above, the two lieutenants on the gun-deck had relaxed, assuming the capture to be a mere formality once the intelligence of the privateer's turn had been passed to them. Despite the shot from a bow-chaser the Dane had not slackened her pace, but run to leeward of the *Patrician* and the sudden broadside that Lieutenant Mylchrist's battery had been ordered to fire had been ragged and ineffectual, only succeeding in puncturing the privateer's sails.

Once to windward the Danish commander sailed his nimble vessel like a wizard. Though Drinkwater turned in his wake, the Dane beat upwind with an impressive agility. Whenever the *Patrician* closed the range to cannon shot, the Dane tacked, keeping a press of canvas aloft so that the momentary disadvantage he suffered while he gathered way on the new tack was compensated for by the attention the *Patrician* had to pay to going about.

With two hours to sunset the privateer had slipped into Sanday Sound, taking advantage of the weather tide that sluiced through the rocks, islets and Orcadian islands with which her commander was more familiar than either Drinkwater or Hill. In the end, as darkness closed over the *Patrician* and caution forced her to haul off the land, the Danish privateer had escaped.

It was not Hill, but Drinkwater himself who turned the deck over to Quilhampton.

'Well, James, you have the ship.' Isolated by the howl of the wind, Drinkwater unwound with uncharacteristic informality. He fixed the younger man with a perceptive stare.

'Sir?' said Quilhampton, puzzled.

'You have not spoken of it, James . . . the matter upon which you solicited my advice in Leith Road . . .' Drinkwater prompted, 'the matter of matrimony, damn it.'

'Oh . . . no, sir . . . no. But as you said, 'tis likely to be a damnably long voyage.' Quilhampton's answer was evasive and he avoided the captain's eyes, searching the horizon with an expression of despair.

34

He wondered if it were an accident caused by the violent motion of the ship as Drinkwater went below, or whether the slight pressure against his shoulder had been a gesture of commiseration.

Manhunt

The islands of Juan Fernandez bear no resemblance to my impression of Crusoe's refuge . . .

Drinkwater wrote in his journal, then laid down his pen, leaned back in his chair and stared rapturously out of the stern windows. The sashes were lifted and the gentle breeze that wafted into the cabin bore the sweet scent of a lush vegetation dominated by the sandalwood trees. He closed his eyes and drew the air in through his nostrils, a calm contentment filling him. For the first time in weeks his cabin bore a civilised air, being upon an even keel. Drinkwater turned back to his journal, rejected the idea of an attempt to rival Defoe and continued writing.

We sighted the peak of El Yunque on the 3rd instant, a fair landfall but occupied by the Spaniards, and, unwilling to advertise our presence upon the Pacific coasts of America, took departure for Farther-out Island, thirty leagues to the westward where we found anchorage in nine fathoms with a sandy bottom, wood and water in plenty, an abundance of pig and goats. There are seals and sea-elephants and several species of humming-bird. The men have been exercised at their leisure, a circumstance which gives me great heart after our recent difficulties . . .

He laid his pen down again and rose, stretching. They lay at anchor within half a mile of the beach and he could see the launch drawn up on the sand, the two boat-keepers paddling like children in the shallows. The warmth of a sun almost overhead lay over the anchorage like a benediction, filling the ship with a langorous air.

'Lotus-eating . . .' he murmured. Leaning his hands on the sill of the window he looked up at the rugged volcanic summit of the island rising precipitously from foothills that were covered in rich vegetation. Unlike the main island of the archipelago, Más-a-Fuera, Farther-out Island, did not possess the anvil-peak of El Yunque, but it was impressively beautiful to men whose eyes had been starved of the sight of green leaves.

An occasional shot echoed up the ravines, evidence of Mount's hunting party flushing the wild pig from the undergrowth. The thought of dining that evening on roast pork brought the juices to Drinkwater's mouth in anticipation and further enhanced his feeling of contentment. They could take a short break here, give the men a run ashore, replenish their wood and water, dine all hands in the very lap of luxury and even, perhaps, if they could find someone among the crew conversant with the process, make some goat's milk cheese.

He returned to his table, picked up a pen and began to write again. The breeze ruffled his shirt and through the skylight the sunshine beat down, warming the old ache in his mangled shoulder.

The mood of the people is much improved since our arrival. Their faces wear smiles this day and I am sanguine that the outbreaks of sporadic drunkenness, of petty-theft and brawling that accompanied our passage of the Atlantic, will cease now that we are brought into better climes and the men become resigned to their task . . .

He looked up and saw the launch coming off, its waist full of filled barricoes of sweet water. Through the skylight he heard orders being given to the watch on deck in preparation for hoisting the casks into the hold. If they worked well today and to-morrow he would give each watch a day's leave of absence and they could scramble about the island like children on holiday.

By noon they had reached the tree-line. Quilhampton in the lead gave a great whoop, like a Red-Indian, for it was to be the halting point of the expedition. Drinkwater was panting with the unaccustomed exertion, watching Frey and Belchambers scamper about the increasing number of rocky outcrops that made their appearance as the valley had narrowed and risen.

As behove the intelligence of naval officers it had been considered necessary to make some purpose of the day. Not for

37

them the wild and aimless wandering of the men, whose liberty infected them like quarts of unwatered rum. Far below they could hear the shouts and laughter of their unconfined spirits as they chased about the ferny undergrowth. Besides, if the men were to give vent to their pent-up emotions, it was incumbent upon the officers to make way for them. So it had been Quilhampton who had decided the walk ashore should become an expedition, and Drinkwater who had suggested they traced one of the streams upwards to its source.

Accompanied by the second lieutenant, the two midshipmen, Mr Lallo the surgeon and Derrick the Quaker clerk, they had set off after breaking their fasts and parading divisions. Those left aboard had worn glum expressions, despite promises of their turn tomorrow, such was the liberating infection of the island upon those destined to run amok today.

The officers began their expedition at the watering place where the stream ran sluggishly out over a bed of pebbles and sand, spreading itself into a tiny delta and carving miniature cliffs and escarpments through the foreshore. But it soon narrowed, its bed deeper and its current swifter, passing beneath a cover of sandalwood trees which already showed evidence of the axe marks of man.

'The oleaginous qualities of this species,' pronounced Lallo, patting one of the dark red tree-boles with a proprietorial hand, 'produces an oil which may, I believe, be substituted for copaiba oil as well as forming an admixture for Indian attars . . .'

'What the deuce is an attar, Lallo?' enquired Quilhampton.

'Perfume, perfume, that fragrance so often necessary to the fair sex in warm weather to render them desirable to men. I should have thought you would have known that, Mr Q, given your strong desire to become a benedick.'

Quilhampton flushed scarlet and Lallo cast a mischievous glance at Drinkwater. 'Is that not so, sir?'

'I fear you embarrass Mr Q, Mr Lallo, but perhaps you would tell me to what use *you* would put such an oil.'

'Well, as for copaiba, it is a specific in certain complaints of the urinary tract . . . it occurs to me that the sandalwood tree might provide us with oleaginous matter with similar properties.'

'Very well. We can gather some chips on our return, but our young friends here are anxious to continue, I suspect. They are too young for complaints of the urinary tract.'

'Very well, sir. *Adelante!*'

Laughing, they pressed on, ever upwards. The trees thinned to scrub, the ferns that grew prolifically alongside the stream now sprouted from rocks and mosses and the water, no longer dark under the trees, sparkled and ran white, leaping and boiling over rocks and into deep, mysterious pools.

After an hour they came to a waterfall, where the stream dropped almost thirty feet over a sheer lip of grey rock. The silver trail roared downwards, sending up a cloud of spray through which a rainbow curved. On either side dense foliage grew, pierced by the heavy heads of several exotic blooms.

'Sir! Look!'

Drinkwater turned to where Mr Midshipman Belchambers, a bright-eyed and excited child, pointed. Frey was beside him, his pencil already racing over the sketch-block he was rarely without.

'God's bones, a humming bird!' Drinkwater recognised the tiny bird from a print he had once seen in Ackermann's, the extravagant result of the print-maker capitalising on the public interest in such exotic subjects roused by Captain Cook. The blurred whirring of the bird's wings as it held its head motionless at the bell of a flower, was a jewel of pure cinnamon.

For several minutes they stared in wonder at the creature, until the lust for achievement drew them further upwards. When they cleared the undergrowth and the scrub, they emerged onto a steep, rocky scree. Here the grass was sparse, hanging in tussocks, rooted in shallow hollows where rain and humus had collected to produce a soil from the volcanic core of the island. They flung themselves down, sprawling in the sunshine, and broke open the sparse stock of provisions they had brought from the ship.

The view was stupendous. Below them the vegetation spread, giving way to the water of the anchorage, blue-green from the sand and coral reflecting light upwards through it. Upon the limpid water, the frigate sat like a toy, her dark brown sides with the cream strake pierced by the open gun-ports through which fresh air dried out the milldew, damp and rot of the Horn. Her spread sails hung drying in loose festoons. At the stern the white ensign lifted languidly, reflecting the luxurious lethargy of the ship. Beyond the anchorage the ocean spread to the horizon, utterly empty, the pale blue of the sky dotted with an occasional cloud, except to the north-west where a greater massing of cumulus marked the distant peak of El Yunque, dominating Más-a-Tierra (the Nearer Island), mainland of the group.

'D'you intend an attack on the Spanish settlement, sir?' asked Quilhampton, nodding at the distant indication of the island and munching on a slab of purser's cheese that was almost inedible.

'No . . . Ah, Derrick, come sit here with us, man, unless you wish to eschew the company of the ungodly . . .'

They watched the quiet Quaker, awkward in the presence of the officers, squat stiffly with them.

'I knew one of your persuasion, Derrick, when I was in the Arctic. D'you recall Captain Sawyers, Mr Q?'

'The master of the *Faithful*, sir?'

'Yes. A fine seaman and one of nature's gentlemen.'

'I am glad to hear you say so, Captain,' the Quaker replied solemnly.

'Is it to be Panama then, sir?' persisted Quilhampton.

'Ah. The wardroom have sent you to find out my intentions, eh Mr Q? And I was giving you the credit for wishing to discover the source of this river.'

'Well sir, I have to admit that curiosity is getting a trifle out of hand . . .' Quilhampton's voice rose at the end of the sentence, so that he left it hanging, like a question. Drinkwater looked round the circle of faces. They were all looking at him expectantly. The mood of the day was too good to spoil.

'Very well, you shall take tablets down from the mountain, gentlemen, beggin' your pardon, Derrick, but you see what curious fellows I am set about with.'

''Tis a sermon on the Mount that we're getting,' muttered

Lallo in a stage-whispered aside that gauged Drinkwater's mood to a nicety.

'Your lese-majestie will be overlooked, Mr Lallo,' he grinned. 'Very well, gentlemen, I will confide in you and parade the hands at sunset, so that your period of privilege is brief.'

'It's a galleon, sir . . . the Acapulco galleon . . . like Lord Anson!' Lallo's lese-majestie was infectious. Midshipman Belchambers was bolt-upright with excitement. The party laughed indulgently.

'As a matter of fact it ain't, Mr Belchambers. Matter of fact it ain't Panama either . . . at least not directly. Initially we shall strike . . .'

'What the devil's that?' Lieutenant Quilhampton was the first on his feet. They stared down at the ship where the wind carried the disintegrating puff of white smoke gently to leeward. They stood stock-still for an instant and then the second gun came, reverberating up the ravine like the first and prompting them to sudden action. Instinctively, Drinkwater cast a glance round the horizon. The sea was as empty as before; the signal of recall was concerned with some internal matter. They gathered up their odds and ends and began to make their way down the mountain.

'Fine bloody banyan day this turned out to be!' Lieutenant Mylchrist muttered between clenched teeth as Lallo bent over his shoulder. The light from the lamp, held aloft by the elderly loblolly 'boy' Skeete, caught the edge of the catling and Skeete grinned, revealing carious teeth and malodorous breath.

'Now, Mr Mylchrist, d'you care for my rum, or the wardroom's brandy?'

'Get on with it, you damned windbag,' panted Mylchrist, waves of pain spreading from his shoulder where the bruised and rough-edged wound showed the entry point of the musket ball.

'You know, it doesn't do to insult one's physician in such a dependent state, Mr Mylchrist, does it Skeete?'

''Deed not . . .'

'Damn the pair of you . . .'

41

'Hold your tongue, Johnnie, and let the surgeon get on with his work.' Mount patted the young officer's shoulder and he lay face down, for the ball had entered his shoulder from the rear.

'You're not the first gentleman to be the victim of a hunting accident,' remarked Lallo, 'now hold still.'

Mount bent, to assist in holding Mylchrist down. Anxiety and responsibility played on his face. 'Trouble is, Bones, I don't think it *was* an accident.'

Mylchrist grunted and Skeete drew the leather pad into his mouth as the catling began to probe the wound. 'You don't?' asked Lallo without pausing in his task.

'No . . . one of my marines reported his musket missing when we halted and not half an hour later Mylchrist here was shot. As far as I know there was no one near him that belonged to the hunting party.'

'Does the captain know all this?'

'No, not yet.'

'Then I suggest you tell him.'

'Your men to spread out, Mr Mount. They know the two men missing, Hogan and Witherspoon.'

'Sir.'

'Very well. Let's get on with it.'

Drinkwater checked the priming in the pans of his two pistols, loosened his sword and nodded to Quilhampton. The second lieutenant waved the cordon of picked seamen forward. At intervals along their front petty officers and midshipmen were posted to avoid the searchers colluding with the deserters. Thanks to Hogan and Witherspoon this was likely to be the only walk ashore the remainder of the crew were going to have. Captain Drinkwater was in a dark and vengeful mood.

They moved forward, trampling the undergrowth and flushing out birds and small scampering things as they moved inland. Drinkwater looked back to where a party of the gunner's mates carried some sulphur bombs, enlargements of the alchemical concoctions Old Blue Lights made up for stumming the casks; Drinkwater was fairly certain of where his quarry had gone to earth, for he had seen movement on the open scree, spied from his cabin through his glass. He was confident it had been one of the deserters watching the ship for signs of retributive landing parties leaving her. To the right of the spot, overhanging crags opened fissures in the vertical faces of sections of the mountainside and some of these looked large enough to be caves.

It was Drinkwater's party that reached this area and he called up the gunners.

'Let's have a portfire to those sulphur-bombs, lively now.'

There was a sputtering of fuse and then an ochreous discharge of acrid smoke.

'Hoy it then, laddie,' coughed one of the gunner's mates, and a pungent missile was hurled into the first cave that seemed to offer sanctuary. Drinkwater moved to the next and bawled his ultimatum into the impenetrable darkness.

'Give yourselves up at once . . . come now Hogan and Witherspoon, you'll be left otherwise.'

No sound came out of the cave, beyond a disturbed flapping and the emergence of a pair of fluttering bats. Drinkwater nodded to the gunners and a second sulphur bomb was pitched.

'Sir . . .'

They turned and saw Lieutenant Quilhampton pointing. 'There's yellow smoke coming from the hillside above . . . must be a rock fall inside.'

The party began scrambling up beside the cave. On the bleak hillside a hole in its roof had formed a natural chimney, funnelling the sulphur fumes clear. It was an unwitting distraction, for no fugitives ran from the smoke-filled cave.

'Hey! Look!'

Again they turned, this time to the right, looking back downwards to where, some twenty yards away, two men were scrambling down into the cover of the scrub and trees. Drinkwater had guessed correctly. The fugitives had holed up in a cave, but one further along the ledge.

'After them!'

There was a general chase of excited men slithering, scrambling and cursing as they went in pursuit. Drinkwater fired his pistol as a signal to Mount and then forsook his dignity and joined the manhunt. After ten minutes he recognised the steep valley of the stream they had followed that morning; he could hear the roar of the waterfall somewhere not far below but, apart from broken branches, the fugitives had vanished.

The roar of the waterfall seemed to act as a magnet to the men. They were already thirsty after their climb and there were now sprained ankles and torn skin to add to their moaning. Drinkwater was well aware their hearts were not in the chase, but he could not afford to let Hogan and Witherspoon escape.

'Halt there! Stand easy . . . you may drink. Mr Frey?'

'Yes sir?'

'Take Belchambers . . . get word to Mr Mount to leave Sergeant Blixoe and his marines at the watering place. He himself is to come up here.'

'Aye, aye, sir.'

Drinkwater watched the two midshipmen scramble down the steep ravine, slashing at the ferns with their dirks. He entertained a moment's apprehension for their safety; they could be hit like Mylchrist . . . then he dismissed the thought. He was almost certain the missing men were now behind him. He looked across the pool. The men were bent over, scooping the water up into their faces. There was about them an air of levity, borne out by suppressed laughter and sly glances cast in his direction. He watched two in particular . . .

Drinkwater turned to Quilhampton.

'Mr Q, I want you to spread the men out and continue down to the beach. Comb this valley and remuster by the boats. We've wasted enough time as it is and it will be sunset in an hour.'

'Aye, aye, sir.' Quilhampton turned and began to shepherd the men down the mountain. 'Come on then, lads . . .'

Drinkwater bent himself to drink from the stream. The two men were watching him, a covert look in their eyes. He stared at them pointedly and, with an obvious and eloquent reluctance, they moved away after the others. With a beating heart Drinkwater remained behind.

Mount found him sitting on a rock, checking the locks of his pistols.

44

'Sir?' The marine lieutenant was gasping with the effort of his climb.

'Sit down, Mr Mount, take a drink slowly and listen to what I have to say . . .'

Mount sat and drank and listened, looking sharply at Drinkwater as the Captain explained his suspicions, his voice lost in the roar of the waterfall. 'You understand, Mr Mount?'

'Perfectly, sir . . . if you'll give me a moment . . .'

Mount checked his own flintlock, a heavy horse-pistol.

'Why Mylchrist, Mr Mount? D'you know?'

'He's the youngest and most vulnerable officer, sir.' Mount's voice lacked its usual conviction.

'Does he ride the men . . . when I am not there, I mean?'

'I have not noticed so, sir.'

'No . . . and why Hogan and Witherspoon?'

Drinkwater recalled Hogan, a handsome Irish giant whom he remembered now, hearing utter mutinous remarks the night they sprang the foretopmast off Cape Horn; and Witherspoon, by contrast a dark young man, agile as a monkey and one of the *Patrician*'s prime topmen, noted for his daring aloft. Another suspicion came to Drinkwater as he waited for Mount's signal of readiness. It was darker than the first and he cursed himself for not thinking of it sooner, aware that it had been hovering just beyond his consciousness for some time.

'Ready.'

Stooping and moving from rock to rock Mount crossed the stream. On the further bank he looked back at Drinkwater and nodded. Lifting their pistols both men advanced cautiously on opposite sides of the pool. Between them the silver cascade of water fell from above, sluicing over the polished rock lip of the escarpment to fall into the hollow with a roar, the smoking spray of its motion cut by the advancing shadow of the high western bank which terminated the glittering rainbow like a knife.

Ten yards from the foot of the fall, where the rocks were broken, cemented by moss and tiny fern-fronds, and the cliff rose sheer above, both men stopped.

'I command you to come out!' Drinkwater roared above the noise of the fall. The spray was already soaking the two officers whose hands covered the pans of their cocked pistols. Drink-water's demand produced no response.

'In the King's name . . .'

'Bollocks to your focking King!'

Mount and Drinkwater exchanged glances.

'Come out Hogan, damn you, otherwise you're a dead man!' Drinkwater's eyes studied the overhang. He could just see the opening in the rock which gave access to the hollow space behind the fall.

'And have ye hang me, Cap'n Drinkwater? I'll not die for your mad raddled King, nor for your damned causes. God damn you, Cap'n Drinkwater, God damn you to hell!'

'Hold your tongue, you Fenian bastard!' Mount roared from the far side of the fall, moving precipitously forward so that Drinkwater was forced to wave him back.

'What about you, Witherspoon? D'you wish to hang? Come, lad, show some sense!'

''E stays with me, so help me!'

'D'you wish Hogan to answer for you, Witherspoon?'

'Aye, sir . . . I do . . .' Witherspoon's voice cracked into a squeak. There was nothing more to be done. Drinkwater nodded and began to edge forward, wondering how much Hogan could see and knowing that, at least, looking from the darkness into the light, the Irishman had the undisputed advantage. He also had a loaded musket.

The base of the waterfall streamed over a rock lip, a great slab of cooled lava that had slipped sideways to form an architrave in the heap of rocks which formed the lower slope of the escarpment. At either end it seemed supported, and softer deposits had been washed out by the water so that, beneath and behind it, a great void opened up, floored by more rock underfoot. Alongside lay the deep pool into which the fall tumbled ceaselessly, its roaring noise buffeting the senses to make thinking difficult. Light entered the cave through the wide silver curtain of the waterfall. Cautiously, Drinkwater moved forward.

As he saw the cave opening up he realised access was obtainable only from his side. Mount could do nothing beyond cover Drinkwater as long as the captain remained outside the fall. But it was too late for such considerations. The deserters knew of their presence; Drinkwater hoped they also thought the area was surrounded by Mount's marines, but, if that were the case, Drinkwater himself was unlikely to be the person sent in to winkle them out.

His eyes were accustoming themselves to the shifting light. The westering sun helped; the rapid tropic sunset was upon them.

Deep within the cave he saw a movement. Instinctively he brought the pistol up and pulled the trigger. The gun kicked in his hand and he saw a scuffle of reaction deep within. Quickly he moved forward, drawing the second pistol from his waistband and finding firmer footing within the cave.

Suddenly he was confronted by Hogan; the man held a levelled musket, its bayonet glittering wickedly in the strange, unreal light.

Drinkwater fired the second gun, but despite having its frizzen on, moisture had seeped from his shirt and been drawn into the powder by its hygroscopic qualities. The hammer clicked impotently and Hogan lunged.

His own gun-lock must have been rendered equally useless for he was relying on cold steel. Drinkwater stepped backwards and reached for his sword. The footing was slippery with slime; both men recovered. Hogan was an immensely strong and powerful man and he had Witherspoon somewhere in the darkness to aid him. Outside Mount was shouting something but Drinkwater paid him no attention, his eyes were fixed on the Irish giant. Somewhere behind Hogan, Witherspoon was suspiciously silent. Drinkwater flicked his eyes into the darkness but could see nothing. Hogan shifted his feet and Drinkwater's attention returned to the Irishman.

'Don't be a fool, Hogan . . . you can't get away with this . . .'

'You're alone Cap'n . . . that's enough for me. Sure, Oi'll fix me own way to die.'

'What about Witherspoon?' Hogan grinned. It was clear he knew of Drinkwater's fear of the other man.

'Or Oi'll fix yours for you, Cap'n!' Hogan lunged again. His reach was long and Drinkwater fell back, slipped and swiped

47

wildly with his sword. He felt the blade crash against the bayonet and the strength of his opponent as Hogan met the pressure. Drinkwater's mangled right arm was unequal to the contest. He saw victory light Hogan's eyes and felt the resistance of rock against his back.

'Now, you English bastard!'

Hogan drew back the bayonet to lunge, his teeth bared in a snarl that bore all the hatred inherent in his heart. Desperately Drinkwater flung himself sideways, falling at his adversary's feet, the wet slime of the rocky ledge fouling him. He rolled madly, aware that he was somehow in contact with Hogan's feet. He kicked, and suddenly found the edge of the cave. A second later he felt the icy cold of water close over his head. The sudden shock electrified him. An instant later a great, irresistible pressure bore down upon him, punching and bruising him so that, for a moment he thought he was being beaten by Hogan until the roaring in his ears proclaimed the source of the pain was the waterfall itself. Then he was subject to an immense rolling motion and vast pressure. Darkness engulfed him as the force of the water thrust him down, rolling him over yet again, but this time in an involuntary way, shoving his aching body so that his lungs began to scream at his brain to let them have air.

He was drowning!

Such were the powerful reflexes tearing at the muscles of his chest that opposition to them was impossible. Blinding lights filled his head, the roaring of the water became intolerable. He could resist no longer. He opened his mouth and dragged water into his lungs.

Mount saw a figure suddenly rise, bursting from the surface of the dark pool some five yards below the fall itself. He levelled his gun, but his finger froze. So far out of the water was the man flung, welled up as strongly as he had just been thrust down, that Mount saw instantly that it was the captain.

A few minutes later Mount had dragged his gasping commander to the side of the pool. Drinkwater lay over a rock, his body wracked by helpless eructations as he spewed the water from himself. After a few minutes, as Mount alternately stared from Drinkwater to the ledge beside the waterfall on the far side of the pool, Drinkwater's body ceased its painful heaving. He looked up, pale and shivering, a mucous trickle running down his chin. His shirt was torn and Mount saw the scars and twisted muscles that knotted his wounded shoulder. Instinctively he saw the captain incline his head to the right, indicating the shock of the chill in those mangled muscles.

'Hogan's got your musket . . . his powder's spoiled . . .'

'What about Witherspoon?'

'Didn't see him . . . think I may have winged him with my first shot . . .

'I'll get support, it's getting dark . . .'

'No! We must . . .'

But he got no further. A loud bellow, a bull-roar of defiance, it seemed, came from the waterfall. Both men looked round and Mount scrambled to his feet.

From behind the silver cascade, glowing now with a luminosity that it seemed to carry down from higher up the mountain where the last of the setting sunlight still caught the stream, Hogan emerged. He bore the musket in one hand and in the other the limp figure of Witherspoon.

It seemed to the still gasping Drinkwater, that the darkest of his suspicions had been correct. The bull-roar had not been of defiance, but something infinitely more elemental. It had been a howl of grief, animal in its intensity. The drooping body of Witherspoon was undoubtedly that of a dead lover.

Such was instantly obvious to Mount too. Without hesitation the marine officer raised his big pistol.

'Sodomite!' he snarled, and took aim.

In the almost complete gloom the two officers were quite hidden from Hogan. The Irish giant had no thoughts now, beyond the overwhelming sense of loss. The desperate venture on which he and his lover had set out that morning had seemed worth the hazard. *Patrician* would not stay. Hogan read his commander for a man of resolution, and nothing waited for Hogan over the Pacific horizon beyond the chance of death by wounding, death by disease or death from one or another of the multiple foulnesses that haunted His Britannic Majesty's fleet. The

49

island, though, offered a bold man everything. He could have outwitted fate and lived, like Crusoe, upon such a spot until he met death in God's time, not King George's. It would have worked but for Lieutenant Mylchrist.

His frame was wracked by monstrous sobs as he dragged the dead body of his lover out of the cave. It only seemed another paroxysm of grief when Mount's ball shattered his skull, and smashed his brains against the cliff behind him.

Shaking from cold and shock Drinkwater followed Mount gingerly back across the stream. Once again he approached the entrance to the cave. In the last of the daylight the two officers stood staring down at their victims.

'God's bones,' muttered Drinkwater crouching down before his legs gave under him. His first shot had indeed hit Witherspoon, hit the breast and heart. Witherspoon must have died instantly, so silently that even Hogan himself had not realised until after Drinkwater's escape, the damage that single shot had done. For Witherspoon's breast was exposed as Hogan had desperately sought to stem the bleeding wound. The shirt was torn back and the two officers stared down at the shapely breasts of a young woman.

CHAPTER 4

The Chase

'I'm damned if I understand why we're not cruising off the Isthmus,' complained Mount as he lounged back in his chair and awaited the roast pig whose tantalising aroma had been permeating the ship for much of the forenoon. 'It is common knowledge, even to Their Lordships, that Panama is the focus of Spanish power.'

'I think you jump to conclusions, Mount,' replied Fraser, cooling himself with an improvised fan fashioned from a sheet of discarded cartridge paper. The wardroom was insufferably hot, even with a windsail ducting air from the deck, and its occupants were as frayed as the end of the canvas pipe itself. 'Besides, preoccupations with opportunities for prize-money are an obstruction to duty.'

'Don't preach to me, Fraser . . .'

'Gentlemen, gentlemen . . . such querulous behaviour . . . it's too exhausting by far . . . be so kind as to leave the preaching to me.'

'God save us from that fate,' said Mount accepting the glass from King, the negro messman, and rolling his eyes in a deprecating fashion at Fraser. Both officers looked at the temporiser in their midst.

The Reverend Jonathan Henderson, chaplain to His Britannic Majesty's frigate *Patrician*, laid a thin, knotted finger alongside his nose in a characteristic gesture much loved by the midshipmen for its imitable property. It invariably presaged an aphorism which its originator considered of importance in his ministry. 'I am sure they know what they are about and it will avail us nothing if we quarrel.'

'What else are we to do, God damn it?' said Mount sharply.

'Come, Mr Mount, no blasphemy if you please.'

'I'm a military man, Mr Henderson, and accustomed to speak my mind within the mess, and I've been too long at sea to have much faith in the wisdom of Their Lordships.'

'If you're referring to my relatively short career . . .'

'*Short?* Good God man, you've not been at sea for a dog's watch! What the devil d'you know about it.'

'Come sir, I was chaplain to the late Admiral Roddam . . .'

'Admiral Roddam? He spent the American War swinging round his own bloody chicken bones and port bottles until they had to move the Nore light to mark the shoal . . . Admiral Roddam . . . hey King, refill my glass and deafen my ears to sacerdotal nonsense.'

Henderson looked furiously at the grinning negro and rounded on Mount.

'Mr Mount, I'm a man of God, but I'll not . . .'

'Gentlemen, pray silence . . . you raise your voices too loudly.' Fraser straightened up from the rudder stock cover from which vantage point he had been trying to ignore the petty squabble.

'There has been a deal too much argument since that business at Juan Fernandez . . .'

'There is usually a deal too much argument when empty vessels are banging about.'

'Very well, Mr Lallo,' snapped Fraser at the surgeon who, until that moment, had occupied a corner of the table with his sick-book, 'belay that.' Lallo shrugged and pocketed his pencil. 'Tell us how Mylchrist is.'

'He'll live, but his shoulder'll be damned stiff for a good while.'

'Like the captain's.'

'Aye, like the captain's.'

'But he's over the worst of the fever?'

Lallo nodded and a silence fell as they considered the events on the island. In the days that had followed their departure from Juan Fernandez the echoes of the affair had petered out except when conversation aimlessly disturbed it. Among the people it had lit another portfire of discontent, for two-thirds of the ship's

52

company had not enjoyed the liberty of that first watch-ashore. Nevertheless, the nature of the incident had had less lasting impact on the men than upon the officers. The hands had preoccupations other than sentimental considerations over a pair of love-lorn deserters. In the collective wisdom of the crew there was an easier acceptance of the vagaries of human nature. Their lives were publicly lived, crude in their exposure and therefore the revelation of Witherspoon's sex came as less of a shock than the vague realisation that they had, perhaps, been made fools of.

Among the officers the reaction had been different. It was to them truly shocking that a woman, even a woman of the lowest social order which it was manifestly obvious that Witherspoon was not, should be driven to the extremity of resorting to concealment on a man-o'-war. Many and various were the theories advanced to explain her action. None was provable and therefore none was satisfactory. To some extent it was this inexplicable nature of the affair that made it most irritating. Unlike the people, the living conditions of the officers were such that they could function as individuals. The solitude of their tiny cabins enabled them to think in privacy and in privacy thoughts invaded unbidden. Of them all James Quilhampton had been most deeply stirred.

It had been Quilhampton who had climbed back up the dark valley and found Mount and Drinkwater, and the dead bodies. It had been Quilhampton who had organised the burial party and stood beside the chaplain as he performed his first real duty since recovering from the sea-sickness induced by the doubling of Cape Horn. The two lovers had been buried that night and the sky above the lantern-lit burial-party had been studded by stars. This involvement had revived thoughts of his own hopeless love affair, left far behind on the shores of the Firth of Forth and long-since repudiated when the news that *Patrician* was bound for the distant Pacific had plunged him into extreme and private depression.

Now he rose from his cot, disturbed by the squabble in the adjacent wardroom, and emerged from his cabin into the silence that had followed it.

53

'You make as much noise as a Dover-court,' he muttered sleepily, slumping down in his chair and staring at the table cloth before him, his nose wrinkling to the smell of roast pork.

'You shouldn't be sleeping James, my boy, when you can be drinking,' said Mount, pushing an empty glass towards him and beckoning King.

'Fill Mr Q's glass, King.'

'Yes sah . . . Missah Q?'

'Oh, very well . . . have you shrub there, King? Good man . . .'

'I was just saying, James, that it's damned odd we aren't attacking the Dons on the Isthmus . . .'

'Oh, for God's sake don't start that again . . .'

'Hold on, Fraser, it's a perfectly logical military consideration, isn't it James?'

Quilhampton shrugged.

'He's still dreaming of the lovely Catriona MacEwan,' jibed Fraser grinning.

'Well, he's precious little to complain of since he was the last of us to have a woman in his arms,' agreed Mount.

'Except Hogan,' said Quilhampton.

'Ah, you see, he *was* thinking of the fair sex . . . an inadvisable preoccupation in the middle of the Pacific Ocean. What you should be considering is what the devil we're doing so far north . . .'

'If I remember correctly, Mr Q,' broke in Lallo, 'the captain was about to confide in us when the recall guns were fired on the desertion of those two . . .' Lallo hesitated.

'Persons, Mr Lallo?' offered Henderson.

'Exactly, Mr Henderson . . . now tell us . . . that confidence was interrupted, but you are in the captain's pocket enough to get furlough in Edinburgh town . . . What's this about Russians?'

'I've no more influence over the captain than you, Mr Lallo; indeed I've a good deal less, I dare say . . .'

But their deliberations were cut short, for faintly down the cotton shaft of the windsail came a cry: 'Sail . . . sail ho! Two points on the larboard bow!'

54

They forgot the roast pork and the glasses of shrub and sherry. Even the Reverend Mr Henderson joined the rush for the quarterdeck ladder adding to the clatter of over-turned chairs and the noise of cutlery as the dragged table-cloth sent it to the deck. King stood shaking his head and rolling his eyes in a melancholy affectation. Only Quilhampton remained impervious to the hail of the masthead lookout.

His only reaction was to bring his wooden hand down on the table in a savage blow, bruising the pine board and giving vent to the intensity of his feelings. For underneath his personal misery, below the strange disturbance caused by the desertion on Juan Fernandez, lay the knowledge that most oppressed him and of which he had been dreaming fitfully as he had dozed on his cot. More than any other officer, it was James Quilhampton who best understood the smouldering mood of the men. It had been Quilhampton alone who had defused the incipient mutiny aboard the *Antigone* the previous summer. Very little had happened to placate the men since Drinkwater's bounty, paid out of the captain's own pocket, had eased tension for a while. But the money had been paid to the whores of Sheerness and any good that Drinkwater's largesse had achieved had long since evaporated. Somehow the affair at Juan Fernandez had crystallised a conviction that had come to him as he had held the tawny-haired Catriona in his arms on his departure from Edinburgh, the conviction that *Patrician* was unlucky and that she would never return home.

Captain Drinkwater had been more relieved than otherwise at the discovery of Witherspoon's sex. No captain, particularly one engaged on a distant cruise in the Pacific, relished the discovery of sodomitical relationships within his crew any more than he relished the problem of desertion. The fact that Witherspoon was a woman made Hogan's action understandable and lent a measure of reason to the twin absenteeism that stemmed from passion, not mutiny. What Drinkwater had dreaded when he learned of the failure of two hands to muster, was a sudden, unpredictable revolt among the men. His orders were difficult enough to execute without the ferment that such a disorder

55

would cause, a disorder which might threaten not merely his command, but his very life. He was not untouched by the tragedy that had happened beneath the waterfall, but he perceived again the workings of providence and when he had entered the initials *D.D.* against the two names in the ship's muster book, his sense of relief had been very real. In the margin provided for remarks, he had added: *Killed while resisting arrest, having first Run.*

It was a poor epitaph. A poetaster might have conjured up a romantic verse at the tragedy; a venal commander might have kept the two names on the ship's books and drawn the pay himself, or at least until he had repaid himself the cost of the sword he had lost in the pool beneath the waterfall. But Drinkwater felt only a further sadness that Hogan and Witherspoon had gone to join those damned souls who awaited judgement in some private limbo, watched over by the guardian angels of the Admiralty. Such, at least, had been the incongruous core of Mr Henderson's homily on the subject. Drinkwater had begun to doubt the wisdom of Their Lordships in soliciting the aid of the Established Church to subdue the convictions of men forced into His Britannic Majesty's Navy. Drinkwater considered such solecisms foolish; ignorant diversions from the grim realities of the sea-service. He was concluding his private remarks in his journal when he heard the cry from the masthead.

'He has a wind, by God!'

'By your leave, Mr Hill, a rest for my glass on that stanchion.'

'Of course sir . . . he has a wind . . .'

'So you said . . . a devil's wind, too, what d'you make of him?'

'I reserve my judgement, sir.'

'Eh? Oh, you refer to that fellow we saw off the Horn?' Drinkwater caught the stranger in his image glass. To whatever the sail belonged, it was not a black-hulled two-decker. 'By the spread of her masts and her stuns'ls, I'd wager on her being a frigate . . . and Spanish?'

'Yes . . . yes, I'd not dispute that, sir.'

'Spanish frigate, sir.'

Drinkwater looked aloft. In the mizen top Mr Frey looked

down, smiling broadly and Drinkwater was aware that the deck was crammed with officers and men milling about, awaiting news from the privileged few at posts of vantage or with glasses to their eyes. He caught the ripple of eagerness that greeted the news, saw the smiles and sensed, despite everything, the metamorphosis that transformed his ship at the sight of an enemy.

'Very well, Mr Frey, you may come down and hoist Spanish colours! Clear for action and beat to quarters!' Then he raised his glass again and studied the enemy, hull up now, crossing their bow from the west. 'Mr Frey should know a Don when he sees one, Mr Hill, given his time watching 'em at Cadiz . . . oh, for a breeze!'

'Would to God hers would carry down to us . . . she's seen us, throwing out a private signal.' Hill looked at the masthead pendant and at the dogvanes. They barely lifted in the light airs that slatted *Patrician*'s canvas.

'Shall I hoist out the boats and tow, sir?' asked Fraser, suddenly impatiently efficient.

'No, Mr Fraser, that'll exhaust the men . . .'

The marine drummer was beating the tattoo and the hands were scrambling about the ship. Below, the bulkheads were coming down and aloft the chain slings were being passed, while along the deck sand was being sprinkled and the gun-captains were overhauling their train tackles and their gun-locks. Above their heads fluttered a huge and unfamiliar ensign: the yellow and gold of Spain. Then Drinkwater had a happy inspiration.

'Mr Henderson!' The thin face of the chaplain turned towards him. The fellow was showing a very unclerical interest in the enemy. 'Do you *pray* for a wind, sir.'

Henderson frowned and Drinkwater saw the men pause in their duties and look aft, grinning.

'But sir, is that not blasphemy?'

'Do you do as I say, sir, *pray* for a wind, 'tis no more blasphemous than to pray for aid on any other occasion.'

Henderson looked doubtful and then began to mumble uncertainly: 'Oh most powerful and glorious Lord God, at whose command the winds blow . . .'

'D'you think it will work?' asked Hill, grinning like the mid-shipmen. Somewhere in the waist a man had begun to whistle and there came sounds of laughter.

'I don't know, but 'tis a powerful specific against dispirited men by the sound of it . . .'

'How goes the chase, Mr Fraser?'

'To windward, sir, like a wingèd bird.'

'I had no notion you had anything of the poet in you.'

''Tis not difficult on such a night, sir.'

'No.'

'It has a Homeric quality . . . the warm wind, the moon, and a windward chase.'

'Yes.'

They had got their wind, though whether it was attributable to the praying of the chaplain or the whistling that breached the naval regulations, was a matter for good-natured conjecture throughout the ship as the men settled down for a night sleeping at the guns. *Patrician* was a big ship, a heavy frigate, a razée, cut down from a sixty-four gun line-of-battle-ship, but she spread her canvas widely, extended her yards by studding sail booms and hoisted a skysail above her main royal when the occasion demanded.

'Turn!' Midshipman Belchambers turned the glass and the log-party watched the line reel out, dragged by the log-chip astern.

'Stop!' called the boy, the line was nipped, the peg jerked from the chip and the line hauled in.

'Nine knots, sir.'

'Very well . . . like a wingèd bird indeed, Mr Fraser.' Drink-water smiled in the darkness, sensing the embarrassed flush he had brought to the first lieutenant's cheeks. 'But do we gain on our chase?'

Fraser turned. 'Mr Belchambers . . . my quadrant, if you please.'

'Aye, aye, sir.' The boy ran off.

'How do you find our youngest addition?' Drinkwater asked.

'Eager and agile as a monkey, sir.'

'Hmm. But he's too young. There seems no shortage of such boys with parents eager enough to send 'em to damnation while they are still children. I doubt they can know what their offspring are condemned to endure.'

'Your own son is not destined for the sea-service, sir?'

'Not if I can find him a fat living in a good country parish!' Both men laughed as Belchambers returned with Fraser's quadrant. The first lieutenant hoisted himself up on the rail, bracing himself against the main shrouds and took the angle subtended by the white shape ahead of them.

Drinkwater watched. The pale pyramid of canvas would be much more difficult to see within the confinement of the telescope and it would take Fraser a moment or two to obtain a good reading. Drinkwater waited patiently. *Patrician* lay over to the breeze, close hauled on the larboard tack. Above him the studding sails bellied out, spreading the ship's canvas and bending the booms.

The sky was clear of cloud, studded with stars and the round orb of a full moon which laid a dancing path of silver light upon the water. The breeze was strong enough to curl the sea into small, breaking crests and these, from time to time, were feathered with phosphorescence.

Fraser jumped down from the rail.

'Aye, sir, I can detect a slight enlargement o' the angle subtended by the enemy.'

'Good; but it's going to be a long chase and this moonlight will discourage him from trying to make a sharp turn . . . 'tis a pity he rumbled us so early.'

'I expect he knew well enough what ships to expect hereabouts.'

'Yes, the Dons are apt to regard the Pacific Ocean as their own.'

They fell to an easy and companionable pacing of the deck. It was astonishing the difference the chase made to the atmosphere on board. All grumbling had gone. Men moved with a new-found confidence and bore themselves cheerfully even in the dark hours. There was a liveliness in the responses of the helmsman, a perkiness about those of the watch ordered to perform the many small tasks as the officers strove in succession to get the best out of the ship. Fraser sought to gain something from the captain's obvious desire to chat.

'Sir . . . I was wondering if you would be kind enough to confide in me. As to our orders, sir . . . if . . . er . . .'

'If anything should happen to me in the next few hours you'd like to know how to act . . . I know, I know . . . damn it, Mr Fraser, the truth of the matter is that I ain't sure myself. We've to damage the Dons and their trade, to be sure, but our main purpose here is to prevent what Their Lordships are pleased to call "incursion into the Pacific" by the Russians.'

'The *Russians*, sir?'

'Ah, I see that surprises you. Well they have settlements in Alaska, though what possible influence that might have upon the course of the war is something of a mystery . . .'

'And we are making for Alaska now, sir?'

'In a manner of speaking. It seemed the best place to begin exhibiting His Majesty's flag.' Drinkwater felt Fraser's bewilderment. Perhaps he should have confided in the younger man earlier in the voyage, but Fraser had had his own problems and the life of a first lieutenant was, Drinkwater knew, not an easy one.

'You are too young to remember the Spanish Armament in ninety-one, eh?'

'I remember it vaguely, sir. Wasn't war with Spain imminent?'

'Yes, the Channel Fleet were commissioned, a lucky thing as it happened, since, as I recall, we were at war with the French Republic within a year. Let me refresh your mind . . . when Cook's seamen brought high-quality furs from the polar seas off Alaska and Kamchatka and sold them in Canton they attracted the notice of the Honourable East India Company's factors. A former naval officer named Mears . . . a lieutenant, I believe he was, together with a merchant master named Tippin took out two ships across the North Pacific on a fur-hunting expedition. Tippin was cast up on Kamchatka, but Mears wintered somewhere in the islands. The following spring, about eighty-eight, or eighty-nine I forget which, he discovered Nootka Sound, a fine fiord on the west coast of what is now known as Vancouver Island and he opened a fur trade between the Indians indigent upon the coast, and the Company's factors at Canton. In ninety the Spanish sent a naval force, seized the four British ships anchored in the sound, but left two belonging to the United States of America. The British ships were plundered and their seamen sent, on Spanish orders, to Canton in the American bottoms. Once the "haughty Don" had disposed of us, he planted his flag and claimed the whole coast across the whole bight to China!'

'Good Lord!'

'At home we armed for war, but eventually the Dons climbed down. The *sanculottes* obliged us by executing King Louis and depriving His Most Catholic Majesty of the support of His Most Christian ally . . . Their Lordships sent George Vancouver out to receive the surrender of the Spanish commander, a Don Quadra, or some such, and Vancouver spent the next year or so surveying . . .'

'And now we go out to prevent some such measures being repeated by the Russkies?'

'That would seem to be about the size of the thing, Mr Fraser.'

There was a brief silence between them, broken only by the low moan of the wind, the hiss of the sea rushing alongside the frigate, the creak of her fabric and some chatter amidships, where the watch congregated, chaffing the dozing gun-crews.

'That ship we saw off the Horn, sir . . . I believe you expressed the opinion she was a Russian.'

'Ah, Hill's been gossiping again, has he?' Drinkwater chuckled good-naturedly. 'Yes, yes I believe her to have been bound for the Pacific, like ourselves . . . if she was ordered out as soon as hostilities were declared between Petersburg and London, she would be expected to reach the extremity of America at the same time as ourselves.'

'She was a two-decker, sir.'

'Yes. And if there's close co-operation between the Dons and the Russians . . .' Drinkwater let the import of the sentence sink in by implication.

61

'I begin to see your problem, sir.'

'Well, Mr Fraser,' remarked Drinkwater drily, 'if I'm knocked up when we overhaul that fellow ahead of us, it'll be *your* problem.'

The wind backed a point towards dawn. Midshipman Wickham came below to where Drinkwater lay on his cot, fully dressed.

'. . . It's increasing too, sir, Mr Quilhampton says, going large we've the legs of him, sir. She reeled off twelve at the last cast of the log.'

Drinkwater yawned. 'Twelve, eh? Very well, Mr Wickham. I'll be up directly.'

Quilhampton was worried when Drinkwater reached the quarterdeck a few moments later.

'She's carrying too much canvas, sir . . .'

Drinkwater gauged the strength of the wind and the feel of the ship beneath his boot-soles. Yes, there was a tendency of the ship to lay down, drowning her lee bow and building up a resisting wave there. He looked ahead. They were overhauling the Spanish ship perceptibly; it would be foolish to risk her escaping by carrying away spars aloft when they might delay the action an hour and break their fasts.

'Very well, Mr Q. Rouse all hands and take in the stun's'ls. Pass the word to the cook to fire up the galley range and boil some skillygolee, and the purser to order "up spirits"; we've a brisk forenoon ahead of us!'

Drinkwater watched the ship burst into life. It was damned odd what the appearance of an enemy did to a ship's company.

'Gives 'em a sense of purpose, I presume,' he muttered to himself, breathing in the fresh air of the dawn and watching the red ball of the sun break the eastern horizon ahead of them, dragging its lower limb like some huge jelly-fish, as though reluctant to leave its resting place, and climb up into the lightening sky.

And then he remembered he had left his sword in the pool beneath the waterfall on Más-a-Fuera.

The Spanish Prisoners

Drinkwater hesitated in the space his cabin usually occupied. The bulkheads were down, the chairs and table had been removed together with his cot, sea-chest, books and the two lockers that turned the after end of *Patrician*'s gun-deck into a private refuge. Even the chequer-painted canvas that served for a carpet had been rolled away. Only the white paint on the ship's side and the deck-head, gleaming in the reflected light that came in from the gaping stern windows from the ship's wake and sent patterns dancing across it, served to remind its new occupants that it was the hallowed quarters of *Patrician*'s captain. For the purpose of the cabin now became apparent; with the removal of the furniture the obtrusive 24-pounder cannon stood revealed and even the lead sink that served Drinkwater's steward in his pantry was filled with water in readiness to sponge those after guns.

'Where's my cox'n?' he asked of the waiting gun-crews who eyed the unexpected intrusion with some wariness.

''Ere, zur . . .' Tregembo shuffled aft, his old face seamed by a ragged scar, his back stiff from former floggings. 'You'm be looking for this . . .' It was a statement, not a question, and Tregembo held out a sword, a new hanger, by the look of it, with the lion's head pommel of a commissioned officer's weapon.

'Who lent it to you?'

'Mr Mylchrist, zur . . .'

'Ah, yes, thank you, Tregembo. And my pistols?'

'Your clerk's taken 'em to the gunner, zur, for new flints. I tried knapping the old uns but they was too far gone . . . 'ere's your sword-belt . . .'

Drinkwater grinned. He could imagine the Quaker's distaste for his task. He pulled the sword from its scabbard. Beneath the langets he read the maker's name: *Thurkle and Skinner*.

'I must thank Mr Mylchrist . . . have my pistols taken to the quarterdeck as soon as they are ready.'

'Aye, aye, zur.'

Drinkwater passed through the berth deck to the orlop. In the stygian gloom he found Lallo with his loblolly boys laying out the catlings and curettes, the saws and pincers of his grisly trade. A tub waited to collect the refuse of battle, the amputated legs and arms of its victims. Drinkwater suppressed a shudder at the thought of ending up on the rough table Lallo's mates had prepared. For a moment he stood at the foot of the ladder, accustoming himself to the mephitic air and watching the preparations of the surgeon. Lamplight, barely sustained here, in the bowels of the ship, danced in pale yellow intensity upon the bright steel of the instruments and illuminated the white of Lallo's bowls and bandages. The contrast between these inadequate preparations below for rescuing men from death and the bright anticipation of the gun-deck above struck Drinkwater with a sudden sharpness. He threw off the thought and coughed to draw attention to himself.

'Ah, sir . . . ?' Lallo straightened up under the low beams.

'You are ready, Mr Lallo?'

'Ready, aye, ready, sir,' said Lallo, somewhat facetiously and Drinkwater caught the foul gleam of Skeete's caried grin.

'How is Mr Mylchrist today?'

From the far end of the space Mylchrist lifted a pale face from the solitary hammock that swung just beneath the heavy beams.

'Much better, sir, thank you . . . I wish I could assist, sir . . .'

'You stay there, Mr Mylchrist . . . you've had a long fever and Mr Wickham is doing your duty at the guns, you wouldn't deny him his chance of glory, would you now?'

Mylchrist smiled weakly. 'No sir.'

'I promise you yours before too long.'

'Thank you sir.'

'And thank you for the loan of your sword.'

'The least I can do . . .'

64

Drinkwater smiled down at the wounded officer. Mylchrist had been very ill, avoiding gangrene only by providence and the application of a lead-acetate dressing whose efficacy Drinkwater had learned from the surgeon of the *Bucentaure* when held prisoner on Villeneuve's flagship.

'The employment of your sword guarantees you a share in the day's profits, Mr Mylchrist.'

Mylchrist smiled his gratitude at the captain's jest. If they received prize- or head-money for their work in the coming hours, the third lieutenant's share for a fine Spanish frigate would better his annual salary.

Drinkwater returned to the quarterdeck to find Derrick awaiting him. The Quaker held the two pistols as though they were infected and it was obvious he had tried to leave them in the charge of someone else. The others were enjoying his discomfiture. Fraser was positively grinning and the first lieutenant's levity had encouraged the midshipmen and the gun crews waiting at the 18-pounders on the quarterdeck. Even the sober Hill, busy with his quadrant determining the rate they were overhauling the Spanish ship, seemed amused.

'Thank you Derrick.' Drinkwater took the two pistols, checked the locks were primed and stuck them in his belt.

'Mr Meggs loaded them for you, Captain.'

Drinkwater looked at the Quaker. In the months they had been together he had conceived a respect for the man. Derrick had refused to call him 'sir', tactfully avoiding the familiar 'Friend' of his faith, compromising with 'Captain'. Drinkwater did not object. The man was diligent and efficient in his duties and only took advantage of his position in so much as he asked to borrow the occasional book from Drinkwater's meagre library. When he had borrowed Brodrick's *History of the War in the Netherlands*, Drinkwater had raised an inquisitive eyebrow.

'Your interest in that subject surprises me, Derrick.'

'A physician studies disease, Captain, in order to defeat it, not because of his liking for it.'

Drinkwater acknowledged his own defeat and smiled wryly.

'Well sir,' he said in a low voice, 'the moment has come . . . you had better go below to the orlop. The surgeon has no assistant, only his two loblolly boys, perhaps you might be able to help.'

'I would not have my courage doubted, Captain,' Derrick flicked quick glances at the inhabitants of the quarterdeck, 'but I thought my post was at your side.'

Drinkwater had never had the luxury of a clerk before and had given the matter little thought, though he recollected Derrick's post in action was 'to assist as directed'.

'Very well, Derrick, but it is glory on the quarterdeck. Courage is a quality you will find at Mr Lallo's side.' He turned and raised his voice, 'Very well, Mr Fraser? Mr Mount?'

'All ready, sir, ship's company fed, fires doused, spirits issued and the men at their battle-stations.'

'My men likewise, sir,' added Mount.

'A little over a mile, sir,' said Hill, looking up from his calculations.

Drinkwater cast an embracing glance along the deck and aloft.

'Very well. Pass the word to make ready. We'll try a ranging shot.'

But there was no need. A puff of smoke shredded to leeward of the Spanish frigate's stern and a plume of water rose close under *Patrician*'s larboard bow. The wind-whipped spray pattered aft and wet them.

'*Olé!*' remarked Mount, dashing the stuff from his eyes.

'We shall make a running fight of it, then,' said Drinkwater raising his glass.

For the next hours they endured shot from the Spaniard's stern chasers, trying to gauge the weight of metal of the balls. Drinkwater held his hand; to return fire meant luffing to bring a bow chaser to bear on their quarry; to luff meant to lose ground. The morning was already well advanced by the time they could read the enemy's name across her stern: *Santa Monica*.

Drinkwater spent the time pacing up and down, occupying the leeward side of the quarterdeck where he had a direct view of the Spanish ship and felt no discomfort from the down-draught from the maintopsail in such a balmy climate. From time to time he paused, rested his glass against a hammock stanchion and studied the *Santa Monica*. She was a relatively new ship, built of the Honduran mahogany that made Spanish ships immensely strong and the envy of their worn opponents. Her spars, too, gleamed with the richness of new pine and Drinkwater recalled Vancouver's words about the slopes of the coasts around Nootka Sound 'abounding in pines, spruces and firs of immense height and girth, being entirely suitable for the masting of ships'.

Slowly their view of the enemy altered. As they overhauled her, they began to see the whole length of the *Santa Monica*'s larboard side. Studying the Spaniard, Drinkwater could see her gun barrels foreshortening with a greater rapidity than they overtook. His opponent was preparing a disabling broadside as soon as all his larboard guns bore, while Drinkwater was hampered by his starboard broadside being on the leeward side of the ship. Even with full elevation, the list of the deck was such that his cannon might have trouble hitting their target. In addition there would be the problem of water pouring in through the gun-ports as *Patrician* lay down under the fiercer gusts of a strong breeze that was fast working itself up into a gale. Yet Drinkwater could not reduce the list by taking in sail without losing his chance.

If the Spanish commander succeeded in his design of disabling *Patrician* his escape was guaranteed. If he was a man of unusual energy the consequences might be worse, he could conceivably hold off and rake *Patrician*, for all Drinkwater's superiority in weight of metal. The vision of Lallo's instruments of agony and those empty limb-tubs, sprung morbidly into his mind's eye. With an effort of will he dismissed the thought. He would have to think of some counter-stroke and act upon it with a nicety of timing, if he was to disarm the Don's intention. For a moment longer he studied the *Santa Monica* as her bearing opened upon their bow with an almost hypnotic slowness. Then he shut his telescope with a snap.

'Mr Hill! Mr Fraser! A moment of your time, if you please . . .'

*   *   *

He was not a moment too soon. So parallel were the courses of the two ships that the angle of bearing for both of them to fire upon the other with any chance of achieving maximum effect, was coincident within a degree or two. Drinkwater had noticed an officer bent over an instrument by the Spaniard's larboard dogvane and made his preparations accordingly.

'Run out the guns!'

When he had passed his orders he heard the rumble of *Patrician*'s 24-pounders as their forward-trained muzzles poked from the heeling frigate's side. His heart was beating, hammering in his chest as, beside him, Fraser sighted along the barrel of one of the quarterdeck eighteens.

'About two degrees to go, sir . . .'

Drinkwater grunted. There had been some movement on the *Santa Monica*'s deck at the appearance of *Patrician*'s guns. Would his opponent react?

For a long moment the question seemed to hang, then he saw the officer by the dog-vane bend again. Perhaps they too were waiting in suspense.

Leaning over, the two ships rushed along, *Patrician* ranging slowly up to windward of the Spanish ship, gradually overlapping her larboard quarter close enough to confuse the sea running between them. Above their decks the yards were braced hard-up upon the leeward catharpings, the sails strained against the strength of the wind, driving the foaming hulls relentlessly through the water. From the high-cocked peaks of their spanker gaffs the opposing ensigns of their contending nations snapped viciously, while beneath them the lines of men at their guns, the groups crouching below the rails ready to haul on bowlines and braces, the red-coated marines aiming their muskets from the barricades of the hammock nettings, and the knots of officers on the quarterdecks and at their posts throughout the ships, waited for the orders from the two captains that commanded the destinies of five hundred souls.

'Infernal machines . . .' Drinkwater heard someone whisper, half-admiringly, and smiled grimly when he realised it was Derrick, caught up in the stirring excitement of this insanity.

'Bearing coming on sir,' said Fraser matter-of-factly, still bent over the dispart sight of the 18-pounder.

Drinkwater saw the Spanish officer by the *Santa Monica*'s larboard dogvane straighten up purposively. Without taking his glass from his eye he gave the order: 'Fire!'

Gun-locks snapped like the crackle of grass as a squall strikes, then came the immense roar of artillery, the trembling rise of the deck as the ship reacted to the recoil and the sudden burst of activity throughout *Patrician* that followed his order. On the gun-deck below, the heavy 24-pounders belched flame and shot, trundling inboard and snapping their tackles together as their crews swarmed round them, sponging and reloading the monstrous things. On quarterdeck and fo'c's'le the 18-pounders and the brutal 42-pounder carronades swept the deck with powder smoke and the enemy with a hail of iron and langridge.

'Up helm!'

Behind Drinkwater, Hill was standing by the wheel, shouting through his speaking trumpet while Fraser, released from his duty bent over the dispart sight, was leaping across the deck whence Drinkwater followed him.

'Smartly there, my lads, stamp and go!'

Patrician's bow swung towards the *Santa Monica* as the Spaniard's hull disappeared momentarily behind the smoke of her own broadside. The fog of her discharging guns would, for a moment, blind her officers to much of his manoeuvre.

Above his head the braces were easing the yards and then there was a rending crash from forward. Drinkwater felt a slight tremble through the hull, but *Patrician*'s turn was unimpeded and then, leaning from the larboard hance, he could see the stern of the *Santa Monica*.

There was a rent in her spanker and her ensign was fluttering down, its halliards having parted as *Patrician*'s jib-boom slashed across her deck. Her stern boat was a wreck and hung down from the davits by a single fall.

'Larbowlines . . . !'

Drinkwater's voice was drowned in the thunder of the larboard guns, fired by their captains as they bore, double shotted and topped with canister they blasted into the starboard quarter of the Spaniard as *Patrician* sliced obliquely across the *Santa Monica*'s stern.

As the smoke cleared Drinkwater caught a glimpse of Comley, the boatswain, wielding an axe on the knightheads, where he fought to free *Patrician* of the obstruction of her smashed jib-boom.

'Hard on the wind again, Mr Hill!'

'Aye, aye, sir, full an' bye it is!'

Patrician turned back to larboard again. She had given ground to the enemy and was now in her lee, but her guns still bore and they were being worked like fury by their crews; flame and smoke roared from her larboard ports as the cannon pointed high. A quick glance aloft showed Drinkwater that barely a shot of the enemy's had told, that their most serious damage had been sustained forward, from their own manoeuvre in crossing the *Santa Monica*'s stern to rake her. Drinkwater dismissed that, raising his glass to assess the damage his ruse had effected.

The enemy were hoisting their shot-away ensign into the mizen rigging, and holes were appearing in her sails, but hardly a gun replied to *Patrician* from *Santa Monica*'s starboard broadside. Then, as he watched he heard a cheer. Shifting his glass from the enemy's starboard quarter where he could see the splintered remains of her gallery, he caught the toppling main-topmast. For almost a minute it stopped falling, leaning at a drunken angle, held by its rigging to the fore and mizen masts, and then it broke free, crashing downwards and bringing the mizen topgallant with it. The Patricians were whooping about their guns and the officers on the quarterdeck wore broad grins. Drinkwater could see they were rapidly shooting ahead of the Spaniard.

'Stand by to tack ship!'

But Drinkwater had no need to range up to windward, subjecting the *Santa Monica* to a further raking broadside from ahead. As he watched, he saw the red and gold lowered from the mizen rigging in token of submission.

'She strikes, sir!'

The news was reported from a score of mouths and more wild cheering broke out from the exhilarated crew of the *Patrician*. All the pent-up frustration of the past months, all the ill-feeling and resentment, the hopelessness of pressed men, the self-pity of dispirited lovers and the petty hatreds of men confined together for weeks on end, seemed burst like an abcess by the violent catharsis of action.

His eyes met those of the sailing master. 'I think our sailing was of sufficient superiority on this occasion, Mr Hill,' Drinkwater remarked, repressing his sudden triumphant burst of exuberance.

'For a Spaniard, sir . . .' replied Hill cautiously and Drinkwater felt the reproach in the older man's tone. He nodded.

'Yes. You are right; for a Spaniard . . .'

They did not board the prize until the following morning, for the wind threw up too rough a sea for them to launch a boat safely. And when they were successful they discovered their triumph to be short-lived.

Their first broadside had been fired from the starboard guns on a lee-roll. The iron shot had hulled the *Santa Monica*, and damaged her so badly that by the following noon it was clear that her pumps were unable to stem the inrush of water. She began to founder under the feet of her prize crew. Lieutenant Quilhampton, sent aboard the Spanish frigate as prize-master, sent this news back to the *Patrician* by Midshipman Frey.

Reluctantly Drinkwater ordered the prize abandoned and by that evening found himself host to two hundred unwilling and darkly threatening prisoners. They consisted of Spaniards, mission-educated Indians and a large proportion of *mestizos*, a lean and hard-bitten lot led by a tall, gaunt officer who wore the epaulettes of a captain in the Royal Navy of Spain.

'I am Captain Nathaniel Drinkwater, *Señor*, and I compliment you on the gallantry of your defence. I regret the loss of your ship.' He bowed formally and took his opponent's offered sword.

He met the Spaniard's eyes and found in them more than resignation at the fortunes of war. The deep-set expression of anger and hatred seemed to burn out from the very soul of the man, and Drinkwater recognised in the lined and swarthy face

71

the man who had bent over the *Santa Monica*'s rail and whose order to fire Drinkwater had pre-empted by a split-second.

'Don Jorge Méliton Rubalcava . . .' The Spanish commander broke off. Drinkwater had no idea whether Rubalcava understood English from this bald announcement.

'Have I your word that you will not raise a revolt, Captain Rubalcava?' Drinkwater asked, turning the sword-hilt and offering it back to its owner. Rubalcava hesitated and swung to an accompanying officer whom Drinkwater assumed to be his second-in-command. But the other seemed only to be awaiting the completion of the formalities of surrender, before declaring himself a greater man than Rubalcava.

'He was throwing papers overboard, sir,' Quilhampton volunteered, 'a fellow of some consequence.'

Drinkwater was watching the two Spaniards. They seemed to be in some disagreement and Rubalcava's anger was suppressed with difficulty. His companion, however, turned to Drinkwater with an unruffled expression, and addressed him in strongly accented and broken English.

'*Capitán*, Don Jorge he give you his parole and express for him the honour of you give his sword. *Gracias*.' The sentence was terminated by a low bow which Drinkwater awkwardly returned.

'You speak excellent English, *señor*, perhaps you could tell me whom I have the honour of addressing?'

'I . . . Don Alejo Joaquin Arguello de Salas, aide-de-camp to His Excellence, Don José Henrique Martin Arguello de Salas, *Commandante* for San Francisco . . .'

Again there was an exchange of bows.

'Perhaps gentlemen,' Drinkwater invited, 'you would do me the honour of dining with me and my officers this evening.'

'*Gracias* . . . what is it you think to do, *Capitán*?

'We can discuss that matter later, gentlemen. And now, if you will excuse me, I have much to attend to in seeing to the comfortable accommodation of your men.'

There was a further mutual acknowledgement and Drinkwater found himself favouring the simple directness of Derrick's mode of address above this extravagant over-worked charade of elaborate bows. He ordered the incredulous Quaker to see the Spanish officers quartered below and turned to Mount to issue orders for the confinement of their seamen.

Mount concealed his grin with difficulty. The bobbing head and sweeping gestures of the quarterdeck had provoked an outburst of merriment along the deck as ill-concealed as the hostility of Captain Rubalcava.

CHAPTER 6 March 1808

Of Wine and Women

'Your allies . . . they make for you good wine . . .' Arguello
raised his glass and held it so that the candles shone through
the rich, dark Portuguese *bual*. Drinkwater had a few dozen
bottles of the Madeira, his only really decent wine, bought
from the commander of an East Indiaman which had been lying at the Nore. Its broaching was the culmination of a satis-
fying meal the main course of which had consisted of the last
pig from Juan Fernandez. The unfortunate animal had lived
on scraps in the manger forward of the ship's breakwater and
been slaughtered before they went into action.

'*Gracias*, Don Alejo . . . you have the same name as the
Commandante . . .' Drinkwater phrased it as a question.

'*Sí*, 'e is my old brother.'

The wine seemed to have relaxed Don Alejo, though
Rubalcava's dark features continued to brood on his defeat.
Despite its quality it had been a difficult meal and it was
obvious that neither Fraser nor Quilhampton had enjoyed it.
Out of courtesy they had drunk toasts to their respective
sovereigns and to their own mutual gallantry. There had been
a stilted enquiry into the *Santa Monica*'s losses that revealed
some difference of opinion between the two Spaniards, and
Drinkwater was becoming suspicious about the Spanish
frigate's task. He was toying with various expedients as to
how to pursue his enquiries when Rubalcava spoke with a
sudden, low urgency to Arguello. Don Alejo nodded, leaned
forward to light a thin cigar from the candles and blew smoke
at the deckhead.

'*Capitán* . . . please, I ask you question . . . what you do with *Capitán* Rubalcava and his men, eh? For you too much prisoner a big . . .'

'Risk?'

'*Sí, Capitán*, a big risk.'

'Of course, Don Alejo, I do not make war upon unfortunate and gallant opponents. Assure Don Rubalcava that I am at his service. To deprive a brave officer of his ship is enough injury to inflict upon any man of spirit . . . where does the good captain wish to be landed?'

It took Arguello a few moments to digest this noble speech, moments in which Fraser writhed in his chair and Quilhampton fixed his commander with an odd, penetrating stare, filling the glass in front of him and hurrying the decanter round the table.

Another low exchange took place between the two Spanish officers. It was clear that Rubalcava had a point of view; it was also clear that Arguello disagreed with it. His exchange with *Santa Monica*'s captain again became sharp, though once the naval officer had been suppressed and had relapsed into a tense and bitter silence, Arguello turned to his host with an air of unimpaired and courtly civility.

'*Capitán* Rubalcava thank you for your much kind express of honour and receive it . . . it is for me to ask you to take us to San Francisco . . .'

Rubalcava drew in his breath, in obvious opposition to this proposal, and there was something tense about Arguello now, something eagerly expectant, as though he wished Drinkwater to answer enthusiastically in the affirmative. Drinkwater met his gaze, as though reluctantly considering his request.

'Of course . . . you will have truce . . . I will, myself, see that you have water . . . anything . . .'

The gesture with the cigar was airily obliging; Drinkwater watched the heavy trail of blue smoke languidly lift in the hot air around the candles. Arguello was begging.

San Francisco; that was where Arguello wished to go. Rubalcava had other ideas. Why? And where had *Santa Monica* been bound when *Patrician* intercepted her?

'Where were you from Don Alejo? The Philippines?'

'*Sí, Capitán*, Manila . . . excellent for tobacco . . .' He held up

75

the cigar and smoke dribbled from his mouth.

'And where were you bound, Don Jorge?' Drinkwater flung the question directly at the Spanish captain. It was a phrase which any seaman would comprehend, even in a foreign language, and, while Drinkwater spoke with professional interest, yet he sought to exploit the rift he had detected between the two men.

Rubalcava's dark head came up and his eyes flashed at Drinkwater with a ferocity that reminded Drinkwater of an Arab he had known once in the Red Sea. Rubalcava pronounced his destination with a kind of contempt, as though he had thought no more of it before his capture than he did afterwards: 'San Francisco.'

'And the purpose of your voyage, *señor?*' Drinkwater thrust the question quickly; he was entitled to ask it.

'*Aviso* . . .' Drinkwater recalled the reported destruction of documents.

'A despatch vessel, with Don Alejo as your courier . . . ?'

'*Qué?* Don Alejo . . . ?' Rubalcava's voice tailed off as Arguello broke in.

'*Sí, Capitán*, I was courier . . . it is my duty . . . I am for the *Commandante* of San Francisco, his chief courier.'

A hiss of dissimulation came from the subsiding Rubalcava.

'You speak excellent English, Don Alejo, please accept my compliments,' Drinkwater coaxed.

'I was prisoner some time, taken off Cadiz but I make exchange. I live at Waltham Abbey.'

'How very interesting . . . perhaps you wish to retire now, gentlemen . . . ?'

Drinkwater rose and his silent officers sprang obediently to their feet. 'Mr Quilhampton, please be so good as to see our guests to their quarters before returning for your orders.'

Quilhampton hesitated, perceived Drinkwater's meaning and acknowledged the instruction. As the Spaniards withdrew from the cabin bowing, Drinkwater motioned Fraser to stay. They were about to leave the cabin when Arguello halted and indicated the portrait of Elizabeth, replaced lovingly by Tregembo on the re-established bulkhead.

76

'Is this beautiful lady your wife, Captain?'

'Yes . . .' Drinkwater watched Arguello address a remark to Rubalcava and he stiffened, sensing an insult, but it was obvious that it referred to the disagreement that existed between the two men, for Rubalcava's expression bore no trace of that complicity of men sharing a coarse jest at another's expense. Nevertheless Drinkwater bridled at the odd reference to Elizabeth.

'Don Alejo!' he called sharply after the departing Spaniard. Arguello turned in the doorway.

'*Capitán?*'

'It is not permitted to smoke beyond my quarters!'

Arguello shrugged, dropped the stub of his cigar and with an elegantly booted toe, ground the thing into the painted canvas on the deck.

Fraser expelled a pent-up breath as the door closed behind the prisoners.

'Another glass, Mr Fraser, you've earned it by your patience, by God. I've passed word to Tregembo to sling you a hammock in here while Arguello occupies your cabin. Mount has the business in hand?'

'Yes, sir. Mount won't let them move. We've the dagoes battened well under hatches.'

'Good. We should be rid of them in . . .' Drinkwater dragged a chart onto the table from the drawer beneath and cast a quick look at it, 'three days, if this wind holds.'

There was a knock at the cabin door. 'Come in!'

Quilhampton rejoined them and Drinkwater pushed the decanter towards him and re-seated himself. 'Well, gentlemen, what did you make of that?'

'There's bad blood between them. Rubalcava doesn't want to go to San Francisco, that's clear enough.'

'Good, Mr Q. I agree . . . but he didn't want to go to San Francisco *before* they fell in with us, which argues a longer animosity than has been caused by our unexpected appearance in the Pacific.'

'Perhaps they just didna get along too well, sir,' said Fraser.

Drinkwater nodded and refilled his glass. 'But from his

latitude and course we can suppose their landfall at least was San Francisco, or the coast thereabouts. Now it is one thing to assume that they were not friends, but let us suppose you are a Spanish officer, bearing despatches from the authorities in the Philippine Islands. Where do you suppose you would be taking them?'

'To the principal naval base in the Americas?' said Fraser.

'Yes, I think so. And that is not San Francisco. That is Acapulco . . .'

'For which he had a fair wind.'

'Correct, Mr Q. Now, to continue the hypothesis; suppose a British frigate appears out of the blue. What would you do, Mr Fraser?'

'If I was running?'

'Yes, as he was.'

'Well, I suppose I would see it as paramount to inform my superiors. From what you told me earlier about the "Armament" of ninety-one they seem to resent intruders in the Pacific.'

'Exactly. And to do that you would lay a course for Acapulco, or Panama, but *not* San Francisco.'

A ruminative silence fell on the three officers which Drinkwater broke.

'So, gentlemen, we have Don Alejo Arguello determined, for some reason, to get to San Francisco *at all costs*, rather than inform his principals at Acapulco that a British frigate is loose in the Pacific.'

'But, sir, though I dinna disagree with your argument, *his principal* is at San Francisco, he said he was aide to the *Commandante* there . . .'

'Who is also his "old brother".' They laughed at the Spaniard's awkward phrase. 'Well perhaps that argues some collusion, who knows?' Drinkwater yawned. 'It's all pure supposition,' he added dismissively. 'I think it's time we turned in. I suggest you both keep loaded pistols handy. I've no mind to lose the ship while I sleep.'

It was an uneasy three days. Every morning and evening the Spaniards were brought on deck in batches, guarded by the marines and allowed to air themselves in the sunshine. The *Santa Monica's* officers were herded in sullen little groups and quartered in odd spaces. Curiously, the presence of the Spanish prisoners improved the morale of *Patrician's* people. The sight of others, more unfortunate than themselves, over whom they could enjoy a sense of triumph, seemed a tonic to their spirits. They did not worry over-much about the loss of prize-money asserting, so Drinkwater heard, that since the proportional loss fell most heavily on the officers, it was a greater hardship to them. There might have been a mutinous component in this dog-in-the-manger attitude, but if there was it was accepted as being part of the black humour of Jack, and to be overlooked. Certainly it amused, rather than alarmed Drinkwater who, as he expressed himself to Fraser, 'had been too much knocked about in the sea-service to do more than acknowledge the rough justice of the men's opinion'.

The officers themselves had little time to dwell on their ill-luck, for the presence of two hundred prisoners left them no time for brooding. Fraser and Quilhampton shared Drinkwater's cabin, a circumstance which exasperated them all despite the curtain that Tregembo had hung about the captain's cot-space, for what men most desire aboard ship is real privacy. No one on board was sorry when the masthead lookout raised the cry of land and an hour later the blue trace of tree-clad hills surmounted by a necklace of cloud lay on the eastern horizon.

Drinkwater was pacing the long quarterdeck, reluctant host to Arguello who walked beside him maintaining a difficult conversation.

'Capitan Rubalcava and myself, we were much surprise to see your ship, *Capitán* Drinkwater.' Arguello had been at obvious pains to improve his fluency in English during his captivity. 'You come to make war upon His Most Catholic Majesty's dominions?'

'You did not expect a British ship in the North Pacific, Don Alejo?'

Arguello shrugged. The gesture, though non-committal, was eloquently negative.

'I was five hundred miles from any of His Most Catholic

79

Majesty's dominions, Don Alejo.' Drinkwater stopped pacing and turned to the Spaniard, watching for his response. Again there came the shrug. 'If I wished, I might have devastated the trade of Peru, Panama . . .' It was Drinkwater's turn to shrug and wave his arm to the south, as though the whole Pacific seaboard of America lay at his mercy.

'So *Capitán*, you come to the Pacific, you do not attack our trade ships, you keep from the land so we do not know you have come. I ask myself why, eh? I think you come to make bigger trouble. I see *Capitán* Vancouver come. I am with Quadra when we made to leave Nootka . . . now you come back.'

Arguello's face was a mixture of dislike, frustration and eager inquiry. It seemed a good fiction to encourage. Nothing as positive came with his orders; as usual governmental parsimony prevented the effort of colonising. All he had to do was to prevent others from accomplishing it, yet such a firmly implanted suspicion in Spanish minds might work to his advantage. He smiled, tight-lipped and read the gratification in Don Alejo's eyes.

'You may find, *Capitán*, more difficult than you think . . .'

'Perhaps,' Drinkwater said dismissively, 'but tell me about *your* voyage, Don Alejo. What was the purpose of your voyage?' He lowered his voice with the air of a conspirator and saw Don Alejo's glance shift to the figure of Rubalcava, leaning disconsolately against the rail, gazing ahead at the approaching shoreline. 'I see that Captain Rubalcava does not wish to come to San Francisco . . .'

He caught the quick, shifting glance of surprise that Alejo shot him glaze with dissimulation. Then Don Alejo raised his hands in an urbane gesture of helplessness. 'As the French say, *Capitán, cherchez la femme.*'

'A woman? Ah, I see, between you . . . I see . . .'

The high-flown theories of grand strategy propounded in his cabin a few nights earlier dissolved in the face of earthier causes. Don Alejo looked puzzled and then laughed, an unfeigned amusement that made Drinkwater slightly uncomfortable and Rubalcava look up from the rail.

'No, no, *Capitán*, not between us . . . *Capitán* Rubalcava does not want to come to San Francisco because of the *hija* of Don José, my brother . . .'

'*Hija?*'

'*Sí* . . . er, I do not know how you say in English, er . . . ?'

A flash of intuition crossed Drinkwater's mind. He recalled the jibe Don Alejo had made at Rubalcava indicating the portrait of Elizabeth on his cabin bulkhead. Arguello had been taunting the Spanish captain. Rubalcava was clearly being put in his place.

'Your brother has a daughter.'

'*Sí*, daughter . . . Rubalcava wishes to marry the Doña Ana Maria Conchita . . . it is impossible.'

'Impossible? The lady is already promised?'

'*Sí Capitán*, and *Capitán* Rubalcava is not high-born . . .'

Drinkwater looked across the deck at the lounging Spanish officer.

'Rubalcava has much hate in his heart, much hate. And you have destroyed his ship, *Capitán* . . . in Acapulco . . .'

Don Alejo ended his explanation there, the words tailing off into that expressive, Hispanic shrug of immense possibilities, and Drinkwater understood. In Acapulco were the means of Rubalcava's revenge.

San Francisco

Under her huge topsails *Patrician* ghosted inwards between the two great headlands that guarded the entrance of San Francisco bay. Half a league apart the high, tree-clad steeps of Bonita and Lobos Points rose sheer from the sea on either side of the frigate as the onshore breeze wafted her eastwards; the blue water chuckled beneath her round bow and trailed astern. Small sea-birds dipped in her wake, screaming and fighting for the minute creatures her passage disturbed, a contrast to the rigidly ordered silence upon her decks.

At her fore-masthead the British ship flew a white flag of truce, but her guns were cleared for action, all but the saluting battery shotted. Slow matches burned in the tubs in case the locks should fail, and every man stood at his post, tense for the slightest sign of hostility from the Spanish ashore.

'They're buggers for red-hot shot, me lads . . .'

'Look there's a battery below those trees, see . . .'

'And there's two man-o'-war brigs at anchor.'

'Lick those bastards wi' one hand up our arses, Jemmy.'

'Shut your fuckin' mouths!'

The whisper of comment, risen like the beginnings of a breeze in dried grass, died away.

Below, under an even stricter watch, the Spanish prisoners were confined until the proposed terms of the truce were ratified by the Spanish authorities and they could be released. Among them the silence was expectant, for no one ashore could know they were mewed up on board and the authorities might suspect the bold approach of the British cruiser was no more than an elaborate ruse to decimate the merchant shipping loading the hides and tallow, hemp and wheat upon which the fortunes of the settlement depended.

Drinkwater stood at the starboard hance, Fraser and Hill close beside him. The three of them listened to the leadsman, waiting to find the bottom and watching the Spanish lieutenant deputed to pilot them into soundings and the sand of an anchorage as the frigate moved ponderously into the vast embrace of the bay. Señor Lecuna, the Spanish lieutenant, was the only one of the prisoners on deck, both Don Alejo and Rubalcava being confined below until the ship had exchanged courtesies with the fort and established the nature of her reception.

'Fog, sir,' said Hill, sniffing the air like a hound.

It descended upon them like conjuror's magic, suddenly blotting out the surrounding landscape and instantly replacing the warm sunshine with a dripping, saturated atmosphere that darkened the decks and chilled the skin.

'*Pasarán . . . Siga el rumbo!*' said Lecuna. '*Siga el rumbo . . . vigile el compás!*'

'Compass . . . *rumbo*? Ah! Rumb line . . . hold your course, Mr Hill,' snapped Drinkwater in sudden comprehension.

'*Sí . . . sí*, hold course!' Lecuna nodded.

'Aye, aye, sir.'

For ten long minutes *Patrician* held on through the fog, her ropes dripping and the condensation collecting upon the guns.

'Look to your primings,' warned Fraser and prudent gun-captains turned to the match-tubs and whirled or blew on the sputtering saltpetre coils. Above them the sun reappeared, swirling through the nacreous vapour.

'*Caiga a estribor . . . er*, starboard, *Capitán . . .*'

'Starboard helm, Mr Hill, if you please,' amplified Drinkwater, watching Lecuna's hand. The leadsman called out that he had found the bottom, shoaling fast as *Patrician* crept into the anchorage.

'*Si, bueno . . . arrie las escandalosas . . .*' he pointed aloft, cut his hands outwards in the universal gesture of completion, and then waved them downwards.

'Tops'l halliards, Mr Fraser! Stand by forrard!'

On the fo'c's'le, the grey shapes of the carpenter's party stood ready to let the anchor go. The seabed had levelled out and Drinkwater wondered how close Lecuna would anchor them to the guns of the fort.

And then, with the same magical effect and as suddenly as it had come, the fog lifted, rolling away to shroud the great northern bight of the bay, produced by some local anomaly of temperature variation. *Patrician* found herself within the entrance to the southern arm of the huge inlet. A group of islands were visible, one a colony to the extraordinary pelican, while the bay forked, reaching deep inland to the north and the south. San Francisco lay on the slopes and hills of the southern headland, Point Lobos. To starboard, less than long-cannon shot away, rose the first of its green bluffs, a spur of that Point Lobos, surmounted by the white walls of the *Commandante*'s residence and the colours of Castile. Beneath the languidly flaunting red and gold, the ramparts of a fort beetled upon her, muzzles of heavy artillery trained on her decks from their embrasures.

Patrician was turning as she emerged from the fog-bank, her topsails bellying aback against their tops, slowing the ship and imparting a sluggish sternway to her. As she gathered way astern, the anchor was let go, the topsails lowered and the hands piped aloft to stow them. With the cable running through the hawse, the saluting battery opened fire.

Patrician brought up to her anchor as the last echoes of the final gun-shot echoed round the bay. Putting off from a small boat jetty beneath the embrasures of the fort was a smart barge, decorated with scarlet and gold fancy-work. At her stern flew a miniature Spanish ensign and at her bow stood an officer with a white flag.

Drinkwater closed his glass with a snap and nodded his thanks to Lieutenant Lecuna. 'Pass word to bring up Don Alejo and Captain Rubalcava.'

The next hour was going to be difficult.

It had long been a contention of Drinkwater's that contact with the shore was the bane of a sea-officer's professional life and today had offered him no reason to change his mind. Now, as he stood on the wide, paved terrace of the *Commandante*'s residence in the company of Midshipman Frey, awaiting the summons to meet the governor, he tried to relax.

Below them, the bluff was already casting its shadow across the southern arm of San Francisco Bay, the last rays of the sun disappearing over the Pacific behind him, beyond the entrance to the harbour. Skeins of brown and white pelicans flew in to roost, brilliantly lit, for the last of the sunshine illuminated the harbour in a wide swathe from the entrance. He watched the ships in the anchorage preparing for the ceremony of sunset, paying particular attention to his own *Patrician*, and the pair of Spanish brigs-of-war below him. Further away some dozen merchantmen lay off the town, their lower yards cock-billed as they worked cargo out of lighters alongside. Drinkwater could see the stars and stripes of the United States and the diagonal cross of Russian colours. But the big, black Russian line-of-battle-ship he had seen off Cape Horn was not in evidence. He cursed his over-anxiety, aware that he had been too-much worked upon by the cares of the day. And what a day it had been!

A day of constant arguments. First the Spanish officer who had boarded them on arrival had argued with Drinkwater over his blatant disregard for Spanish sovereignty by entering the port with his guns run out, demanding to know, in the name of King Carlos, what the devil he was doing in Spanish waters. Drinkwater had countered these intemperate demands and expostulations by coolly awaiting the arrival of Don Alejo Arguello and Captain Rubalcava.

Captain de Soto, the boarding officer, having made formal apologies for the peremptory mode of his address at the appearance of these gentlemen, then fell to arguing with them, insisting that he was acting on the *Commandante*'s strictest instructions and exploding with rage at the news that the *Santa Monica* had been destroyed. De Soto's anger released a storm of fury from Rubalcava which was incomprehensible to the watching Britons, but which drained the colour from de Soto's face and sent his right hand flying to his sword-hilt. Don Alejo's temporising interruption calmed things down, but it was clear that Rubalcava was a deeply embittered man and the source of his

85

disaffection stemmed from more than a matrimonial disappointment. There was an air of alienation about Rubalcava that seemed to Drinkwater's perceptive eye to go beyond the odium associated with the loss of a ship. Perhaps it was just the fruit of an active rivalry between officers on a colonial station, perhaps de Soto expected command of the *Santa Monica* or had always rated himself higher than Rubalcava; perhaps, Drinkwater thought, his mind running wild as the two Spaniards postured before the calming influence of Don Alejo, it was de Soto who had won the affection and hand of the *Commandante*'s daughter. He gave up the vain speculation with the recollection that Don Alejo had indicated Rubalcava was of low-birth. How much that meant in the Spanish colonies, Drinkwater could only guess. He had heard that the results of miscegenation were less frowned upon by the passionate Spaniards than the British in India, and that it was possible for able half-castes to rise in government service. Perhaps Rubalcava was one such man, though in his appearance he seemed to fit the Quixotic image of the Hispanic man of action.

When this purely domestic contention had finally died down, Drinkwater had found himself drawn into further argument following repudiation of his terms. The wood and water promised by Don Alejo were not available, said de Soto; upon that the *Comandante*, Don José Henrique Martin Arguello de Salas, was adamant. The lie of the land persuaded Drinkwater that both were readily available elsewhere, except that the point had become a matter of honour. De Soto's insistence compromised Don Alejo, despite the mandate of the *Commandante*, and Drinkwater sensed the Spanish *hidalgo*'s loss of face before his juniors. He decided to intervene.

'Don Alejo,' he interrupted, 'I am willing to forgo the wood and water.'

Don Alejo's face brightened. '*Capitán*, you are a man of honour . . .'

The indispensable formula of bow and counter-bow threatened to reassert itself and Drinkwater cut it short. 'All I ask, Don Alejo, is a written undertaking that Captain Rubalcava, his officers and the seamen taken out of His Most Catholic Majesty's ship *Santa Monica*, will not bear arms against the forces and possessions of His Britannic Majesty for the duration of the present war.'

'*Qué?*' The vehemence of Rubalcava's interjection suggested he understood the gist of Drinkwater's demand. Rubalcava had been watching Drinkwater closely, knowing him for a wily opponent and now asked what the heretic commander demanded under the very guns of Spain!

'Otherwise,' went on Drinkwater unperturbed, 'we will have to discuss the terms of ransom. You are my prisoners, Don Alejo, I have treated you as men of honour after you struck your country's colours in the face of superior force. You bear your swords and I offer you your freedom. All I ask is your parole not to serve again in the present war. It is nothing.'

He shrugged, aware that the gesture was catching, and feigned to dismiss further argument. Nevertheless it broke out with renewed violence, but in Spanish and detached from Drinkwater. In the end Don Alejo agreed, but it was clear that Rubalcava did not intend to adhere to whatever the others committed him.

De Soto had departed to confer with the *Commandante*, and the prisoners had resigned themselves to wait. Drinkwater had not agreed to Don Alejo's accompanying de Soto; the muzzles of those Spanish guns were too damned close.

De Soto returned an hour later. He was much changed, an affable, effusive and courtly man who requested the honour of Captain Drinkwater's presence at the *Commandante*'s table that evening. An hour later they had begun to disembark the prisoners. They were still landing them as Drinkwater and Frey looked down into the dark cusp of the bay where, like a giant water-beetle, *Patrician*'s long-boat made its way to the quays of the town.

'You are spared that tedious task, Mr Frey,' he nodded down at the labouring boat.

'Yes, sir.' Spruce in his new coat, its white collar patches bright in the twilight, Frey grinned back from the unaccustomed throttling of his formal stock. He had heard something about meeting a lady tonight. The occupants of the

87

gunroom thought a great deal about meeting ladies.

Drinkwater moved his right shoulder beneath the heavy material of his own full-dress coat, glad of its weight in the evening chill. A touch of mist trailed across the dark foliage of the trees below them and the sudden concussion of the sunset gun made him start. It was echoed smartly by *Patrician* and the two brigs as their colours fluttered down. Night fell on the great bay, the lights of the ships twinkling across the smooth water. Two more beetles crept out from *Patrician*'s side and began to circle her darkening bulk languidly.

'And that duty too, Mr Frey,' Drinkwater nodded, and both watched the two cutters begin to row the night's guard round and round the frigate.

The wait was beginning to tell on Drinkwater's patience and he sighed impatiently. He was tired, exhausted by three days of vigilance and today's largely irrelevant exertions. He had wanted only to disencumber himself of the damned prisoners, not to fence endless words, to be caught up in the parish-pump politics of a colonial outpost. He detested such futile activities, longed for the fresh air of the open sea. He straightened his back, eased his shoulder and drew in a long breath of the damp, aromatic evening air.

'Ah, *Capitán*, please forgive . . . His Excellency will receive you . . .'

Don Alejo Joaquin Arguello waved his arm for Drinkwater and Frey to follow.

Lieutenant James Quilhampton nodded a curt farewell to Lieutenant César Lecuna of the *Santa Monica*. Upon these two officers had fallen the duty of co-operation during the landing of the prisoners. He looked briefly at the signed receipt.

'*Adios . . . vaya con Dios . . .*' Lecuna turned to his own men. '*Adelante!*'

Quilhampton turned to walk back along the quay to the waiting long-boat, almost bumping into Midshipman Belchambers who ran up at full tilt.

'Sir! Sir! The men are running!'

'What? God damn! Why didn't you stop 'em?' Quilhampton

clapped a hand to his hat and began to run. It was the hour of *corso*, the promenade. The draggle-tailed society of San Francisco was airing its social pretensions. Amid such a crowd, many of whom gathered to hiss and barrack the English sailors, he knew his seamen would melt like snow on a hearthstone.

'We couldn't stop 'em, sir . . . not without firing into this crowd.'

'No, of course not,' Quilhampton replied sourly to the marine corporal whose three men looked down sheepishly. The Spaniards had not liked the presence of the armed marines on their soil and Quilhampton had been obliged to admit they were appointed to the boats for his own protection and to prevent his men deserting. When that news had been communicated to Captain Rubalcava it had brought the first smile to the Spanish commander's face. Doubtless a few dollars had been spread amongst the boat's crew. Now only four men remained on board, studying the bottom boards under Quilhampton's withering glare.

'Did these lubbers try and run too?' he asked, and the question went unanswered. Behind him he felt a stir of hostility among the crowd of idlers. Some unfriendly shouts followed.

'Get in the boat,' he snapped at the marines, 'and take an oar each.'

It was going to be a damnably long pull back to the ship with so few oarsmen, but soon the night would shroud their humiliation. He followed Belchambers and the marines into the longboat, took his place aft and tucked the tiller underneath his arm.

'Toss oars, bear off forrard!'

The crowd surged to the edge of the quay, abuse rising like a wave behind them. Someone spat, provoking a burst of expectoration and fist-shaking. A stone plopped alongside. A gobbet of spittle struck Quilhampton's neck.

'Pull you buggers! Put your bloody backs into it!'

The heavy boat moved with ponderous slowness; Quilhampton endured further humiliation, but dared not turn and face his tormentors.

'Pull!'

As he sat hunched and swearing over the tiller his mind

ranged over the wisdom of remaining in the harbour an hour longer. It had seemed to him as they had glided into the bay that the *Patrician*'s presence within the dark embrace of those great headlands touched off some primitive suspicion in his mind. Intuition told him that despite her massed cannon, despite her state of readiness and the precautionary guard-boats pulling round the ship, she lay in mortal danger.

He could not explain this theory. The terms of the truce seemed water-tight, and it was unlikely that the Spanish authorities would break their word. But these new desertions combined with his suspicion of the connivance of Rubalcava, triggered off his nervous conviction that the ship was ill-fated, and he doomed with it. It was a far more serious matter than the desertion of the two lovers at Más-a-Fuera, and he had yet to explain it to Captain Drinkwater.

Drinkwater exchanged bows with the *Commandante*, Don José Henrique Martin Arguello de Salas. His Excellency was a tall, heavily handsome man with a thick-set figure that was rapidly running to seed. In contrast to his brother he seemed of a more indolent character. Like Don Alejo he spoke a little English and he had a formally easy manner which, in the circumstances, put Drinkwater on his guard. He disliked being manipulated and Don José seemed an expert in the matter.

'Ah, *Capitán*, Don Alejo speak of his misfortune to meet you. You are come to make trouble for us, no?'

'I have come to do my duty, Your Excellency.'

'And what *is* your duty, *Capitán*?'

A servant appeared bearing a tray of glasses. Drinkwater took one and sipped from it before replying, meeting the *Commandante*'s inquisitorial stare with his own.

'A most excellent sherry, Señor . . . I command a cruiser, Your Excellency,' he said slowly, feigning a greater interest in the wine. 'It is the duty of a cruiser to wreck the enemy's trade . . .'

'We 'ave ships of other nations 'ere in San Francisco.'

'You have ships of nations with whom Great Britain is at war, Excellency, nations who until recently were our allies and received payments from our Treasury. You are a man of honour, Your Excellency, and understand such treachery is intolerable.'

'The Russian ships?' Don José asked, frowning, clearly having difficulty with Drinkwater's English.

'That is correct, yes.'

'And the ships of the United States, *Capitán*? Would you fire on the flag of the United States?'

'Great Britain is not at war with the United States, Excellency,' Drinkwater said, noting the quick glance between Don José and his brother, 'but of course,' he added, 'we should find it necessary to search even neutral vessels for contraband cargoes.' He smiled as courteously as he could in the knowledge that they were contemplating such a ruse. 'I would not like to imagine my reactions if I discovered that, for example, a *Spanish* ship was sailing under false, American colours. I am sure you take my meaning.'

The cloud hanging over Don José's brow lifted as Don Alejo hissed a few words of explanation at his elder brother. Don José nodded and met Drinkwater's smile with one of equal falsity. Drinkwater looked about him.

'Is Captain Rubalcava to join us this evening, Your Excellency?' Drinkwater asked. 'He was a gallant enemy . . .'

'No,' put in Don Alejo sharply, 'Don Jorge will not be joining us . . .'

Further enquiry or explanation was cut short by the major domo's announcement. The gentlemen turned towards a heavy door and Drinkwater and Frey exchanged glances, then imitated the Spaniards' low bows. They were aware of the rustle of skirts and the subtle waft of perfume filling the candle-lit room. As he straightened up Drinkwater heard the faint rasp of sharply indrawn breath from Midshipman Frey. His face was flushed with a sudden wave of long-suppressed concupiscence and Drinkwater smiled, for the object of his sudden lust was overwhelmingly beautiful.

'May I present the lady Doña Ana Maria Conchita . . .' Don Alejo recited the young woman's names and titles, but Drinkwater distilled the information that she was his niece and Don

91

José's daughter. Whilst the long absence from the society of women would have made memorable an hour spent in the company of any young woman with good teeth and a bosom, Doña Ana Maria's presence promised an evening of pleasing enchantment.

Tall, like her father, she wore the wide skirt and tight bodice of Spanish fashion. Her carriage was regal and her bare shoulders rose above the swirl of a shawl which was drawn together below her breasts. About her neck a necklace of Chinese jade reflected the candle-light, rising and falling with her breathing.

But there was far more to her beauty than mere sexual allure, for her face was as intelligent as it was lovely. Her eyes were of such an umbral brown that they appeared bronze in the light from the candles. Her flawless cream skin was unpowdered and her lips were soft, wide and red without the artifice of carmine. Above her straight nose and wide forehead, long black hair was oiled like jet, drawn back in the severe mode of her class and beneath the swept-back waves at the side of her head, jade earrings depended from the lobes of her ears. Suddenly Rubalcava's embitterment made shattering sense. Drinkwater relinquished her hand and turned to his companion.

'*Señorita*, I have the honour to present Mr Midshipman Frey.'

It was clear that Frey was devastated by the lady, fighting an overwhelming desire fuelled by the gross appetites of the starved, and ready to die for her in the next moment if she had asked it of him. His hand shook as he bent over hers and he straightened up with an idiot look of rapture. She could not fail to be aware of the turmoil she was causing and Drinkwater turned to Don José. Both he and Don Alejo were clearly studying the effect Doña Ana Maria was having on the two British officers. Was there something premeditated about this attention?

'My uncle,' she said in an English that contained an elusively familiar inflection, 'tells me you have come to San Francisco with many cannon, *Capitán*.'

She had turned those wonderful eyes on him again.

'I have come on an act of humanity, *Señorita*, to repatriate the

92

gallant Captain Don Jorge Rubalcava and his men, whom the fortune of war made my prisoners.'

There was no trace of reaction to the name of her former suitor, the tiny reactive muscles about the eyes that could reveal the quickening impulses of the brain remained unmoved. Presumably Rubalcava meant nothing to her. 'You speak excellent English, *Señorita*, please accept my compliments.'

'Thank you, *Capitán*. I learn it from my duenna, Doña Helena.' She indicated an elderly woman who wore a *mantilla*, whom Drinkwater had taken for Doña Ana Maria's mother and the *Commandante*'s wife. If his senses had not been so mesmerised he would have recognised the folly of such a supposition. It was inconceivable that he should have entertained it, even for an instant. Doña Helena stared at him from a wizened face with a pair of fiercely blue eyes.

'Your servant, ma'am,' Drinkwater bowed, aware of the ferocity of her scrutiny.

'Aye, honoured ah'm sure, Captain.' There was venom in the reply, a sharp hatred bred in the bone and born of popish origins, and the mystery of Doña Ana's acquired accent was cleared up. In her native Scotland, Doña Helena would have been called Mistress Helen, though it was uncertain when she had last seen her native land.

Only the sombre figure of the priest remained to be introduced. He had come in with the women, an emaciated young Franciscan in a heavy wool habit. His crucifix and rosary chinked gently as he moved and his presence adumbrated the room. There was clearly no Doña José; the *Commandante*, it seemed, was a widower. The Franciscan's introduction as Fra Alfonso terminated the pre-prandial formalities and Drinkwater found himself leading the beautiful Doña Ana Maria in to dinner.

Drinkwater willingly surrendered to the charms of the young woman during the meal as he knew he was intended to do. His host, Don José, was on his left and seemed content to allow his daughter to practise her near-fluent English upon the British captain. There were a few initial questions about Drinkwater's career which he avoided exploiting, paying his host the compliment of reporting on the gallant conduct of the Spanish fleet in the momentous action off Cap Trafalgar, during which he had been a prisoner aboard the French flagship, *Bucentaure*.*

'You speak with the Marquis de Solana, *Capitán*, at Cadiz?'

'Yes, Your Excellency, I was received by him several times, concerning the matter of British prize-crews cast up on the coast after the great gale that followed the battle . . .'

The meal passed delightfully, though Midshipman Frey had a less happy time of it, seated next to the Scottish companion, Doña Helena. Yet he would not have traded his place for all the gold in Eldorado, for he could not take his eyes off the beautiful Doña Ana Maria opposite. Aware of Frey's sheep's eyes, Drinkwater began to feel sorry for the young woman, realising she was a victim of her own extraordinary beauty. It was not difficult to see how Rubalcava's proud spirit had been so enslaved. Something of an even darker alchemy was brewing in the unholy eyes of the silent Franciscan.

'You have children, *Capitán*?' The timbre of her voice was low and mellifluous.

'Yes, *Señorita*, I have two; a son and a daughter.'

'Ahhh. That is, they say, the choice of kings.' He watched her face as she added, 'I . . . I would like children . . .'

It was an impropriety, an intimacy, a mark of the isolation her beauty caused her, made in a low voice to a complete stranger.

'I understand you are to be married soon, Señorita,' he replied quietly.

'Yes . . .' She smiled and he sensed her excitement and the strength of her love for Rubalcava's rival which was prompting these confidences, confidences that were earning glances of disapproval from her duenna opposite. 'As soon as Nicolai arrives,' she ran on, her dark eyes glowing, 'he commands a great ship, like yourself, *Capitán* . . .'

'Nicolai?' Drinkwater was suddenly alert and cast a quick glance to his left where Don José seemed to be speaking in a low voice to Don Alejo.

'Aye, Cap'n, Nicolai Rezanov will be here soon tae clip your

* See *1805*

94

wings . . .' Doña Helena's blue eyes were chips of ice, chilled by ancient enmities. Her outburst attracted the attention of the Arguellos and turned them from their private conclave. In the sudden silence Drinkwater exploited the hiatus.

'Rezanov . . . an unusual name for a Spanish officer.'

Don José's face was a mask; Don Alejo made a small gesture to a waiting footman. The door was flung open and de Soto marched into the room and bent to Don José's ear. The *Comman-dante* looked sharply at Drinkwater.

'*Diablo!*' he muttered, then nodded and, as de Soto straightened up, the *Commandante* said, '*Capitán*, there has been much trouble in the town. Some men from your ship . . . they run away . . . there is a *mêlée* and a woman is killed.'

Council of War

'How many?'

In the light from the candle that stood on the cabin table Captain Drinkwater's face was thrown into dramatic relief. His head was cocked slightly, revealing the damaged muscles of his wrecked shoulder, and the single flame emphasised the intensity of his eyes. He was pale with fury.

'Eight, sir.' Quilhampton had never seen Drinkwater so angry and felt like a chastened midshipman. Beside him Fraser fidgeted nervously.

'Eight? *Eight!* God's bones man, you had *marines* in that damned boat! Marines with bayonets, for God's sake, and you let *eight* men run!'

'Yes sir,' Quilhampton mumbled unhappily.

'And do you know what they have done? Do you know what your eight precious liberty-loving English jacks have done, sir?'

'No sir.'

'They swilled *aguardiente* and ran wild in a whore-house! The upshot of their desertion is that they have been accused of causing the death of a woman and . . . and . . .'

Drinkwater brought his clenched fist down on the table-top so that the candle flame guttered. 'They have entirely compromised me, tied me hand and fist, God damn them!'

'Sir?' Quilhampton frowned, not understanding.

Drinkwater let out a long breath. 'Good God, James, can you offer me nothing in extenuation?'

'Only that there were many people on the quay and to shoot would have endangered the local people.'

'Mr Quilhampton was much abused by the crowds, sir,' put in Fraser, 'much spat upon and the like.'

Drinkwater fell silent and then he asked: 'What became of Rubalcava?'

'He left in the first boat after you and Frey had gone ashore, sir.'

Drinkwater shook his head, then moved round the table and lifted three glasses from the fiddles atop the locker. 'Pass that decanter, Mr Fraser . . . thank you.'

He poured the *bual* into the glasses and handed each of the two officers a glass. 'What's it like on deck?'

'Still foggy, sir, and dead calm. You can hear the guard-boats . . . no fear of a surprise. Mylchrist's up there now, reckons his fever's sharpened all his instincts,' replied Fraser who had not long come below.

Drinkwater grunted. 'We've an hour or two, no more . . . well, your health.'

There was a pause and then Drinkwater looked at Quilhampton. 'Ease your mind, James, 'tis I who am the greater fool.'

'You sir?'

'Yes . . . I have played right into their damned hands. I suspected something, but could not lay it by the tail . . . damned if I can now, but I'll wager the whore's death was contrived.'

'Contrived? I'm sorry . . . I don't follow . . .'

It had come to him in his enforced idleness, sitting in his barge as the oarsmen brought him back to the ship from the *Commandante*'s boat jetty below the battery. There had been that vague feeling of something passing between the Arguello brothers, that sensation of their using Doña Ana to distract him. Whether she was a party to this he did not know, but it seemed obvious that the news of the brawl had been engineered and it came to him in the boat that those eight seamen had been lured away on promises of safety, promiscuous sex and money.

'Was there much contact between the people and the Spaniards while they were here?' he asked flatly.

'No sir,' said Fraser, 'no more than one would expect with them cooped up on board.

97

'Mount mentioned he caught two seamen and a marine bartering for tobacco,' Quilhampton added.

'Did he indeed?'

'But there is nothing particularly significant in that, sir,' said Fraser.

'Except that ample opportunity existed for a sum of money to pass to disaffected men,' Drinkwater said, 'and God knows it takes little enough to turn the heads of these poor devils. A gold dollar, the promise of a whore and a drink and a pass through the town . . .' Conviction was forming in his mind.

'And they're in an ugly mood sir . . . simmering below the surface. They fought well enough, sir, but the smell of land . . .'

'Aye, and women,' growled Fraser, and Drinkwater felt guilt fuelling his anger.

'And Don Alejo had gold, sir, a lot of gold.'

'Why d'you say that, Mr Q?'

'He was concealing something on himself when he was compelled to abandon the *Santa Monica*. I thought it was a purse at the time. Then later, when he was quartered in my cabin, I went there by mistake, came below and without thinking, proceeded directly to my cabin. I opened the door before I realised my stupidity. Don Alejo was sitting smoking one of those damned cigars. He was half-undressed, lounging in my chair and on the cot lay his sword, some papers and a leather purse, the same one I had seen aboard the *Santa Monica*. It was bulging, sir, to the extent of revealing its contents . . . gold sir.'

'Dollars, or pistoles or something very like . . .'

'No sir, gold nuggets . . .'

'The treasures of the Manila galleon, eh?'

'I think perhaps only a little . . . a private speculation like the nabobs of the East India Company.'

'H'm. How did he take the intrusion?' Drinkwater asked.

'He was not pleased. I told him the stink of his cigar had attracted my attention and that smoking was forbidden below decks.'

'You should day-dream more often of Mistress MacEwan if it leads you into such adventures, Mr Q. Very well, then, it only serves to confirm my suspicions that some of the men were

98

suborned. More may be preparing to desert at the first opportunity, we shall have to proceed warily . . .'

'Sir, Ah'd be obliged . . .' Fraser frowned.

'Yes, Mr Fraser, I'll explain.' Drinkwater motioned them to sit. He was past mere tiredness, the events of the last hours had stimulated him and his active brain was whirling with the problems that suddenly beset him. He passed his hands over his face, seeking a place to begin his explanation.

'Well gentlemen, the main purpose of our cruise is to dislodge any attempt by the Russians to establish territorial claims northward of the Spanish domain of Nueva España. Since the Tsar repudiated his alliance with us last summer, it is believed that it is the intention of the Russian court to settle southwards from Alaska. Some reports, brought into Canada by *voyageurs* indicated Russian incursions up the Colombia River, further north from here . . . it's all very vague, but as welcome to us as the Spanish claim to Nootka Sound was. Although they have a fur-trading depot at Sitka, in Alaska, the tenuous claims of Captain Vancouver lie between Sitka and here, from whence, if the evidence in the bay is anything to go by, the Russians obtain many necessary supplies.'

'I counted seven Russian vessels in the anchorage, sir, a schooner, three brigs, a barque and a ship, sir.'

'Yes. I saw them last night. They will be expected on the Alaskan coast soon, and now we have arrived, just at the wrong moment for them. Not only have we advertised our presence, but we have destroyed one unit of the Spanish squadron that might have protected their trade.'

'But it's *Russian* trade, sir. I mean, are the Dons that interested in protecting it?' asked Fraser, to whom the matter was still confused.

'I presume they would not want it destroyed,' Drinkwater replied.

'But the Russians, sir, if they are seeking territory, will become a direct threat to the Spaniards, competing for the same length of coast.' Fraser frowned.

'Yes. Eventually they might, once our claims of land and our failure to maintain them are dealt with. But, for the meantime,

99

they are allies of expedience. Besides, this could become a matter of national prestige. I imagine the Dons would like their revenge for the loss of Nootka Sound. They only capitulated before because they lost the French monarchy as a support. Now they have Tsar Alexander. I believe they are about to settle the coast between them.'

'With what force?'

'The destruction of the *Santa Monica* does not draw all their teeth, Mr Fraser. Their main Pacific base is at Acapulco, they will have ships at Panama and, from what I heard tonight, there is a garrison at Monterey. I learnt something else tonight gentlemen, and this is the reason why we have been compromised. The murder, if indeed there has been a murder, is a prevarication, a means to delay us. The *Commandatore* has agreed to meet me to discuss the return of our men after the murderer has been tried. He has made protestations of not wishing to impugn the honour of our flag after our courtesy to our prisoners. In the same breath he is talking of our breaking the terms of the truce, of referring to Monterey for instructions . . . in short, any damned obstruction that will delay us while we are enmeshed in some specious diplomatic tangle.'

'But sir, they have no *force* to keep us here!' expostulated Fraser. 'We can tow out from their guns in a couple of hours and those toy brigs wouldn't knock the marines' shakoes off.'

'You are correct in your specific, but not your diagnosis. We can tow out, Mr Fraser, but we may well meet a line-of-battle-ship coming in.'

'We can outmanoeuvre a Spanish battle-ship, sir,' said Fraser almost flippantly.

'She will be *Russian*, Mr Fraser, we saw her off Cape Horn and by the certainty with which our friends ashore are behaving, I believe her arrival imminent.'

'*Do* we tow out, sir?' Quilhampton asked, that inchoate sense of foreboding closing round him again. He had found its first physical manifestation at Más-a-Fuera and the second had dotted him with the spittle of hostile Spaniards, half-castes and Indians. Now every moment of delay increased its intensity.

'Yes, make your preparations. Let us slip our cable and use the fog to make a virtue of necessity. In an hour then . . .'

They left him, scuttling out to pass word to the watch and turn out those sleeping below and at the guns. They would all be ragged-nerved and foul-tempered by the time they had laboured at the oars of the boats and dragged *Patrician*'s inert mass clear of the bay. He would have to be patient with them and watch for outbursts of disaffection. In the meantime he would have to wait. He could not sleep, although he was haggard with exhaustion. An hour's sleep would make him feel worse than none at all. He poured the last of the *bual* into his glass and went on an impulse to his sea-chest. Rummaging in the bottom he drew out a frayed roll of canvas. Spreading it on the table he looked down at it. It was the portrait of a woman, painted long ago by the French Republican artist Jacques Louis David. In addition to the frayed edges and cracked paintwork, little circles of mould were forming on the canvas, perverting the purity of the colours, and there were three holes, where the tines of a fork had once pierced it.

Hortense Santhonax stared back at him from cool grey eyes. Beneath the studied negligence of her pearl-wound and piled auburn hair, her lovely face held a hint of a smile. He remembered her, years ago, almost as long ago as the Spanish outrage at Nootka Sound, before she married Edouard Santhonax and espoused the Bonapartist cause. She had been a frightened *emigrée* then, Hortense de Montholon, running from the vengeful howl of the pursuing mob, to be rescued by an impoverished master's mate named Nathaniel Drinkwater.*

He had been half in love with her then, before she turned her coat and married his enemy.

He had killed Edouard Santhonax less than a year previously, killed him to preserve the secret he had brought out of Russia. He had widowed her in the line of duty. Or had he and why did he stare at her portrait now? The bare shoulders and the soft breasts were barely concealed by the wisp of gauze artfully placed by the skilled hand of a seductress. She was already rumoured to be the mistress of Talleyrand, a fading beauty he supposed. It made no

* See *A King's Cutter*

sense to be subject to so compelling an urge as had driven him to remove her portrait from the obscurity of his sea-chest.

Except that she was providence, an ikon, presentient as his dream and an impulse to be obeyed in those rare moments of hiatus when his tired mind was in revolt. An ikon: an apt simile. He was unable to shake off that old superstition of his destiny. She had become the embodiment of the spirit of France, inhabiting the subconscious recesses of his imagination and marrying the man whose fate had become inextricably bound up with his own. The dice had fallen his way last, it had not always been thus as his wrecked shoulder testified; but he was not yet free of Santhonax's ghost. The secret from Russia still haunted him, even here in the Pacific.

'Witchcraft,' he muttered and let the margin of the canvas go. It coiled itself like a spring and he looked up to see the faithful, pale oval of Elizabeth's portrait staring at him from its frame. 'Witchcraft,' he repeated and, hiding the canvas again, he drew on his cloak and went on deck.

In some strange way he felt relieved by the power the portrait of Hortense possessed. There was a reassuring quality of normality about it: a familiar neurosis. He had not been too much overcome by the beauty of Ana Maria.

The Leak

'If you wish to say something Tregembo, for God's sake say it and stop fiddling with those damned pistols!' Drinkwater snapped irritably. Mullender's duster and Tregembo's fidgeting had driven him on deck where a sleeting rain had turned him below again. *Patrician* bucked to the onset of the rain-bearing squall and gusts of cold, damp air rattled in through the sashes of the stern windows.

'You'll be needing 'em 'fore long zur, if I ain't mistaken,' Tregembo growled.

'The pistols? Would to God I needed 'em instanter! That damned convoy should have appeared by now . . .'

'I didn't mean for that, zur . . .'

'Eh?' Drinkwater frowned, looking at his coxswain with sudden attention. 'What the devil *did* you mean then?'

Tregembo laid the pistol down in its box and waited until Mullender had gone into the pantry. His old face, lined and scarred as it was, bore every indication of concern. 'Zur . . .' The door to the tiny pantry stood open behind him. Drinkwater crossed the cabin and closed it. 'Well?'

'The people, zur . . . you know they're disaffected . . . 'tis common enough upon a long commission an' they mean no harm to you, zur . . . but . . .'

'Spit it out Tregembo, I'm in no mood for puzzlements.'

''Tis the men you left behind, zur . . . 'tis scuttlebutt they're to hang, an' such rumouring is having a bad effect, zur . . .'

'For God's sake Tregembo, those men *deserted* . . .' Drinkwater sat and stared gloomily at the old Cornishman.

'There are stories of women, zur . . . the boat's crews saw

women ashore, an' there are grog shops a-plenty . . . those merchant-seamen were three sheets to the wind, they'm saying . . . they be powerful reasons for making a man run, zur.'

Drinkwater nodded. 'I know all this, Tregembo . . . why tell me now?'

'Because it won't be single men, zur. Next time it'll be a boat's crew, zur, an' the word, as I hear it, is to hell with the officers . . .'

There was a peremptory knock at the cabin door. Instantly Tregembo turned away, picked up the pistol case, shut it and slid it into its stowage in the locker.

'Come!'

It was Fraser. He was followed by the elderly Mr Marsden, a wizened and wrinkled man skirted with a leather apron which hid bandy legs but revealed a powerful torso, muscular arms and hands of immense size. The sudden irruption of the first lieutenant and the carpenter into Drinkwater's cabin indicated something serious had happened.

'Begging your pardon, sir, but Mr Marsden has just made an urgent report to me concerning water in the wells.'

Drinkwater looked sharply at the carpenter. 'Well, Mr Marsden?'

'Three feet, sir, in two hours, and making fast.'

'When were the wells last pumped? At the change of the watch?'

'Yes, sir, an' nothink much in 'em bar what you'd expect.'

'Something adrift below, then?'

Marsden nodded. 'Seems likely, sir.'

'Any idea what?'

'No sir . . .'

'No shot holes . . .'

'Not that I can see, sir . . . 'sides we engaged that Spaniard wi' the larboard broadside . . .'

'Aye, and now we're on the larboard tack! Mr Fraser, put the ship about on the instant! Mr Marsden pump the wells dry, let's see if the other tack makes any difference.' He rose, perversely relieved in the need for action, potentially disastrous though the news was. For the ship suddenly to make so much water could be due to any one of a hundred reasons, none of them easy to

104

determine, let alone overcome. 'Come gentlemen, let us be about our business!'

Grabbing hat and cloak Drinkwater hustled Fraser and the carpenter out of his cabin and followed them on deck. Alone in the cabin Tregembo watched the surge of the smooth wake as it rose, bubbling green from *Patrician*'s transom. A long-tailed Bosun-bird slid across his field of view, quartering the wake for prey. 'Don't you forget what I told 'ee,' he muttered after Drinkwater.

On deck the watch were running to their stations to tack ship. Drinkwater took no part in the manoeuvre, instead he fished in the tail-pocket of his coat for his glass then levelled it to the eastward.

Banks of slate-coloured clouds rolled to leeward dragging dull curtains of rain behind them, blotting out sections of the faint blue line of the coastal mountains of California. From one such shroud the low line of Punta de los Reyes was emerging. *Patrician* had spent nine days keeping station off the point round which any convoy from San Francisco must pass on its way to the Alaskan settlements of the Tsar. They had kept well to seaward of the long, low arm of sand-dunes and marram grass, lurking out of sight to avoid either of those two man-of-war brigs that might be sent to see if the coast was clear. Even allowing a week for the tardiest merchant ship to complete her lading, it would be reasonable, Drinkwater argued to himself, for them to have intercepted some trading vessels moving north by now.

Patrician jibbed up into the wind and the foreyards were swung on the word of command.

Unless, Drinkwater mused, those merchantmen were waiting for something more puissant than a pair of brigs; something like a Russian line-of-battle-ship! Not for the first time Drinkwater cursed the brevity of his aptly-styled briefing from the Admiralty. Again he felt that sense of abandonment by Lord Dungarth, the very man from whom he would have expected the most comprehensive elucidation of the state of affairs in the Pacific. He knew his orders originated from British spies in the Russian service, agents whose access to the most secret intentions of the Tsar had been preserved at a prodigious cost, as Drinkwater had good reason to know.

Supposing, he reasoned, he had been utterly mistaken in that glimpse of another man-of-war off Cape Horn. Suppose that brief spectral image had magnified itself in his imagination and the vessel had been, at worst, a Spaniard. He knew that the Russian-American Company, under whose auspices Russian ships traded down the coast from Alaska, had armed vessels at their disposal. He knew, too, that at least one frigate had been built on the Pacific coast of North America for the purpose of reinforcing Russian claims upon the shores of what Drake, Cook, and now the Admiralty, were pleased to call 'New Albion'.

Patrician forged ahead, gathering increasing way on the new tack. The hands were busy coiling the braces on the pins and on the fo'c's'le the weather fore-tack was hauled down to the bowing bumpkin. Shafts of sunlight fanned down through the clouds, dappling the surface of the sea with brilliant patches of dancing water. Off on the quarter a school of dolphins abandoned the chase of a shoal of bonito and gambolled in their tumbling wake. Neither the brightening weather nor the appearance of the cetaceans lightened Drinkwater's gloom. All his ponderous considerations were of little consequence now. Marsden's report postponed them indefinitely. The leak and its cause superseded all other matters and it did not help his temper to realise that the trap he had baited by towing out of San Francisco Bay would now be useless. His nearest dockyard was in the West Indies, with the Horn to double to get there. He had only one course of action open to him: Hobson's choice of a careenage.

'Well?'

As Marsden came aft Drinkwater stopped at the after end of the starboard gangway, his cloak flapping round him in the wind, his hands clasped behind his back. The carpenter's face was still clouded by concern.

'She's still makin' water, sir . . . perhaps a little less, but 'tis bad enough, sir.'

'Damn! Very well, Mr Marsden, very well. I'll be below myself shortly. Mr Fraser!'

'Aye, sir?'

'Steer east-nor'-east and fetch me the coast directly.'

Below the waterline the hull was a vast stygian cavern of noise. He followed Marsden and his two mates with their lanterns guttering in the stale, mephitic air, trying to shut out the natural noises of the creaking and groaning space to hear those unnatural sounds the better. It was a hopeless task, one that he was less qualified than Marsden to execute, yet one which demanded his attention. How far below the waterline was this leak? Any remedial action he took depended upon some rough location. To careen *Patrician* properly would render her utterly defenceless should she be taken by surprise, for all her guns and stores would have to come out of her and be safely landed. Drinkwater had himself led an attack on a French frigate in such a supine state, and carried her safely out to sea from her bolt-hole on the Red Sea coast of Arabia. To be served himself in similar fashion, dished-up to an enemy without the chance of defending himself sent worms of apprehension crawling about his belly. But he had to know the worst and he stumbled along the carpenter's walk, a narrow space maintained free of stores just inside the ship's skin, by which access was provided to plug shot-holes and maintain the water-tight integrity of the ship.

'Mind, sir, this grating be a bit loose . . .'

'Yes, thank you . . .'

In the yellow pools of lamp-light he could see the ship's inner skin, discoloured with the traces of mould. The thick air was heavy with the multiple smells of this great warehouse of the cruiser's wants. Here powder and shot were stored in magazines and lockers; locked store-rooms housed spirits and flour, fish and dried peas. Tier upon tier of barrels stowed bung up and bilge-free, held the potable sweet-water; casks of dubious age contained the salt-pork and cheese provided by a munificent Victualling Board; the oats and dried fruit, the wood-store and oil-room, all fitted below the waterline, above, abaft or forward of the hold proper. The platformed section of the orlop along which they worked their way showed no ingress of water. Amid the creaks and groans of the ship's timbers, the slosh of

107

bilge-water and the hiss of the sea beyond the inner and outer wales and the massive futtocks, they strained their ears for sound of a roar, a spurt, even a trickle of incoming water. But all they could make out above the working of the ship, was the squeal of disturbed rats.

Drinkwater escaped to the upper deck, scanning the horizon and again finding the sea bereft of any sign of a ship. A mile to leeward a whale fluked, slapping the water with its gigantic tail before sliding into the depths of the ocean. Somehow that brief appearance of leviathan only served to emphasise the emptiness of the scene.

Slowly *Patrician* approached the coast; the yellow line of Punta de los Reyes spread across the horizon ahead, the clouds hanging over the coastal mountains fused into mist and falling rain. Drinkwater crossed the deck to where Fraser, his odd, sandy features wearing a comic expression that bespoke his anxiety, waited to hear what Drinkwater had to say with as much patience as he could muster.

'Hae ye any luck, sir?'

'Little enough Mr Fraser.'

'No, I couldna find anything either. I thought it might be the hood-ends . . .'

Drinkwater considered the suggestion. The hood-ends were where the butt ends of the strakes, or planks, met the timbering of the stem. Here, the constant working of the sea round the bow could disturb the fastenings and loosen the planks. Leaking about the stem was very difficult to determine at sea and was increased by the ship continuing to make headway.

'That's an informed guess, Mr Fraser. Whatever the cause we cannot ignore the matter. I intend to get the ship into sheltered water and lighten her. We may have to careen, which will mean the devil of a lot of labour. Whatever expedient we are driven to we'll require a boat guard. If there *is* a Russian battle-ship in the offing we had better lie low. God help us if we are caught.'

'Amen to that sir.'

'For heaven's sake it'll be like being caught in a whore-house on Judgement Day . . . begging your pardon, Mr Henderson.'

'I appreciate the strength of your metaphor, Mr Mylchrist, and deduce therefrom that we can expect an exceedingly great wrath to descend upon us should the event come to pass.'

'Well we can't ignore the matter. Three feet in the well ain't a lot, but it came in damned quick and I think something fell out, a trenail, perhaps,' said Quilhampton, leaning on the wardroom table, his head in his hands, 'that's the only logical explanation.'

'D'you think we're up against logic, James?'

'What the hell else d'you think we're up against?' Quilhampton jerked up.

Mylchrist shrugged. 'I didn't get my wound from an enemy . . .'

'No . . . no more you did . . .'

Mylchrist's gloomy implication chimed in uncannily with Quilhampton's superstitious foreboding.

'A nail from the hull – another in our bloody coffins . . .'

'Oh, for God's sake Johnnie . . .'

'Gentlemen, perhaps a prayer is apt while we wait for the first lieutenant.'

'What are you going to pray for, Mr Henderson?' asked Mylchrist sourly. 'Three hundred pairs of feet enabled to walk upon the water?'

'Mr Mylchrist, I am outraged! If God abandons us in our extremity, your blasphemy will give him cause enough . . . happily His mercy is infinite and able to accommodate a miscreant as wretched as you.'

'Ah, I forgot the quality of mercy,' remarked Mylchrist sarcastically, 'the recollection comes as a great relief to me.'

Henderson drew from his nose the spectacles he kept in almost permanent residence there, a habit which intimated he was never far removed from the devout perusal of Holy Scriptures. Such a deliberate and portentous gesture augured ill for the bantering inhabitants of the wardroom as they lounged about, waiting for their orders from the first lieutenant.

'Johnnie, what exactly did you mean just now?' Quilhampton interjected, a preoccupied look on his lean face.

'About what?'

'About the leak. Did you mean to imply someone may have had a hand in the matter?'

'Well, yes, of course . . .'

'Gentlemen, I have your orders . . . pray pay attention. You may require to make notes . . . we're in for the devil of a hard time.' Fraser's burr ended the conversation as the worried Scotsman hurried into the wardroom and waved aside the negro messman and his coffee pot. 'Nae time for that, King, nae time at all . . .'

It was not ground of his own choosing. A light mist trailing in the wake of a rain shower was clearing as they closed the coast. *Patrician* stood shorewards under a single jib and her three topsails, a cable bent to her sheet anchor and a leadsman chanting from the forechains. Balanced on the rail, braced against the mizen shrouds, Drinkwater scanned the littoral ahead. He sought an anchorage beyond the flats that extended northwards from Punta de los Reyes. A long, comparatively low-lying spit of land extended for fifteen miles northward of the headland, behind which, his charts suggested, lay an inlet running deep into the countryside. He had little real knowledge of its suitability, but the preoccupation of a worried mind convinced him that to delay, to seek a more ideal spot, would be foolish.

Ahead of him the mist had resolved itself into a low cloud of spray that hung over the pounding white of breakers where the long Pacific swells toppled and thundered on the sands of the Californian foreshore. Behind the beach low sand-dunes ran to the southward and, somewhere beyond the horizon, terminated at Punta de los Reyes. At intervals along this sand-spit higher eminences rose and, at the distal point, a low but prominent hill marked the termination of the land. The white of breakers pounded on the low bar around which Drinkwater hoped to work *Patrician* and seek an anchorage beyond the spit, in the safety of the long lagoon of Tomales Bay.

The wind had fallen light, a gentle onshore breeze that ruffled the sea. The promise of sunshine earlier in the day had failed and cloud had closed off the heavens and given the sea's

110

surface a leaden colour, as it lifted itself to the easy motion of the incoming swells.

'Noooo bottom!' The leadsman's chant had become monotonous, though they were within a league of the shore and then, sharply insistent: 'By the mark twenty!'

The breakers were suddenly nearer, drawing out on the starboard bow. The gentle pitch of the ship was steepening as she reacted to the shortening of the heaving wave-length compounded of the rise of the sea-bed and the back-swell, beating seawards from the rampart of the land.

'By the mark thirteen!'

Worms of anxiety were crawling in Drinkwater's belly. Hill came across the deck and stood below him. Without words they shared their apprehension. Tomales Point was opening all the time. A guano-stained rock had detached itself from the land as it changed its appearance with their close approach.

'Bird Rock, sir,' Hill remarked, though Drinkwater knew the comment was an expression of caution, not topographical interest. He felt a swell gather itself under *Patrician*'s stern, lifting it and thrusting the ship forward so that her bow dipped sharply. The sudden elevation and clearer view ahead alarmed both captain and sailing master. They were in shoal soundings now, the leadsman chanting the deeps of nine and eight fathoms. Behind the smoking barrier of the long sand spit, the narrow placid opening of the lagoon stretched away to the southwards. On its far shore the low-lying land rose gradually, hazing into the distance and the rain covered mountains. But across the entrance to Tomales Bay lay the whitened fury of the thwarted Pacific, roaring and thundering upon the sand-bar that blocked their intended refuge.

Then the swell rolled under them, the stern dropped and the bow reared up, the long bowsprit stabbing almost vertically. Drinkwater felt himself jerked by the mast-whip shaking the mizen shrouds. Ahead of them the smooth back of the swell culminated in a great arch of water, soon to disintegrate in hundreds of tons of roiling water as one more breaker on the coast. It entirely blotted out their view, but both Drinkwater and Hill had seen enough.

'Stand by the braces!' Drinkwater roared, leaping from the rail. 'Down helm! Larboard tack! Hands aloft, let fall the courses and t'garns'ls! Lively there! Afterguard, leggo spanker brails! Haul aft the spanker! Come Mr Mylchrist move those lubbers smartly there . . . Fo'c's'le . . .'

'Sir?' Comley stood, four-square, facing aft expectantly.

'Hoist your jibs, sir!'

Hill had moved across the deck to stand by the binnacle. He shot glances at the compass, then aloft at the masthead pendant and at the larboard dogvane.

'Full and bye, Mr Hill . . .'

Patrician began to swing with an infuriating slowness, bringing the swell onto her beam and rolling to leeward. As her bowsprit pointed round to the north it seemed to trace the curved shore of Bodega Bay. Drinkwater anxiously watched the thundering breakers get closer; the air was full of the roar of them, the air damp with the spray of their destruction upon the sand-bar. Beam-on, *Patrician* lifted on a mighty crest; the huge, oily swell passed beneath her and she rolled violently into the following trough. The sails slatted impotently, slapping back against the masts with a rattle of blocks and slap of buntlines. The wind dropped and, for several minutes, Drinkwater considered the necessity of anchoring, to avoid grounding in such an inhospitable spot. But the ship carried her way and the wind filled her sails sufficiently for her to maintain steerage. Crabbing awkwardly to leeward *Patrician* clawed slowly to the north and westwards, rounding Bodega Head, the far end of the bay, with a cable's length of deep water to leeward.

As the head-land dropped astern, relief was plain on everyone's face.

'A damned close thing, sir,' said Hill, shaking his head.

'Yes,' replied Drinkwater curtly. 'Stand the leadsman down now. We'll tack ship and haul to the s'uthard in an hour.'

Drinkwater saw Marsden approaching him, his hat in his hand.

'Yes, Mr Marsden, I presume you have bad news? Troubles never come singly?'

'Yes, sir . . .'

'Well?' Drinkwater could hear the slow, solemn clank of the pumps, sluicing water from below and out through the gun-deck ports. 'How much water is she making?'

''Tis about the same, sir . . . the pumps can cope . . . it's something else, sir?'

'The devil it is!'

'It's an auger, sir . . . there's an auger missin' from my shop!'

'Are you sure?'

'Aye, sir, an' both my mates agree, sir . . . gone missin' recent, like.'

'Anyone else know about this?'

'Well . . . my mates, sir . . . that's all at present but . . .' he looked round helplessly. News such as the theft of a drill-bit from the carpenter's shop following so hard on the discovery of a leak could lead to only one conclusion: the leak was a deliberate act of sabotage.

'Very well, Mr Marsden. Tell your men to hold their tongues.' Drinkwater was pale with anger and Marsden happy to quit the quarterdeck under the captain's baleful glare.

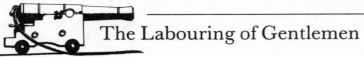

The Labouring of Gentlemen

'Drake's Bay, gentlemen.'

Drinkwater laid the point of the brass dividers on the chart, a facsimile of George Vancouver's survey supplied by an unusually obliging Admiralty whose largesse had been prompted by the desire to see him and his frigate gone from home waters. Captain Drinkwater was, under no circumstances, to have been permitted to plead any of the customary excuses for delay. The folio of copies of Vancouver's and Cook's charts had arrived by special messenger with a smooth but pointed letter from Mr Barrow: *Every consideration is being extended to facilitate the speedy departure of H.M. Frigate under your command* . . .

Drinkwater shook off the obsessive recollection to concentrate upon the task in hand as his officers clustered round. The spur of Punta de los Reyes jutted into the Pacific, doubling back to the eastward in a distal point behind which re-entrant lagoons, sand dunes and an occasional hill formed the border of a bay within which shelter from the prevailing winds and the Pacific ground-swell might be sought. Here, more than two centuries before, driven as Drinkwater now was by necessity, Francis Drake had refitted his storm-battered ship. Drinkwater had rejected the place earlier because there was a danger of its being exposed to view from the south-east, a mere thirty miles from the hostile Spaniards at San Francisco. Now, it offered them their only accessible refuge.

'Ideal, gentlemen,' he said with more confidence than he felt, 'let us hope the ghosts of Drake and his people look kindly upon us, for we have much to do.'

'Why didn't he go into San Francisco, sir?' asked Quilhampton, pointing at the great arms of the harbour as it wound inland amid sheltering hills.

'Because, Mr Q, he sailed right past it, without discovering the entrance. Now, this is what I intend we should do . . .' He paused to get their attention. They straightened up from the chart, coughing and shuffling. Fraser and Quilhampton had notebooks ready.

'Immediately upon coming to an anchor we will hoist out all the boats and lower the cutters. I want Mr Q to land Mount and a detachment of marines with seven days' rations to occupy this hill . . .' Drinkwater pointed to a neatly hachured cone depicting a summit some two miles inland from the eastern side of the bay. 'You will establish a signal station, Mr Mount. We will give you a boat-mast and a few flags and Mr Belchambers with a couple of seamen. I want a daily runner to meet a boat with your report. Understood?'

'Perfectly, sir,' nodded Mount.

'Good. Usual signals for enemy in sight . . . any approaching ship is an enemy.'

'I understand, sir.'

'Very well. When you have landed the marines, Mr Q, I want you ashore here, on the point, with an hour-glass and a tide-pole. We know the moon is waxing and the tides with it, but I want to know the maximum rise and fall as soon as possible.'

'Aye, aye, sir.'

'Good. Now Mr Fraser and you, Mr Hill, the greatest burden of the task falls on you. We will send down our topmasts and bridge the boats. I want the spare spars used for that . . . then I want two anchors laid out astern. We will shoe these, for I want no risk of them coming home . . .'

'Your pipe, Mr Comley!'

The boatswain straightened up from the rail and a piercing whistle rolled over the smooth waters of the anchorage. Above the heads of the men in the cutter, all activity aboard *Patrician* ceased. The deck parties getting the topmasts down and the spare spars over the side into the long boat, launch and barge, the details beginning to shift stores in the hold, the running messengers, the labouring landsmen and toiling cooks all stood stock still, pending the pipe to carry on.

Under the larboard bow the cutter bobbed, bowsed in to the ship's side by a boat-rope. In shirt sleeves Captain Drinkwater and Mr Marsden leaned inelegantly over the side, each with a musket ramrod placed against the ship's side; they put the other ends to their ears. The operation had been repeated several times and the men, having been exhorted to work as they had never done before were heartily fed up with the periodic whistled injunctions to stop and keep silent.

The cutter's crew strove to hold the boat as motionless as possible, the bowman bracing his boat-hook against the downward thrust of the larboard bumpkin, an oarsman stilling the rumble of a rolling loom.

'Got it, sir!' Marsden's eyes gleamed with triumph and Drinkwater withdrew his ramrod, shuffled further forward while the boat lurched dangerously and crouched next to Marsden, his ramrod replaced against *Patrician*'s spirketting alongside that of the carpenter's.

Drinkwater put his ear to the small, expanded bell that was designed to tamp the charge and ball in the breech of a Brown Bess. The dull, formless sound that was part the resonating of the ship, part the blood in his ear was dramatically displaced. It was low and indistinct, but instantly recognisable as the sound of water running through a constriction. His eyes met those of Marsden and he nodded.

'Very well, Mr Marsden, mark it . . .'

Marsden look at the hull, reached out and scored a mark with a lump of chalk. The problem still remained to discover how far below the waterline the sea was gaining ingress. Not far by the clarity of the noise. Less than a fathom? Drinkwater fervently hoped so. He nodded at Marsden again.

'Well?'

Marsden was looking up at the hull. Above them the curved head-rails swept from the fo'c's'le to the massive stem timbers and *Patrician*'s gilded and painted figurehead. Bright splashes of colour and limned streaks of gilt were encrusted with salt and the chips and chafing of ropes, while overhead stretched the gratings that formed the shitting place for the crew. Suddenly the carpenter turned to Drinkwater, comprehension widening his eyes.

'The shot locker, sir . . . the forrard shot-locker!'

'By God, Marsden, you're right!' Drinkwater turned and the boat lurched again. 'Haul her back to the ladder there, and be quick about it!'

Neither Drinkwater nor Marsden could contain their impatience as the boat was hauled aft along the ship's side. Noting the sudden flurry of activity below him, Comley leaned over the side.

'Permission to carry on, sir?'

'Yes, Mr Comley, carry on . . . and get two lanterns ready!'

Again the pipe whistled over the placid water of the bay, but now it was not the imperious single note of the 'still'. Now the note hopped down a tone and men swung to work again, cursing and bantering according to temperament and the liberty that the leading hand, or petty officer, midshipman, mate or lieutenant allowed them.

The cutter ground alongside the long-boat and launch which were being lashed into one huge raft, purlined with the spare spars to form a platform for heavy gear and guns. Drinkwater and Marsden scrambled out of the cutter.

'Thank you, Mr Frey,' Drinkwater called to the midshipman in command, 'you had better return to assist the first lieutenant to get that second anchor laid out astern.'

Without waiting for a reply and waving aside a pretended and half-cocked formal welcome, Drinkwater ran below with Marsden waddling in hot pursuit. It had been his strict instruction to his officers, and one which he himself saw no reason to disobey, that the urgency of the work over-rode everything else and that they would borrow the phrase of the English navigator who had first charted the careenage, for the gentlemen should labour with the mariners.

With the activity and eagerness of a man half his age, Drinkwater sped below. Every moment that his ship lay defenceless in the bay cost him agonies of worry; now, with almost certain knowledge of the location of the leak, he was at once nervously eager and apprehensive to see it for himself. If Marsden was right, the leak might not be so very difficult to get at. If it was an act of deliberate sabotage, some ease of access could be assumed; on the other hand anyone contemplating such a deed would run in fear of a discovery that could hang the perpetrator.

'Here, you men,' he hailed a working party hauling cable aft for bending on the spare anchors, 'belay that and come below.'

The shot locker Marsden referred to was right forward, a deep, narrow, inward funnelling space immediately abaft the massive timbers of the stem. This otherwise useless space was one of several voids about the ship in which iron shot was stowed. In the case of the two shot lockers at the very extremities of the ship, they served a double purpose and indeed, so wet and corroded did the shot in them become, that it required extensive scaling and was rarely used for action. Instead, while it formed a reserve, its chief purpose was to provide manageable concentrations of weight at the ship's ends by which, with facility, her trim might be altered.

Two or three men might, in such a remote corner of the frigate, shift the contents of the locker and get at the skin of the ship undetected. Drinkwater conceded the lead of the impromptu procession to Marsden who had grabbed a lantern. Dropping from the orlop into the hold they worked their way forward. Now the ship lay tranquilly at anchor, Drinkwater fancied he heard the haunting trickle of water long before they reached the hatch to the forward shot locker, but there was no doubt half-an-hour later when the seamen he had commandeered sweated below the faint flame of a lantern he held above their labouring heads. The pungent smell of disturbed and powdery rust cut through the thick stench of bilge as the shot was handed up and rolled like reluctant footballs aft, clear of the small square hatch-coaming. Gradually the grunting men worked themselves lower until one swore and suddenly they could see the dark gleam of running water in the lamplight.

'Look!' Marsden hissed. Drinkwater could see for himself. A partially rotten section of the ship's inner skin had been removed, the lighter colour of exposed wood showed clearly. Ten minutes later Marsden and one of his mates had swapped places

118

with the gasping seamen and levered off the broken inner planking. The jet of water that squirted inwards from the outer hit
them like a fire-hose.

They were lucky. Lucky in the mist that lay offshore, shrouding
their activities from all but the eyes of a few curious Indians and
a drunken *mestizo* that rode, legs swinging, on the swaying back
of a decayed *burro*. Lucky in the location of the leak, deliberate
though it was, for by discharging only eight guns and shifting
stores and cannon aft, they raised it above the waterline where it
could be properly repaired. And they were lucky that the wind
held light, that no disturbing swells rolled around Punta de los
Reyes to dislocate their tender situation.

But luck was something realised in retrospect, or perceived
solely by degrees. Nothing at the time could mitigate the excori-
ating anxiety that churned the pit of Drinkwater's stomach and
sent him about the deck to direct, encourage and chivvy. Periodically he cast an eye at Mount's distant flagpole. Once the signal
for an enemy in sight lifted limply above the post, and marine
runner and midshipman met at the appointed rendezvous to
learn that the ship was passing to the south and appeared not to
have seen the *Patrician* skulking with lowered masts in the bight
of Drake's Bay.

But it was not simply the dread of being caught defenceless
with his guard down and the frigate in a state of disorder, as he
had once caught Edouard Santhonax in the *sharm* of Al Mukhra,
that worried him.* Worse was the underlying anxiety of the
cause of their predicament, that deliberate act of sabotage about
which there was no doubt. He had inspected the hole and it had
been drilled with an auger bit and possibly plugged until an apt
moment arrived with a coast and refuge to leeward to compel
Drinkwater to make for the land.

There was only one explanation for such a calculated act.
Whoever planned it, intended to desert. The country about
them was empty; a desperate man could lose himself in an hour
or two of liberty. In the direction of the distant mountains, the
wooded foothills suggested fast-flowing streams, game and

* See *A Brig of War*

119

freedom. If a few desperate souls succeeded in such a venture it was almost certain that more would follow, that a trickle of stragglers might become a flood. He feared he would be left with a dismantled warship and lack the means of refitting or working her, let alone fighting her.

Such thoughts chased themselves about his weary brain, robbing him of sleep until, when he finally capitulated to exhaustion, they inhabited his dreams, assuming nightmarish qualities in which laughing, drunken seamen taunted him as they caroused with dark-eyed Spanish and Indian beauties, or stalked him through the dense woods, as he had once been stalked through the pine-barrens of South Carolina.* He would wake shuddering and sweating, steadying his nerves with a glass and sitting gloomily in his chair, ticking off the precautions he had taken to prevent desertion. Mount had been instructed to watch for a signal from the ship, so that his marines might cut off any men running from the beach; the officers had been instructed in the matter, and the one boat not needed as a platform or for some purpose concerning the refit such as holding stores, rowed a constant night-guard about them.

There had been one farcical alarm when the marine sentry on the fo'c's'le had fired at an innocent turtle, mistaking it for a swimmer, and there had been an inevitable slackening in vigilance as the days passed uneventfully. But there were Irishmen and papists aboard who were less hostile to the thought of Spanish rule, vestigial as it was; and there was a dissenting faction epitomised by the Quaker Derrick with his innocent and simplistic cant about the evils of war.

Lastly, there was Drinkwater himself, by no means unsympathetic to the aspirations of men driven by the protraction of this interminable war. Such sympathy ran contrary to his duty and his sense of the latter had been powerfully reinforced by the wanton act of sabotage, stripping from his consideration the plight of the unfortunate. In the uncompromising light of day he bore the unaltered burden of command: to bring them safe home again having first executed his orders.

* * *

* See *An Eye of the Fleet*

'Another heave, there, bullies . . . Waay-oh and belay! Fetch another tackle Mr Comley and reeve a bull-rope through the chess-tree sheave and take it to the jeer capstan. We'll get a better lead . . . stand easy a moment there amidships . . .'

Quilhampton wiped his face, smearing his shirt sleeve and feeling the fabric rasp on his unshaven cheek. This was only the third gun to be heaved back into position, though they had been labouring since four o'clock in the morning. They had eight more to drag forward from the after end of the gun-deck, 24-pounders, each weighing two and a half tons and each with an inert brutishness that provoked cursing from the tired men. Another eight of the damnable things had been hoisted off their carriages and laid on the impromptu decking of the raft.

They had lifted the bulkheads and deprived the captain and officers of their privacy, rolling guns aft and moving every possible weight towards the stern in order to lighten the bow. The after ends of both the gun-deck and the berth-deck were cluttered, and on either side of her waist amidships, *Patrician* looked like a merchantman loading from lighters.

'Ready there? Very well. Stand-to!' Quilhampton concentrated again, waving up three men with hand-spikes and shouting to set the tackles tight. Slowly the heavy carriage was manoeuvred along the deck, swung through a right angle and its wheels were trundled into the familiar grooves of its station.

Patrician had started life as a small line-of-battle-ship, bearing sixty-four guns according the establishment of the day. But ten years after her building, when war with France broke out, she was *razée*-ed, cut down by the removal of her upper gun-deck, and converted into a heavy frigate. Her main armament consisted of two dozen of the 24-pounders Quilhampton was engaged in replacing in their ports. Such cannon could be found on the middle gun-deck of first-rates, monstrously awkward things whose movement, even in the tranquillity of a sheltered anchorage, had constantly to be controlled by ropes and tackles.

'A trice more on that bull-rope, there, handsomely . . . handsomely . . . belay! That's well there! Come up!'

Men relaxed, a collective sigh of relief swept the gun-deck

and Quilhampton gave them a moment's breather before bawling, 'Next one, lads . . .'

They had started most of their fresh water casks into the bilge and then pumped out the contents to lighten the ship and lessen her draught. That first day Quilhampton had spent hours watching the tide make sluggishly upwards, marking the pole he had driven into the beach. It had risen little more than a fathom, insufficient to persuade Captain Drinkwater to beach the ship. Besides, thought Quilhampton, looking round him as the tackles were over-hauled and hooked into the carriage ring bolts of number nine gun, the leak had been reasonably accessible and a heavy stern cant had brought it above the waterline. They had been lucky. Damned lucky.

'How do you do, Mr Q?'

The unintended rhyme of Fraser's enquiry provoked a ripple of laughter, laughter that the spent officers left unchecked. It was at least a symptom of good nature.

'Well, enough, Mr Fraser . . . tomorrow should see the guns back and at least we'll have our teeth again.'

'Aye, then we've only to re-rig, ship spars and boats and dig fifty tons o' ballast out o' yon beach, fill wi' fresh water, rattle down and weigh three anchors an' we'll be as fit as fighting-cocks to combat the world again . . .'

Fraser moved off to inspect the parties in the orlop and the hold, preoccupied and almost as worried a man as his commander.

'Set tight there . . . pass word to the jeer capstan . . . right, heave . . . !'

'Well?' Drinkwater looked up from the charts strewn about the table. Fraser noted they were of Vancouver Island and the Strait of Juan de Fuca. He tried to draw encouragement from Drinkwater's optimism.

'Quilhampton estimates the main batteries back in position tomorrow, sir. He has only the guns overside to hoist inboard now.'

'Good. And the hold?'

'Restowed, but wanting ballast and . . .'

'Water, yes, I know. If we ration we'll have sufficient for a week or ten days, by then we shall fetch a bay to the northwards. There are a hundred watering places on this coast.'

'What about here, sir?'

'Too brackish, I fancy,' Drinkwater tried to encourage Fraser with a smile, aware that he could produce nothing more than a wan grimace. 'And aloft?' he prompted.

'Two days, sir, to be certain.'

'Yes, but I didn't like the temper of tonight's sunset. We may not have too long.'

'No, sir. We've been lucky . . .'

'Damned lucky . . .'

Drinkwater woke aware that he was being shaken violently.

'Sir? Sir, wake up . . .'

'What . . . what is it Mr Belchambers? It *is* you ain't it?'

'Yes, sir . . . Mr Quilhampton presents his respects sir . . .'

'Eh? Oh, what's the time?'

'Just before dawn, sir . . .'

The cabin was still dark and Drinkwater felt a surge of irritation. The news of the previous evening that the end of their predicament was in sight had somewhat relieved his mind and the sleep he had fallen into had been profound. 'What the devil are you calling me for?'

'It's a ship sir . . . a ship coming into the bay!'

Rezanov

'What kind of ship, Mr Belchambers? Large? How rigged?'

He was awake now, his heart pumping painfully, every shred of anxiety turned over in the previous days now fully justified. This was the Russian ship, advised of their whereabouts and now enabled to catch them half-armed and trapped in the bay. Nicolai Rezanov had paid court to the lovely Doña Ana Maria, languished awhile to recruit his people and relax from the cares of his voyage. Then he must have received reports from the local Indians and Spanish spies that could not have failed to spot the strange ship, or the unfamiliar red coats of Mount's marines at Drake's Bay. Even by the slowest *burro*, news must have reached Don José Arguello of their whereabouts; even, perhaps, their unpreparedness. A sudden violently bilious spasm of hatred towards the anonymous saboteurs jerked him upright from his cot. By God they were going to pay for their treachery now!

'A ship, sir . . . that's all I am able to say, except that Mr Quilhampton is passing word to call the men, sir, quietly . . .'

'Very well, I'll be up directly, pass the word for my coxswain.'

'Aye, aye, sir.'

The midshipman scuttled away as Drinkwater reached for his trousers. Beyond the curtain he could hear the sounds of the ship stirring, the muted groans of tired men dragged early from their hammocks. Where in God's name were his sword and pistols?

'Where away?' Drinkwater hissed, staring into the grey dawn light. Mist trailed away over the water, luminous from an imminent dawn which already lightened the eastern sky.

'Right astern, sir. See where the masts are outlined against the sky?'

'Yes . . . I have her now.' The final fog of sleep dispersed. He could see the upper masts of a ship. How far was she distant from them? How diminished by perspective?

Others were creeping aft. Fraser and Hill joined them.

'I've ordered a spring passed forrard, sir,' said Fraser, 'we can get the starboard broadside to bear . . .'

'Yes,' Drinkwater acknowledged flatly, simultaneously pleased that Fraser had demonstrated his initiative, and irritated that he had not thought of the thing himself.

'What d'you make of her?' he asked Hill, who peered intently through his glass. Daylight grew by the minute and, Drinkwater thought, they were hidden as yet against the land and the re-treating night. If the intruder was meditating surprise she had better loose it upon them quickly. 'Well?'

'I don't think it is the Russian, sir . . . at least not that two-decker we sighted off the Horn.'

'Then what the devil is it?' Drinkwater snapped testily, abusing his rank and giving vent to his high-keyed state.

'Want me to take a boat and see, sir?'

'Too big a risk . . . but thank you. No, let us wait for daylight and spend the time getting her under our guns.'

A few minutes later Fraser reported the capstans manned. The cable from one of the two stern anchors had been led for-ward and a spring taken to the midships' capstan so that by heav-ing and slacking on the trio of anchors, *Patrician* was turned through almost a right-angle, set within a web of heavy hemp hawsers, her starboard broadside run out and her men at their quarters. In utter silence they waited for daylight to disclose their target.

Details emerged slowly, remarked upon as they were noticed. her ship-rig, her tall masts and the opinion that she was a Spaniard were followed by other intelligence as to the paintwork and the run of her hull, until the disclosure of a mere six gun-ports confirmed she was only a merchant ship.

The mood changed instantly. Instead of apprehension there was cursing that only a single boat remained to seize her, though they might knock her clean out of the water with a single broadside from the eager guns.

'They must have seen us by now,' said Drinkwater, puzzled at the lack of reaction from the strange vessel. As though this thought had taken wing it was followed by a hail.

'Ahoy there! What ship is that?' The question was repeated in bastard Spanish, but the accent was unmistakable. The newcomer was a citizen of the United States of America, a fact confirmed by the hoisting of her bespangled, grid-iron ensign.

'A Yankee, by God!' remarked Hill, grinning. Drinkwater, seeing them hoisting out a boat and unwilling to reveal the chaotic state of his ship, snapped, 'Get the cutter alongside, *I'll* pay *him* a visit.'

'Well now, Captain . . . sit you down and take a glass. I'm damned if I expected to find the British Navy hereabouts . . . you wouldn't be thinking of pressing my men . . . I might not take kindly to that.'

Captain Jackson Grant replaced the short clay pipe between his teeth and fixed Drinkwater with a grim stare.

'I would not drink with you and then steal your men, Captain.'

'There are those of your party that would, Captain.'

'You have my word upon the matter.'

Grant laughed. 'You think that settles the thing, eh?' He removed his pipe and Drinkwater saw that the man possessed eyes of different colours. The left was dark, the iris brown, while the right was a paler blue. The oddity gave his features, which were otherwise heavily handsome, a curious disbelieving appearance.

'You can rest assured, Captain Grant, that your men are quite safe . . .' Drinkwater recalled the hostile looks that had been thrown in his direction as he had come aboard.

'Here . . .' Grant passed a glass, *'aguardiente,* Captain,' Grant drawled, '"burning water", made by the Spanish from local grapes. Not to be compared with the cognacs of France, but tolerably agreeable to rough provincial palates.'

'Your health, Captain.' Drinkwater suppressed the shudder

126

that travelled upwards from his stomach in reaction to the fiery spirit. Grant's tone was bantering, hinting at hostility, a hostility that was, for the moment, overlaid with curiosity. They were of an age; Drinkwater put the next question.

'You fought for your independence, Captain?'

Grant grinned, showing yellow teeth. 'Sure. I served under Commodore Whipple and in privateers. Made a deal of money from my service too. British money. And you?'

'Yes. Under Rodney and ashore in the Carolinas. And against privateers. My first command was as prize-master . . . little schooner called the *Algonquin* of Rhode Island.* We caught her slipping into the Irish Sea to stop the Liverpool merchants resting at night . . .'

'God damn! Josiah King's ship?'

'I do not recall the name of her commander . . .'

Grant's curious eyes narrowed to slits. 'You can have been no more than a boy . . .'

'Nor you, Captain . . .'

Grant's hostility began to melt and he grinned, his face relaxing. 'Goddam it no, we were both just boys!' He leaned forward and refilled Drinkwater's glass. The shared memories and the raw brandy loosened their mutual suspicions; both men relaxed, exchanging stories of that now distant war.

'So what *do* you do in Drake's Bay, Captain, with your masts struck and the look of a surprised wench about your ship?'

'Refitting, Captain, a spot of trouble with a leak. And you?'

'A spot of trade,' he held up the glass, closed his brown eye and focused the blue one on the pale amber fluid. '"Fire-water" sells well, hereabouts. I can't sell it in San Francisco, but *mestizos* and Indians'll be here once they hear Cap'n Jack's anchored.'

'I see,' said Drinkwater wryly, raising one eyebrow. 'And for what do you sell the *aguardiente*?'

Grant grinned again, showing his wolfish teeth. 'California bank-notes, Captain, dried hides, can't you smell 'em?'

Drinkwater sniffed the air. The faint taint of putrefaction came to him.

'Yes . . . and you get the *aguardiente* from where?'

* See *An Eye of the Fleet*

127

Grant shrugged. 'Monterey, San Francisco, San Diego . . .
the damned Franciscans proscribe the trade there, but I find,' he
laughed, 'the customers come to me.'

'From whom do you buy the stuff, then, if the Franciscans
have a hold on the country?'

'Oh, there are plenty of suppliers, Captain. Don't forget I
come from civilisation. I can supply bows, buttons, lace and fur-
belows from Paris faster than the Dons can ship their dull and
dolorous fashions from Madrid.' Grant's smile was knowing.

'Does Don José Arguello trade with you?'

Grant shot Drinkwater a shrewd look and his tone was suddenly guarded. 'Oh, no, Captain. Don José is an *hidalgo*, *Commandante* of this vast and idle province. Spanish governors are
forbidden to trade on their own, or their province's accounts.'
Grant tossed off his glass and refilled it. 'Why do you ask?'

'Curiosity.' Drinkwater paused. It came back to him that
there had been that atmosphere of hidden secrets about the *Commandante* and his entourage. 'His brother then, Don Alejo?'

'You're very shrewd, Captain Drinkwater, as well as being im-
properly named . . .' Grant refilled Drinkwater's glass. 'You have
heard of the lovely Doña Ana Maria Arguello de la Salas, eh?'

'I have heard something of her . . . and also of a Russian . . .'
He let the sentence trail off and sipped the glass. A feeling of con-
tented well-being permeated him. His limbs felt weightless, his
energies concentrating on thinking, of gauging this American
and divining how much truth he was speaking.

'Oh, yeah . . . I heard the damned Russkies had fallen out with
good old King George. Well, he couldn't look after his own could
he? Eh?'

Drinkwater sat quietly, refusing to be drawn, raising his good
shoulder in a careless shrug.

'Sure. Now I know why you're here. An' the damned Russkies. Don Alejo encourages them . . . and he trades . . . who
wouldn't? A man must take something back to Castile better
than button scurvy or mange from this desert of Nueva España.
You've heard of Rezanov, Captain, eh?'

'A little, perhaps. I understand he stands high in the favour of
the lady you mentioned.'

'Arguello's daughter?' Sure, she dotes on him and the match is encouraged by those Spanish apes.' Grant was suddenly serious. 'She's a beautiful woman, Captain, perhaps the *most* beautiful woman. Certainly she's the most beautiful woman Jackson Grant has ever seen. Yes, sir. You haven't seen her . . . by God, she got eyes like sloes, shoulders like marble and a breast a man could do murder for . . .'

Drinkwater stirred uncomfortably, but Grant was oblivious in the fury of his passion. His weird eyes gleamed with an intensity that spoke of the coastal rivalries fired by the unfortunate beauty of Donā Ana Maria.

'Why a man would pass over a score of these damned flat-nosed Indians, even a brace of the best-looking *Ladinos* from Panama with wanton arses and coconuts for tops'l yards, for an hour in that lady's company for all that she only strummed a guitar and wore the habit of a nun . . .' He wiped the back of his hand across his mouth, poured another peg of brandy into his glass, tossed it back and refilled it again.

'And Rezanov?' Drinkwater prompted.

'Ah, Rezanov . . . Nicolai Petrovich Comte de Rezanov,' Grant lisped the name with an aping of a French accent, his eyes glaring with dislike. Then his faced cleared and he laughed, a cruel laugh. 'You have not been in the Pacific long Captain . . . I consider you should not have come at all . . . you damned British have no right here . . . but neither have the damned Russkies . . .' Grant's voice was slurred, his mind shifted briefly to his Anglophobia and then slid back to a more personal hatred. He waved his hand towards the stern windows. The pale streak of the beach rising to dunes and dun coloured hills could be seen beyond the anchorage. 'Nueva España . . . New Albion . . . New Muscovy . . . come Captain, it's not yours, nor Spain's, nor the fucking Tsar's. One day it'll be ours . . . a state of the Union, Californio . . . mark my words Captain, and Jackson Grant'll be a founding fucking father . . .' Again he held up the glass of *aguardiente* and glared through it with one bright blue eye.

'Oh, Rezanov had his ideas . . . big ideas . . . he came out with an expedition under Captain Kruzenstern, accredited ambassador to the Mikado at Yedo, but the little yellow men kept him kicking his heels at Nagasaki before kicking his arse out of their waters.' Grant chuckled. 'Kruzenstern went on his way and left Rezanov in the *Juno* to inspect the factories, forts and posts of the Russian-American Company . . . now what d'you think the Russian-American Company was, eh? Nothing but a damned front for the bloody Tsar to get his claws on this part of the world. They trap the sea-otter and shoot the grizzly bear, but they can't get the bloody furs to Canton faster than Jackson Grant, and the poor bastards live in squalor in Alasky and the Kuriles. You should see them at Sitka, why it'd make your lower deck scum look like lords . . .

'Rezanov thought he could kill all these ills . . . damned odd lot these Russians. Rezanov thought he was a prophet . . . guess that's why the Doña Ana fell for his line of speaking, her being influenced by the papist church . . . Well . . . he came prospecting down the coast . . . Sitka, Nootka, the Colombia River, Bodega Bay and San Francisco . . . and Doña Ana Maria and her father, *El Commandante* . . .'

'And he secured an alliance to trade?'

Grant shrugged. 'Sure, something of the sort, I guess. They say he bettered that Franciscan corpse that passes for a confessor . . . Don Alejo at least had gold from him . . . Tartar gold, and that's fact . . .'

'And from Doña Ana Maria?'

'A promise of marriage . . .' Grant stared gloomily into his glass, the brown eye lugubrious.

'And Rezanov returned to the north?'

'Yeah. I last saw him at Sitka. I heard later he'd set off for Russia to confirm a treaty with the Tsar . . . get it ratified, or whatever the hell they do with these things. He got his own back on the yellow men, too,' Grant laughed, 'sent men and ships and took the island of Sakhalin from them to please his master, I guess. Reckon a Tsar's signature must be worth an island or two, eh, Captain?'

'And when is he expected to return, this Rezanov?'

Grant frowned, the drink clouding his powers of thought. He seemed to be trying to recall a lost fact. Then, as he remembered, he smiled. 'Never, Captain . . . you see Rezanov's been dead a year . . . just heard the news in Sitka . . . he died like a dog in Krasnoiarsk . . . left the field plum clear for Jackson Grant . . .'

Grant chuckled and Drinkwater considered the import of this news. Apart from altering the life of Doña Ana he did not see that it was of much effect to him. There was still that Russian battle-ship.

'Captain Grant, have you seen anything of a Russian man-o'-war on the coast?'

'Sure. The *Juno*'s at Sitka, or was when I left, bound, so word had it, for the Colombia River . . .'

'But the *Juno*'s been in the Pacific for some time, hasn't she?'

'Yeah. She was built on the coast, a frigate . . . maybe thirty, forty guns.' Grant craned unsteadily on one chair leg, staring at the distant *Patrician*. ''Bout the same size as yourself . . .'

'What about a bigger ship? A two-decked line-of-battle-ship with a black hull? Have you seen such a vessel?'

Grant shook his head. 'No . . .'

'And where are you bound from here?'

'San Francisco . . .'

'To tell Doña Ana her lover is dead?'

Grant frowned through his drunkenness. 'They don't know?'

'They were expecting him.'

'What? How the hell do you know that?' Grant attempted to rise, but fell back.

'I was there a fortnight ago.'

'Shit, Captain . . .' He broke off to think, rubbing his hand across his mouth again and then pouring out more brandy. 'How the hell did you get into there and out again without the bloody Inquisition catching you? You're at war with the Spaniards, ain't ya?'

'Under a flag of truce, Captain. I was a cartel . . . returning Spanish prisoners. We took the frigate *Santa Monica*.'

'*Dios!* And Rubalcava? Did you take him a prisoner, or did you kill the bastard?'

'I took him prisoner. I imagine he's pleading his suit with Doña Ana at this moment.'

Grant looked up, fixing Drinkwater with his odd eyes, the one

131

dark and agonised like a whipped cur's, the other flinty with hatred. Drinkwater was surprised at the depth of the wound he had inflicted. 'All's fair, they say, in love and war . . .'

Grant's mouth hung open when suddenly the sound of distant shots came through the open stern windows. Drinkwater rose and peered in the direction of the *Patrician*. Even at this distance he could see the smoke of powder hovering over the deck, and the desperately rowed boat was making for the shore full of men. He grasped the situation in an instant. His men were deserting!

'God's bones!' he hissed through clenched teeth, picking up his hat and making for the door. 'Your servant, Captain Grant, and good luck!'

And the words 'All's fair in love and war' tormented him with their accuracy all the way back to the *Patrician* in the cutter.

Drake's Bay

'How many?' he asked, aware that he had asked the question before. Last time the answer had shocked him, now it appalled him.

'Forty-eight, sir.'

He looked down the list that Fraser handed him and then at the remnants of *Patrician*'s company assembled in the waist. With Mount absent the bayonets of Blixoe's marines seemed a thin defence against a rising of the rest. Forty-eight men lost in a single act of mutinous desertion. And the remainder were in a black mood. How many of them would have run given the opportunity, seduced by over-long a proximity to the shore yet deprived of even the feel of warm sand under their feet? And he was half-drunk and the day not far advanced . . .

'We were heaving her round, sir, as you said, ready to bring her out of the bay and someone cut the after cable. She swung to the wind and the stern's touching the bottom.'

'Thank you, Mr Fraser.' He looked round the deck and coughed to clear his throat. 'Very well, lads, if there's another man who wishes to go I'll not stand in his way. But I warn you I'll hang anyone . . . *anyone* I catch. Those of you that remain need fear nothing. We shall haul the ship off and complete rigging her. We are better off without unwilling ship-mates. Now let's to work . . .'

Drinkwater turned away, sick with despair, aware of the brandy on his breath and guilt-ridden by his absence at a crucial moment.

'Ah'm sorry, sir, I couldna' gie chase, we had just cast loose the barge frae the raft, an' you had the only other boat . . .'

Fraser's acccent was exaggerated by stress. Wearily Drink-water acknowledged his plight.

'It's not your fault, Mr Fraser, not entirely. We must worry about Mount. I hope to God he does not run foul of those men. Have they arms?'

'Two or three were marines, sir . . . aye, they've a gun or two between them.'

'Get a signal of recall up to Mount and then let us haul her into deeper water.'

Suddenly the danger from surprise attack by Russian battle-ships seemed a foolishly mythological preoccupation. *Patrician* herself appeared to carry her own ill-luck.

Drinkwater stared down at the rag tied round the hawser. It had definitely crawled aft an inch or two. By a stroke of misfortune the ship had grounded close to high water, and now she was reluctant, twelve hours later, to come off. Above them a full moon hung in the velvet sky and from time to time the ship lifted and then bumped on the bottom as a low swell rolled in from a distant gale somewhere in the vast Pacific.

'Again, my lads.' He could hear the creak of the capstan, the grunts of the straining men and the slither of their bare and sweaty feet on the planking. The rag moved aft another inch. A feeling of hope leapt in Drinkwater's breast. 'Again, lads, again!'

They caught his tone and the grunts came again. He heard Lieutenant Quilhampton's exhortations. Thank heavens they had shoed the anchors, augmented the palms of the flukes with facing pieces of hard-wood, so that they held better and allowed the anchors to bite and not drag home to the ship before they had hauled her into deep water.

The rag jerked again and then began to move steadily. The ship lifted to a swell, the rag surged aft, there was a dipping in the rope and the men cheered, they could feel the tension on the messenger and the nippers ease, someone had fallen over and a ribald laugh came to him. The swell crashed onto the beach and the ship shook with great violence as the entire length of her keel struck the bottom.

'Heave again . . . heave away!'

She was off now, he could feel it through the deck. The next swell passed under her and, though he waited for it, she did not strike in the low trough that followed. Half-an-hour later they had her safe in deeper water.

'Stand the men down, now, Mr Fraser. Six hours below, then turn 'em out again. I want this ship in fighting trim by this time tomorrow.'

They had not finished by the following night, for the long pre-saged gale burst upon them in the late afternoon. The lurid sunset of the previous evening, green as verdigris, had held its ill-promise by a deceptively mild morning; but gradually cloud had obscured the sun and a damp, misty wind had rolled in from the Pacific. Urgently they had hoisted in the boats and had recovered all but the damaged barge abandoned by the deserters on the distant beach. Even the masts and spars were ready to go aloft again.

As the wind freshened they watched Grant get his ship under-way. There was a flamboyant style to the American com-mander. He loosened his sail and threw his foreyards aback, making a stern-board, until he brought the wind broad onto his starboard bow. Drinkwater watched in admiration, aware that Grant was cocking-a-snook at the British Navy, demonstrating the supreme ability of both himself and his men, men that Drinkwater would fain have had aboard *Patrician* at that moment despite his promises to the American. Grant hauled his fore-yards with a nicety that would have delighted even that old *punctilio*, Earl St Vincent, and stood out to sea, heading south-eastwards for the better shelter of San Francisco Bay. As Drink-water watched in his glass the last thing he saw was the American vessel's name, *Abigail Starbuck*, gold letters fading in the grey mist, above which, conspicuous at the taffrail, stood a single figure. Drinkwater could almost imagine Grant winking that pale and sinister ice-blue eye.

'Do you trust him to hold his tongue, sir?' asked Hill, who had also been watching the departure of the American ship. 'Or will he gossip our predicament through every *bagnio* in San Francisco?'

'I mind someone telling me the word "Yankee" is Cherokee Indian for one who is untrustworthy. In Captain Jackson Grant's case I would certainly judge him to be opportunistic.' Drinkwater wondered if Grant might make use of what he knew to gain access to Don José and, through him, to Doña Ana Maria. 'But that, Mr Hill, is just the opinion of a bigoted Englishman with a deal of things on his mind.'

'Aye . . . the men . . .'

'Or lack of 'em. God's bones, Hill, I wish to God I'd not gone gamming with that damned Yankee!' Drinkwater's tone was suddenly ferocious.

'You'll not go chasing after them, sir?'

Drinkwater turned to the old sailing master. He shook his head.

'Damn it, no. We'll lose the whole festering lot of them once they get ashore. Grant spent yesterday selling rot-gut spirits to the Indians, and I daresay our fellows will soon hear about that. These men will go to the devil if they have half a chance. No, I'll not go chasing after them . . . but damn it, Hill, we've hardly men left to fight. Grant said there was at least a frigate at Sitka . . .'

'But no two-decker . . .' Hill's tone was tolerantly reasonable, like a parent leading a wilful child to a desired conclusion.

'You still don't think that ship we saw off the Horn was a Russian, do you?'

Hill shrugged, almost non-committally. 'No, sir, I'm more inclined to think it was a Don and is presently sitting off Panama. And even if it was a Russian, what in the world makes you think it's hovering over the horizon, like Nemesis?'

'You think I am obsessive, eh?'

'You've had a deal of doings with Russia, sir,' Hill said circumspectly, 'I know that . . .' Drinkwater looked at Hill. They shared past clandestine 'doings' on behalf of Lord Dungarth's Secret Department, and Drinkwater saw concern in the older man's eyes. '. . . But here, in the Pacific, surely it's unlikely . . .'

'*Unlikely?* What's unlikely? That the Russians are anxious to dominate the Pacific? Or that I'm off my head about a ship I saw off the Horn? Damn it, Hill, what the deuce d'you think we're out here for but to lick the blasted Russians before they take advantage of the decaying power of Spain? What better time for 'em with Spain a nominal ally, but the whole damned world knowing that the Dons are under the Corsican's tyranny and rotten at the core. D'you think if the Russians land there, that whoremonger Godoy in Madrid is going to lift a finger? Why, he's too busy lifting the skirts of the Queen of Spain!'

Drinkwater's diatribe descended to crudity for lack of better argument. Though he saw Hill could not dismantle it and was reluctantly conceding his viewpoint. He could not explain to the master that he was haunted by fears of a less logical kind.

Hill had not had that prescient dream off Cape Horn, Hill had not been touched by the strangeness of the incident on Más-a-Fuera, nor by the undercurrents of something sinister between the Arguello brothers, nor by the beauty of Doña Ana Maria, nor the jealous lusts she excited, nor the ghost of Nicolai Rezanov. Some intuition, born perhaps of the blue-devils, of the isolation of command, of too introspective a nature, or too vivid an imagination, but some powerful instinct told him with a certainty he could not explain, that they were in danger.

Its source was, as yet, conjectural, but its reality was as obvious to him as the smell of distant blood to a famished shark.

The gale lasted two days. *Patrician* escaped the worst of it behind the low shelter of Punta de los Reyes, though she snubbed at her cable and rolled in the swells that cart-wheeled into Drake's Bay. They got her topmasts hoisted despite it, and set up her rigging to the upper hounds. A lighter mood settled on the ship as they prepared to face the second night of dismal and howling blackness.

'We're better off without them . . .' said Mylchrist as the wardroom officers relaxed after the day's labours and discussed the matter of the deserters.

'Good God, Johnnie, you ain't going to give us a speech about "we happy few" and "summoning up the blood" are you? For God's sake we're in the Pacific, not on the stage.' Quilhampton slumped in his chair and toyed dejectedly with a biscuit.

137

'James is right, you know, we're in a damned parlous condition,' observed Mount seriously. He too sat downcast at the table, his fingers fiddling with the stem of a wine glass, rolling it and fitting it over the numerous wine-rings that marked the table-cloth. He had taken the defection of his two marines badly and was angry that his detachment to the observation post had occurred at all. In Mount's opinion, the desertions would not have taken place had he been directly in control of the sentries.

'And now there's a gale . . .'

'And a delay . . .'

Hill came into the wardroom, peeling off his tarpaulin and shaking his head. Water flew from his soaked hair as though from a dog. 'A delay that'll ensure the Dagoes know of our whereabouts . . . give me some shrub, for God's sake, that rain makes a man chilly . . .'

'Have a biscuit . . .' Quilhampton pushed the barrel towards the master who occupied a vacant chair. 'Where's the first luff?'

'Wandering about worried sick . . .'

'Och, an' away,' mocked Mylchrist, but no one paid this puerility any attention.

'And what does the Captain think, Hill? You had his ear all morning?'

Hill looked at Mount, aware that the marine officer held Drinkwater to blame for his absence from the ship at a crucial time.

'You know damned well what the Captain thinks; he's as concerned as the rest of us.'

'And this Russian nonsense? He'd do better thinking the Americans have their greedy eyes on this coast . . .'

'We ain't at war with the Americans,' drawled Mylchrist, eager to re-establish his credibility after his rebuff.

'Doubtless we soon will be,' said Quilhampton, *'Britannia contra mundum.'*

'Now who's bleating about "we happy few"?' Mylchrist crowed.

'I think, gentlemen, it's time for sleep . . .' Hill tossed off his pot and rose. 'God grant we're out of this pestilential spot tomorrow morning.'

'Amen to that . . .'

Below his pacing figure the ship slept, exhausted with the seemingly endless exertions of the day. Only the anchor-watch were about, huddled in corners and beneath the boats to avoid the drizzle that hardened from time to time, into heavy showers of torrential rain.

The night was black, the wind tugging at the ship and moaning in the lower rigging, rising periodically to a higher cadence as it shifted a point and freshened. But it always fell away again, never sustaining a promise of abandoned violence, though every time it rose, Drinkwater's heart beat faster in anticipation of fresh disaster. In such a state of mind, sleep was impossible.

So he walked his quarterdeck in the time-honoured tradition, between the main mast and the carved taffrail, for no better reason than it seemed the only way to pass the time of anxiety and to be on hand if the worst of his fears came to pass. He was half-dead with his fatigue, his brain had lost the power of coherent thought, yet was too active to permit sleep. In an unending kaleidoscope it reviewed a tumbling series of images, of monstrous black ships in the mighty combers of the Horn, of yawning caverns of water that threatened to suck him down into the bowels of hell, of the laughing mockery of the white-lady of his nightmare who, inexplicably and with a paralysing abruptness, changed into the dark and lovely vision of Doña Ana Maria. And even as he sank fantastically upon her white and ample breasts he found the scimitar smile of Rubalcava and the triumphant eyes of the Arguello brothers. Above these images the imperious shadow of Hortense Santhonax manipulated the wires of a marionette.

In all this waking, walking nightmare he paced the deck, his senses all but dead to anything beyond the fury of his hallucinating brain, his cloak wrapped round him, his eyes stark staring into the windy blackness of the night, until at last he slept, slumped against a quarterdeck carronade.

* * *

Lieutenant Quilhampton jumped into the shallows and splashed ashore followed by Sergeant Blixoe, four marines and the bow-man of the cutter. As the boat was dragged onto the beach and Blixoe wandered off, following the scuff marks of the deserters' foot-prints in the sand, Quilhampton strode along the beach to the stove barge. He was joined by Marsden, the carpenter. Both of them stood for a moment looking at the split and holed planks in the side of the boat, the results of a few moments' work with a boarding axe.

'Tomahawk,' opined Marsden, laying the finger of a horny hand upon the splintered wood. 'I can patch it to get her back on board.' He patted the gunwhale of the boat.

'Very well . . .'

'I'll need a hand . . .'

Quilhampton called the cutter's crew over to assist and they lifted her gunwhale and braced her at a practical angle with foot-stretchers and bottom boards so that Marsden could plug the hole with a greased canvas patch covered with a lead tingle. While the work progressed, Quilhampton followed Blixoe up the beach.

The marine sergeant had orders not to proceed out of sight of the ship and Quilhampton followed him to the highest sand-dune in their vicinity.

'Bugger-all, sir,' said Blixoe, turning as Quilhampton came up with him.

'Did you really expect 'em to be in sight, Blixoe?' Quil-hampton grinned despite himself, for the marine was itching to fire his musket and dispel the obloquy the returned Mount had heaped upon him. 'No scalps for you, Sergeant, I'm afraid.'

'One 'opes, sir, one 'opes,' Blixoe replied grimly, still search-ing the desolate locality like a hound sniffing the wind. 'What about there?' He pointed. Beyond the dunes stretched the fingers of an inlet, spreading northwards, cut off from the ocean by a long isthmus which culminated behind them in Punta de los Reyes. An Indian village, a miserable collection of adobe dwellings overhung by the wispy smoke of cooking fires, lay some miles to the northwards.

Quilhampton shook his head. 'No . . . do you ensure none of the fellows that came ashore with us run.'

Blixoe turned and they looked down at the huddle of men round the barge. The rest of Blixoe's men stood about, their stocks loosed in the sunshine that burned warm after the passing of the rain and wind, their loaded muskets at the port, the bayonets gleaming wickedly.

'No bloody fear of that, sir.'

They looked at the ship, silhouetted black against the sun's lambent reflection which danced upon the surface of the sea and was diffused by the watery mist that still lay a league offshore. Already the topgallant masts were aloft and they could see the foretopgallant yard being hoisted, its length slowly squaring against the line of the mast as the lifts were adjusted and its parrel was re-secured.

'Not long now,' Quilhampton remarked, a sense of relief pervading him. Their luck had held so far. A few more hours . . . nightfall perhaps, tomorrow morning at the latest, they would feel the deeps of the ocean beneath their keel.

'No sir. We've been lucky.'

'Yes, damned lucky.'

'They say that leak, sir,' ventured Blixoe, taking advantage of Lieutenant Quilhampton's mellow mood, 'well, that it were caused deliberate, like . . .'

Quilhampton looked sharply at the sergeant, but the man was in profile, his bucket hat pulled down over his eyes as he stared at the *Patrician* anchored in her pool of sunshine.

'And what do *you* say, Mr Blixoe?'

Unperturbed, the marine shrugged his white woollen epaulettes. 'How should I know, sir?'

'I'll lay a guinea you've a theory of your own, though.'

Blixoe pulled the corners of his mouth down. 'I reckon we've all got theories, sir. Trouble is, the truth ain't much to do with theories, is it?' Blixoe turned and faced Quilhampton. 'Truth is, sir, that the men are at the end of their tethers. We lost a good prize and we know there's rich pickin's off the bloody Dagoes; there's men as knows the papist's ways, stuffin' their churches with gold and word has it that there is a church somewhere about

141

this coast where they've the bones of some saint all laid out in a casket of jewelled gold . . . and what they're wondering is why, begging your pardon, sir, the Captain ain't batterin' down these bloody Spanish churches, sir . . . by way of an act of war, like? That's the truth of it, sir.' Blixoe paused, then added, 'If you'll pardon me for speaking freely . . .'

'Yes, of course, come, they seem to have finished down there . . .'

They could see the barge being dragged into the water. Men were scrambling into her, ready to pass her painter to the cutter. Quilhampton looked again at the ship. The foretopgallant yard was across.

And then he froze. The heat went out of the sun and his heart suddenly thudded in his chest. 'Look!'

Pointing with one hand he restrained Blixoe with the other. The marine paused and shaded his eyes against the glare. They were insubstantial at first, mere phantoms in the haze, but then their outlines hardened, the sharp, squared edges of topsails, the low hulls of men-of-war standing into the bay. There could be no doubt as to the purpose of their approach.

'Come on!' Slithering in the sand, Quilhampton began an awkward descent.

'Fire those bloody muskets, lads,' Blixoe called to his platoon and a ragged volley of alarm sounded flatly across Drake's Bay.

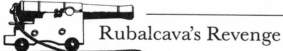

Rubalcava's Revenge

'God's bones!'

Drinkwater swung round and stared at the beach as the sound of the volley echoed across the bay. He expected to see men running but on the contrary, they stood stock-still around the boats, every attitude suggesting they were as surprised as himself at the shots. Then he saw the tiny white figure of Quilhampton in his shirt-sleeves, running ungainly through the soft sand, his arms waving wildly and with the four marines stumbling after him.

'What the devil . . . ?'

'Deck there!'

They swung to the hail from the foremast where topmen sat astride the newly sent up top-gallant yard.

'To seaward, sir!'

Drinkwater and the officers idle on the quarterdeck spun round, following the man's urgently outstretched arm.

'Bloody hell!'

'It's those Spanish brigs!'

'Jesus!'

The two brigs had broken through the vaporous tendrils of the mist and were suddenly recognised as the vessels they had seen last anchored under the shadow of Point Lobos, beneath the *Commandante*'s Residence. They were standing into Drake's Bay, their yards braced and on slightly diverging courses. End-on, Drinkwater did not need glasses to see the bristling lines of cannon piercing their sides.

'Beat to quarters! Man the capstan!'

They had a spring upon their anchor cable; it lay slack in the

143

water and, if they were quick, might give them a moment's advantage.

'Where's my coxswain?'

'Here, zur . . .'

'Sword and pistols, upon the instant! Gentlemen, arm yourselves . . . they will rush us!'

The deck of the *Patrician* presented a spectacle of disorder. Topmen descended from the foremast by the backstays, sliding down hand-over-hand. Officers and men ran, bumping into one another, as they scurried to their posts.

'Man the larboard broadside!'

Drinkwater saw Fraser, his sword drawn, his shirt-tail untucked from some strenuous endeavour at the base of the foremast, run below to command the battery in Quilhampton's absence. Amidships, Hill stood ready by the capstan, pushing spare waisters into place about the splayed bars and then Tregembo was awkwardly hitching his sword-belt about his waist and Derrick was silently offering him his pistols.

He stuck one in his waistband and fisted the other. A thought struck him and he held it out to the solemn Quaker. 'Here, defend thyself, if no one else . . .'

Derrick shook his head and Drinkwater, his mind pressed, dismissed the man for a high-minded fool.

'Guns are bearing, sir,' squeaked Belchambers alongside him, sent by Fraser.

'Are they loaded, damn it?'

'Mr Fraser says to tell you they're loaded, sir as best they can be . . . mixed shot and langridge . . .'

'Then run 'em out!'

The boy skittered off and Drinkwater took one last look about the deck. It was a chaos of flung-down hand-spikes, of uncoiled ropes and stoppered sails rolled in grey sausages of resistant canvas. Spars, half-secured and almost ready for hoisting, lay at drunken angles, like pitch-forks left against a hay-cart. But the men at the quarterdeck guns were kneeling ready, though their breasts heaved from their late exertions, and the dishevelled marines, in unprofessional oddities of dress, leaned upon the hammock nettings, their bayonets gleaming and their muskets

144

levelled. They had not been utterly surprised and, as yet, the Spanish had not a single gun that could bear. Below his feet he felt the 24-pounders rumble out through their ports.

The brigs were close now, perhaps two cables away and he could hear an angry buzz that came from a dense cluster of men about their twin fo'c's'les. They were dark with boarders, heaped like swarming bees.

'You lads there,' Drinkwater called to the quarterdeck gun-captains, 'mark their boarders,' he raised his voice, 'mark their boarders, fo'c's'le!' a wave of comprehension came from Midshipman Wickham forward. If those three carronades did their business, their spreading langridge would tear a bloody and ragged hole through that cluster of men.

As the noise from the brigs grew louder it seemed a grimmer silence settled upon the *Patrician*. Drinkwater pierced it. He would have to loose his cannon soon, or risk his enemies stretching ahead and astern of him, out of the lines of bearing of his guns.

'Stand by for boarders! Fire!'

The thunder of the cannon erupted in orange flames and the white obscurity of reeking powder smoke. The deck vibrated with the recoil of the heavy trucks and, as the smoke cleared, he could see the gun-crews leaping about their pieces as they reloaded. But, it was already too late. So close were the brigs that the most elevated gun had sent its shot no higher than man-height above their rails. Their masts and topsails, shivering now as they checked way to drive alongside, loomed above the shredding smoke and Drinkwater could see the white circles and inter-lacing and expanding ripples that showed more than half his shot had plunged harmlessly between, and far beyond, the Spaniards.

But there were bloody gaps in the clusters of men about the beakheads of the enemy, and there were dots in the water, some inert and some waving, where men died and shrove their souls in agony. He could hear the screams and a weird ululating cry as some unfortunate man spewed shock and horror and the dreadful pain of a mortal wound into the air.

It was a moment of the briefest pause. Below a fast-reloaded

145

gun roared again, followed by another and another and then Drinkwater turned. The first brig crashed into the bowsprit, locking her own in a tangle of splitting wood and torn wreckage. He could see the smoke and stab of small arms and a few bold men beginning to scramble across the interlocked spars as the enemy brig, thus entangled, fell slowly off the wind and along-side the British frigate.

Aft, the second brig loomed close alongside. There was a sickening crash as her cathead struck the *Patrician*'s quarter and the impact of the collision sent a second mighty tremble through the ship. A grappling iron struck the rail and its line was belayed, to be cut through by a marine; but another followed, and another, and the marine fell back, clutching his throat, shot through at close range by a pistol ball.

'Get your men on deck, Fraser!' Drinkwater roared below and swung round, his sword drawn, joining the hedge of bayonets and boarding pikes and cutlasses as the gunners abandoned their now useless pieces and fought to defend themselves.

The Spaniards poured over the rails, jumping like reckless monkeys from one ship to another, and Drinkwater knew that the Dons had emptied every stew and calaboose, every tavern and every vessel with men who had a mind to cut the bloody British intruders down to size. And, God, there were enough of them. If every waterfront idler, and every drunken *mestizo* in San Francisco had come, it did not explain the torrent of men that poured, cutting, slashing and stabbing their way across his quarterdeck.

He recognised the uniform of a provincial Spanish regiment, an officer leading a party of the brig's seamen, together with a ragged rabble of 'volunteers', a mixed rag-bag of races, half-drunk and verminous from the desperate look of them.

But as he fought for his life, he recognised something else, something that his heightened consciousness had half-expected. There were men from the *Santa Monica*, men in clear breach of their parole, and at their head, howling with the triumphant bellow of a *conquistadore*, was Don Jorge Méliton Rubalcava.

*　　*　　*

146

By the time Quilhampton reached the boats, the brigs were alongside *Patrician*. He splashed through the shallows and fell into the stern of the cutter.

'Leave the barge!' He ordered, panting with exertion, 'Oars! Come on, come on,' he chivvied, 'give way together!'

Shoving the tiller across the boat, he swung the cutter's bow round towards the noise and smoke of desperate battle.

Drinkwater was slithering in gore. His right forearm was cut and blood trickled from the graze of a pistol ball across his skull. He hacked and stabbed with his sword and the clubbed pistol in his left hand was sticky with gore. He was aware of beating off a savage attack, of flinging back the first impetuous rush of the Spaniards. He was aware too that Midshipman Wickham had reported from the fo'c's'le that they had succeeded in staving off the inrush of boarders forward. Slewed on their slides the heavy carronades had cut swathes of death through the enemy and dampened the ardour of their attack.

But Lieutenant Mylchrist had been carried below dangerously wounded, and Wickham feared another rush from the regrouping Spaniards. Drinkwater asked where the first lieutenant was, but lost Wickham's reply as he parried a pike thrust and cut savagely at a swarthy cheek, seeing the bright start of blood and the pain in the glaring eyes of a man.

'Mount, bayonets here!' he bawled and threw himself back into the fight as the Spaniards renewed their attack upon the heavily outnumbered British.

Fraser never got out of the gun-deck. From a boat towing alongside, or by sliding down the bumpkins of the after brig, men squeezed through a loose gunport as Fraser obeyed Drinkwater's order to reinforce the upper deck with his gun-crews. This small intrusion quickly became a torrent as two, then three ports were opened. Dark, lithe men with short stabbing knives clenched in their teeth and wet from a partial ducking alongside, hauled themselves inboard to confront the gunners. The gun-crews were tired after days of exertion and the recent labour of hauling out their weapons and it seemed this influx of men was endless, a

147

wildly diabolical manifestation rising from hell itself. They were small wiry, half-caste fellows, who wriggled between the guns and seemed utterly at home in the shadows of the gun-deck, as happy as the nocturnal pick-pockets, scavengers, footpads, pimps and thieves they were. They slipped easily inside the long guards of defenders with rammers and pikes, hamstringing and hobbling men who fell howling, only to be disembowelled and eviscerated by the gleaming knives that flashed dully in the semi-darkness.

His hanger flickering desperately, Lieutenant Fraser was fighting for his very life.

Mr Lallo motioned to Skeete and the loblolly boy dragged the twitching body of Lieutenant Mylchrist to one side. Already the pledget they had just secured was darkening with blood.

'Next!' Lallo wiped a reeking hand across his brow and took a pull at the rum bottle he kept propped against a futtock.

Derrick, the captain's Quaker clerk, heaved the next victim onto the canvas spread on the sea-chests. It was one of the topmen, a big, burly man whose legs were curiously drawn up in the foetal position. His eyes were staring wildly and his lips were rimed with dried spittle. The swaying lantern hooked above the operating 'table' threw dreadful shadows across his features, so that his face seemed to be working in convulsive spasms.

Skeete forced fingers into the man's mouth, prised open his jaw and, with the vicious ease of practice, thrust a damp pad of leather into the topman's gape. The jaws snapped like those of a predator.

'Legs down!' Lallo ordered and Skeete jerked his head at Derrick. The Quaker swallowed hard and took the leg opposite to Skeete, while Lallo forced down the man's shoulders.

'Ahhhh . . .'

Lallo slopped rum into the open mouth and deftly replaced the leather pad as the man went slack.

'Not on the wound, for Christ's sake!' Lallo shouted as Derrick, beholding the complete horror of the injury, gagged uncontrollably.

Lallo slopped rum on his hands, wiped them on his apron,

148

and bent over the ghastly ruin of the man's abdomen. The fetid air of the orlop was filled with the stench of blood, urine, rum and vomit and resonated with the groans and whimpers of the wounded.

'He's lucky,' remarked Lallo to the professionally interested Skeete, 'no rupture of the guts . . .' His finger traced the blue outline of a section of intestine, almost caressed the crinkled mass of a protruding curve of bowel and pointed to the smooth darkness of an excrescent organ.

'Aye.' Skeete agreed with his superior.

'Needle and sutures, Skeete . . .' Lallo began tucking the misplaced viscera back into the hollow of the body. He might have been stuffing a cushion. 'You'll have to help,' he remarked, looking up at Derrick, who had come forward again, his forehead pale as wax in the yellow guttering of the lamp-light. 'You should be used to quaking,' he jested, provoking a snigger from Skeete as he produced the prepared needle.

They drew the two sides of the topman's belly together and, with a swift and deft precision, the surgeon looped a line of sutures down the white flesh.

'Missed his wedding-tackle eh, Skeete?' he remarked, finishing the stitches with a flourish.

'By a mile, sir,' grinned Skeete.

'Next,' said Lallo . . .

Midshipman Frey was on the quarterdeck. He was already wounded in the shoulder and feeling light-headed. He felt a terrible blow in his guts, a blow that drove the wind from his body and he felt himself flung back, crashing against a gun carriage and slumping down, hitting his head on the bulwark. For a long time he lay inert, the noise of battle seemingly miles above him while he fought for his breath in an interminable indrawn gasp that seemed like an enormous and unsuccessful paroxysm that would go on until he lost consciousness.

But he did not lose consciousness entirely. He seemed dimly aware of many things; if he did not succeed in inflating his lungs he would die, but the light was bright in his eyes and he remembered the sunshine, diffused by the golden mist. The upper spars

149

that he had been engaged in hoisting, seemed drawn with a perfect precision against the sky. He had thought of attempting to paint that effect of the light later, and he thought of the resolution again now, only filled with a sadness that he might never be able to try it. If he did not draw his breath soon, his hand would have lost its cunning for ever.

And then the reflex triumphed and air was drawn painfully into his lungs. Agony radiated outwards like a bomb-burst from his chest, stabbing him with fires of red-hot iron and it seemed easier to die than to endure.

There were other things troubling him now. The sunlight flickered before his eyes as the dark and sinister shadows of men interposed themselves. He found he resented this and began to try and call them, to tell them to stop standing in the light, that he wanted the warmth of the sun to die by. He could see clearly now, shoes, and bare feet, and a marine's boots, all dancing in a mad figure. He would have to shout louder to make them hear and then they would stop . . .

Drinkwater saw Frey fall and cut his way through between a Spanish officer and a marine, swinging the sword across the neck of the seaman whose pike butt had been driven into the midshipman's guts. The exposure of himself was foolish for, in his concern, he half-turned to see if the lad was alive and received another nick on the forearm for his trouble. But it was the merest pin-prick, the point of a weapon, a long lunge and he saw the triangular blade withdrawn, following it with his eyes until he found its owner, Rubalcava . . .

'You treacherous bastard!' Drinkwater attempted to bind the grinning Spaniard's blade, but a man fell across in front of him stone dead, and he saw it was a marine, and suddenly he was ringed with steel, standing astride the howling, heaving body of Midshipman Frey with a dozen enemies surrounding him. He gasped for breath and read triumph in Rubalcava's eyes.

He saw the Spaniard lower his sword point and stride across the deck. He brandished the long blade in a single side-swipe, severing the halliards of the ensign.

The wind tugged the huge, St George's cross and the bright

150

Union in its upper canton. Slowly it fluttered downwards to lie across *Patrician*'s shattered rail. The noise of fighting ebbed away, to be replaced by the silence of defeat.

Quilhampton, willing the oarsmen to reach the ship as soon as possible, was watching events ahead of him in a lather of impatience. He did not recall until they were half-way back to the *Patrician*, that he had come ashore unarmed, relying upon Sergeant Blixoe's party to maintain discipline. His chief concern had been to recover the damaged barge. Now he was running full-tilt into action with nothing more than a tiller in his hand.

It was at the moment that this dawned on him that he saw the ensign lowered to the rail in token of submission. Aghast he stood in the boat, staring dumbfoundedly ahead. Seeing him thus, the oarsmen faltered, trailing their oars and looking round.

They were in the shadow of the ship and everywhere swarmed the alien figures of the enemy.

'Fuckin' 'ell, they've taken the fuckin' ship . . .'

'Oh shit . . .'

'Put the helm over, sir . . . let's get the 'ell out of 'ere, for Chrissakes, before those bastards see us . . . come on you lot, backwater starboard and pull like fuck on those larboard oars.'

Quilhampton came to his senses as the boat turned, the jerk of the fleeing oarsmen set him heavily in the stern sheets. He did not interfere with their retreat.

His premonition had been right. They had lost the ship to the enemy.

PART TWO

FLOOD TIDE

'Le trident de Neptune est le sceptre du monde.'
Lemierre

Débâcle

Drinkwater woke in the dawn, disturbed by the throbbing of his wounds and the spiritual nadir of defeat. His cell was a bare room with a small, barred window, a crude table, chair and palliasse, the details of which were just visible in the gloom. The hopelessness that had dominated his thoughts in the night was displaced by the physical discomfort of his body, and this demanded his attention. He was still tired from lack of sleep, but the edge had gone from his exhaustion, and his brain began to seek priorities in the instinctive business of survival.

They had brought him stumbling up what had seemed like thousands of steps before throwing him into this small room. He had no inkling of where he was beyond a vague realisation that Rubalcava had brought his prize into San Francisco Bay. Fatigue, despair and loss of blood had deprived him of rational thought in the aftermath of surrender and it was only just returning to him in the chill of this desolate dawn.

Slowly he dragged himself to his feet and stumbled to the chair, peeling off his coat and laying bare the bloody mess of his forearm. His head ached and he had another wound on his thigh, as well as numerous bruises and a shivering reaction to his plight.

They had left him a plate of bread and a jug of wine. After a mouthful he began to feel a little better. On the table lay the ship's log-book and his journal. He remembered taking them from his rifled cabin. They had also left him tinder and a candle end. He fished in his pocket. His Dollond glass was still there together with a small pen-knife.

He drew out the latter and prised out its tiny blade. Elizabeth had given it to him. For a moment he sat regarding it mistily, fighting off an impulse to weep. He had a second draught of the raw wine and, while the shaking of his hands subsided, he fought to strike flint on steel and catch a light to the candle. It took him several minutes, but he felt much better as he made himself work.

Pulling off his shirt, he removed the tails and tore them into squares, using the wine to clean the superficial head-wounds, scouring them each until some subtle change in their hurt told him no purulent matter adhered to the tissue. Feeling bolder he set to work on his thigh. Like those on his forearm the cut was raised, hot and inflamed. Gritting his teeth he pulled the wound open, releasing a glair flood of matter and shuddering with the pain of the thing. When he had mastered himself he heated the knife blade. He knew he should perform curettage, that much he had learned from M. Masson, the surgeon of Admiral Ville-neuve's flagship, the *Bucentaure*. Only thus could all the morbid flesh killed by the weapon be removed. His own surgeon, Lallo, did not believe the theory, pooh-poohing it for Gallic nonsense and regarding, Drinkwater suspected, his own enthusiasm to be verging on the treasonable.

The knife sizzled on his flesh, sending up a disgusting stink as he watched his own body burn. Only when the pain became unbearable did he stop, sweat pouring off him as his muscles contracted into a rigor of agony. He poured wine across the gaping redness and bound his leg with a piece of shirt. Then he turned his attention to his arm.

When he had finished he felt a curious shift in the nature of his pain. The insistent throbbing had eased, replaced by the sharp, almost exhilarating tingling of butchered nerve-ends. The former had throbbed with the rigadoon of death, the latter the invigoration of life.

Daylight had come by the time he had finished. Carefully he edged the table nearer the tiny window and, gritting his teeth, he clambered up on it. He found he could see out quite easily. He knew instantly where he was and the half-acknowledged familiarity of the ascent of the previous evening came back to him.

Between his prison and the distant mountains to the east, the

156

bay of San Francisco harbour lay awash with mist. The summits of the trio of islands, Yerba Buena, Treasure Island and Alcatraz, the island of pelicans, rose like mountain tops above this low cloud. So too did the masts of ships, the half-rigged top-gallants of *Patrician* and close on either side, the lower trucks of the Spanish brigs. It seemed to him extraordinary that he did not even know their names. But this realisation was submerged in a greater horror. From the jutting peak of *Patrician*'s spanker gaff the damp folds of bunting lifted lazily in the beginnings of a breeze. There were two flags, the one flaunting above the other; the red and gold of Castile superior to the white ensign. Such a publicly visible token of his abject plight took his spirit to new depths. He could not bear to look, and in shifting his gaze saw other masts, those of the merchant ships anchored off the town, and wondered if the treacherous Grant's *Abigail Starbuck* lay amongst them.

But his eyes were drawn ineluctably back to his ship, emerging steadily from the evaporating mist. Raising the Dollond glass he focused it upon the battered rail and relived that terrible hour.

James Quilhampton woke to the barking of a dog and was instantly on his feet. Rigid with damp and cold he and his men had spent a miserable night beside the cutter. They had watched, in utter dismay, as the victorious Spaniards had carried *Patrician* out of the bay. The shame of the British defeat seemed emphasised by the superior size of the captured ship, but Quilhampton had been granted little time for such fancy philos-ophising. His party consisted of himself, Blixoe and his three privates, Marsden the carpenter and a boat's crew of eight sea-men who had been sent to recover the barge. Their situation was desperate. They had no food or water and the mood of the men was by no means stable. It did not take Quilhampton long to realise that several of the cutter's men were ripe for desertion and that his hold on the leadership of the little band was tenuous. Without a sword he felt naked, and without his coat his wooden arm, its articulation and belting exposed to the gaze of the curious, made him feel doubly vulnerable.

They had escaped from the action unobserved, rowed the cutter deep into the re-entrant lagoon behind the bay and bivouacked after a fashion in the lee of the boat. Blixoe had shot two ducks and they had roasted the carcasses over a miserable fire hidden from observers in a small valley between the dunes. After that they had slept, Blixoe and his marines on their guns. When Quilhampton awoke to the yelp of the dog the first thing he noticed was that the man approaching them did not seem alarmed at their presence. This realisation put him on his guard and he called the others awake.

The newcomer sat astride a plodding donkey, his large, horny feet hanging almost to the ground. He wore a dirty cotton suit, his face grimy and unshaven beneath a battered, wide-brimmed hat. He had a long knife at his belt, carried a gun and, Quilhampton noticed, across his curious wooden saddle-bow a wine-skin was slung.

Trying to look casual Quilhampton stood and wished the newcomer good morning.

The man reined in his *burro* and grinned, letting fly a torrent of incomprehensible words and jerking his jutting chin from time to time in the direction of the open sea. He appeared to end his address on an interrogative note. Quilhampton shrugged.

The stranger made the universal gesture of eating and then pointed in the direction of the village they had seen from the summit of the dunes the previous afternoon.

'He's tellin' us we can get food at the village, sir,' muttered Blixoe.

'Yes.' Quilhampton nodded vigorously. The stranger grinned and rubbed his right forefinger tip against the ball of his thumb.

''E wants money.'

Quilhampton shook his head. 'No . . .' he tried to remember scraps of Spanish he had learned as a prisoner at Cadiz, three years earlier, but his memory failed him as the stranger's eyes became less friendly. The man jerked the head of the *burro* round, suddenly suspicious.

Quilhampton had a sudden inspiration. 'Hey . . . *amigo* . . . *agua* . . .' He pointed at his mouth. The mongrel was crouched, as though guarding his master's retreat from these ragamuffin strangers, growling defiance.

But the newcomer was not in a charitable mood. He hefted his gun and kicked the donkey forward. Giving a short bark, the dog turned and followed.

'He had a wine-skin,' said Blixoe, raising his musket.

'No . . .' The powder in the pan flashed and the shot knocked the hat from the *mestizo*'s head. His long legs kicked the donkey wildly and the over-burdened beast broke into an awkward gallop.

'Hold your fire!' Two more of the marines followed their sergeant's lead. The wineskin, jolted or flung sacrificially from its perch, plummeted to the ground while man, donkey and dog disappeared whence they had come.

A howl of triumph went up and the seamen and marines began running forward. Realising what was happening Quilhampton began to run too. He reached the wine-skin just as a seaman picked it up.

'Give it to me, Lacey.' He held out his hands. The seaman looked around, seeking support among his mates.

'Bollocks,' said someone behind Quilhampton and Lacey tore the plug from the neck of the leather bag and squirted the dark fluid expertly into his open mouth. The act was a signal, the men clustered forward and grabbed at the thing, wine spilled about them and some reached eager mouths, though none were satisfied. Quilhampton, Blixoe and Marsden stood back from this unruly mêlée. Then something inside Quilhampton snapped. He strode forward, swung his wooden arm and scattered the drinkers, catching the wine-skin as someone dropped it.

'Sern't Blixoe, get some order into these men . . . you too Mr Marsden . . . pull yourselves together and remember you're man-o'- war men, not scum!'

He raged at them and they, shamefacedly responded, though one or two remained truculent. Blixoe got his men to shepherd them into a rough line.

'Now then . . . that's better. Let me remind you I'm in command and I shall decide what's to be done . . .'

159

'Well what *is* to be done . . . sir?' sneered a man named Hughes.

'That's for me to decide.' Quilhampton faltered. What *was* to be done? There would be food in the village and the inhabitants were, nominally at least, enemies. The marines had their muskets and bayonets, the seamen their knives. Marsden also had his tools, only he himself was unarmed.

'Well . . . I think the first thing to do is to secure some victuals in the village. I'm sure we can persuade our friend to give a quantity of bread as well as the wine.' It was a feeble joke but it brought a laugh to unite them. They turned and began to follow the tracks of the *burro* through the sand.

The Royal Navy had invaded California.

Drinkwater stood as the bolts of his cell were withdrawn. Bread, wine and fruit were brought in and he was reminded of imprisonment in Cadiz in the days before the great battle off Cape Trafalgar. He recognised his guard too, for while the tray bearing his breakfast was carried by a half-breed, de Soto stood in the doorway. His face was expressionless and Drinkwater met his gaze, suddenly feeling his spirit must not submit.

'You are dishonoured, sir,' he snapped suddenly. 'Captain Rubalcava has broke his parole!'

A flicker of anger kindled in the officer's eye as the last word suggested the gist of Drinkwater's outburst. He uttered a word to the *mestizo* who swung a bucket into the cell and retreated, pulling the door behind himself with a crash of bolts.

But Drinkwater felt a renewal of hope. Beyond the confines of the stone corridor he had heard a laugh, a loud, happy laugh and he knew instantly the very curve of the throat from which it had come. He was in a cell below the commandant's residence, a bridewell for special 'guests' of His Excellency, too precious to be mewed up in the common *calabozo* of San Francisco.

'Well Captain, please sit down.' Captain Jackson Grant, speaking fluent and colloquial Spanish motioned Rubalcava to a seat. He grinned at the dark and vicious face of the Spaniard. 'You have come to pay me, eh?' Grant laughed.

160

Rubalcava nodded. 'Yes, I have come to pay you. You are short of men, I have come to pay you in men . . .'

'The devil no! I gave you intelligence of the British . . .'

'You said you were short of men, *Capitán* Grant!'

'Sure, I said I was short of men. I *am* short of men, but I'm damned if I want men for what I told you. I can get my own men in the first cat-house ashore . . .' Grant shouted angrily.

'You will take men, *Capitán* Grant, because that is what you are being paid . . .'

'Damn you Rubalcava, I don't *need* men. I can sail this hooker from here to Baltimore with a mate and a cook!'

Rubalcava's mouth curved in a sneer. 'You have a great reputation for bragging, *Capitán*. You will take men . . . as I give them . . .'

'The hell I will . . .' Grant was on his feet. Rubalcava merely lifted his elegantly booted feet and put the red heels on Grant's table. 'I want gold, Rubalcava, gold . . .'

'We have not yet found El Dorado, *Capitán*, in the meantime, you will settle for men, otherwise . . .'

'Shit, man, there *is* gold in California . . . what the devil do you mean *otherwise*?'

'Otherwise, *Capitán* Grant, we shall have to inform the authorities that you have been selling *aguardiente* to the natives.'

'The hell you will . . . I *bought* the fucking stuff from the authorities!'

'I think you are mistaken, *Capitán*. At least, the authorities know nothing about the matter.'

Grant expelled a long, frustrated breath. 'You will regret getting the better of me, Rubalcava, damn your insolence . . .'

Rubalcava smiled again. 'Perhaps, *Capitán* . . . anyway I have six men for you. All prime seamen, just as you require.'

'Six. Good Good, man, you have a whole frigate's crew imprisoned. You could have let me have more than six!'

'For you to sell to the Russians? No, no, *Capitán*, these are honourable prisoners-of-war. Besides, we need them to work cargo in the merchant ships.' Rubalcava paused, catching the American's eye, 'Or to dig for gold in the hills, *Capitán*, eh?'

Grant laughed, good-naturedly. 'Oh, sure, Captain Rubal-cava, sure.'

'It is thirsty work, discussing business, *Capitán* Grant.'

Grant blew out a breath and reached for two glasses and a bottle of *aguardiente*. He slopped a finger of the brandy into each glass and handed one to to the Spaniard. 'To what do we drink, then? Eh?'

'To the late Nicolai Rezanov, eh *Capitán* Grant?' And with his free hand Rubalcava piously crossed himself. '*Requiescat in pace.*'

Lieutenant Quilhampton waved Blixoe's flanking party forward, waiting with the main body in a slight hollow in the sand. He watched Blixoe and two of his marines edge forward, approaching the strangely silent village. The smoke of cooking fires rose into the air and the clucking of hens could be heard, but the bark of a dog or the squeal of a child was suspiciously absent.

There was a sudden shout and sand spurted up around Blixoe's party. A haze of smoke hung over the wall of a ramshackle hut and Quilhampton could see the rough timber had been loopholed for small arms. Blixoe began to wriggle back in retreat. There was a second volley and then a whoop. Ragged Indians and half-castes, the tiny population of fishermen, ran out of the hut and launched an impetuous charge across the beaten sand towards them. They waved a few muskets and staves and pikes, and they outnumbered the cutter's crew. Quilhampton turned to his men, but they were already in full flight. He made a violent movement of his good hand to Blixoe who needed no second bidding and twenty minutes later they had tumbled into the cutter and were pulling as hard as they could from the desultory shots and the shouted insults of the natives.

When they had opened the range they hung over their oar-looms and those of them that could, laughed at the comic humiliation of their predicament. Others sat and pondered what was to be done.

'It is God's will, friends, we shall have to make the best of it. It is not the first time we have been torn from our places by the rough circumstances of existence.'

162

'For Chrissakes, you witless fool, do you not know that a Yankee packet is hell compared to old Drinkwater's barky.'

'Old Drinkwater don't have a fucking barky, Sam, so let's take Derrick's advice and make the best of it. They say these Yankees pay well and sail like witches.'

'And their women is handsome, their land rich and we shall find the streets of Baltimore paved with gold . . . yes, I heard the same kind of crap from a recruiting lieutenant somewheres . . .'

'Well my lads . . . so you've volunteered for service under the old stars and stripes, the flag of liberty, free trade and sailor's rights and glad we are to welcome you all aboard the old *Abigail Starbuck*.'

Captain Grant came on deck to review his new recruits. Clucking his tongue and pronouncing himself satisfied, he delivered them to his chief mate.

It was towards evening when the bolts of Drinkwater's cell were drawn back again. Don Alejo Arguello entered the tiny room and swept a bow at his prisoner.

'*Capitán* . . . I am so sorry that you have been the misfortunate victim of the bad luck of war.'

'The misfortunes of war have little to do with it, Don Alejo. I had your words that Captain Rubalcava would not serve again . . .'

'*Capitán*,' Don Alejo protested, his tone exaggeratedly reasonable, 'Don Jorge, he is an officer of, of energy, of spirit . . . he was on board with me, one of the four *fregatas* that your navy attacked without declaration of war four years ago . . . Do not talk of civilisation, *Capitán* Drinkwater . . .'

Drinkwater remembered the incident. Their Lordships had despatched a force of four frigates to intercept a squadron of Spanish cruisers homeward from Montevideo with specie worth over a million pounds sterling. Their force had been so equal that the Spanish commander, Rear-Admiral Don Joseph Bustamente, had been compelled to fight to defend the honour of his flag. A superior force would have achieved the same result (which was to provoke Madrid to declare war) and have avoided the loss of many lives and the explosion of the Spanish frigate

163

Mercedes. Governments could forget such things easier than the men whose lives they marked.

'You understand, *Capitán* . . . Doña Ana Maria said you were *simpático* . . .'

'Where are my men, Don Alejo, and my officers? Is the surgeon allowed to attend the wounded . . . ?'

'*Capitán*, I forgot, you are wounded. I will have to send for . . .'

'I am all right, Don Alejo,' snapped Drinkwater, 'it is my men I ask after.'

'My dear *Capitán*,' Don Alejo shed some of his easy humour and his tone hardened, 'we are civilised people. They are being looked after and your officers, they are in the charge of military officers . . . come, I will bring you ink and a pen and send you some meat; we shall look after you. Good night . . .'

And he was gone, leaving Drinkwater alone with his thoughts.

'Belay that sheet and settle down . . . now pay attention. We have only about ten leagues to sail to San Francisco. When we get there we can find out what has become of the ship and our shipmates. Then I will decide what to do. Whatever happens we will have to slip into the harbour unobserved, either at night, or in a fog. I am relying on your loyalty. That's all.'

'I'm hungry . . .'

'Aye and thirsty . . .'

'You can belay that lubberly talk. We're all hungry and thirsty, but tomorrow we will find water at least . . .'

'I bloody hope so . . . for your sake . . . lieutenant . . .'

Quilhampton ignored the sneer. The boat rose and fell on the long Pacific swells that were the aftermath of the recent gale and other, more distant, disturbances. Under its single lugsail the cutter made a good speed and the tiller kicked under his arm. The day was leaching a golden glow across the western horizon behind them as they steered south-east and the first stars were visible against a clear, rain-washed sky.

It was curious, he mused, how the merest chance could comfort a man and how insubstantial a foundation was required for hope. But the disastrous loss of the ship seemed to satisfy some

164

arcane and superstitious foreboding that had haunted him for so long, that its fulfilment had come as something of a relief. And so retrospectively ridiculous had the day's events seemed, that their escape was like an *entr'acte*. This instant was reality; this kick of the tiller, this dying of the day and the chuckle of water along the boat's strakes. He sensed a curious and inappropriate contentment, as of one having turned a momentous corner. The episode on the beach had been one of desperation. He was now engaged on something of purpose. The boat's course was his best chance of seeing Catriona MacEwan once again. And as his men dozed, James Quilhampton hummed gently to himself, and beat time with his wooden hand upon the gunwhale of the cutter.

The Prisoner

Time hangs heavily upon a lonely man who has suffered a great misfortune. His troubles dominate his thoughts and disturb his attempts at sleep. He relives the hours of his disaster in a knowingly fruitless attempt to reverse time; he attempts to shift blame and then to acknowledge his own responsibility. His mind deploys logic and then rejects it in favour of vague, superstitious emotions which play on the very vulnerability of his isolation. Culpability seems his alone; he has dared too much and providence has cut him down to size. Such solitary pits for the soul are dug by circumstance for every commander of ships. In this, Drinkwater was no exception.

Although logic told him the chain of bad luck began when the leak forced him to seek the shelter of a careenage, superstition sought an earlier explanation: the hanging at the Nore, the loss of the Danish privateer, the sighting of the strange ship off the Horn, the incident at Más-a-Fuera. Even the worthless capture of the *Santa Monica* seemed but another malevolent step in a fantastic conspiracy by fate. Such fears, dominant in the small hours, could have been dispelled by a turn on the quarterdeck at dawn while the watch swabbed down and the smell of coffee blew about the ship. The 'blue-devils' was a misanthropy endemic among sea-officers but against which there were known specifics.

Some men played instruments, some invited company, some diverted their minds by reading, writing, sketching. Some drank. All relied upon the routines of the naval day to ameliorate their obsessive preoccupations. Some carried the dissolution of their lives within their characters, some gave way to jealous fits, some to violent abuses of their powers. Some bickered with their officers, some immersed themselves in trivial matters and disturbed the tranquillity of their ships. Most ultimately coped, because demands were put upon them that compelled them to submit to influences beyond their own passions.

Cooped day after day in solitary confinement, allowed no exercise beyond the tiny cell, Drinkwater went unrescued by routine or any demand upon his expertise with which to patch his spirit. He was left alone with the wild fears of his imagination. Logic told him that he was guilty of misjudgement and incompetence, and every view from his tiny window reinforced this opinion as he looked down upon his captured ship. Superstition told him he had been abandoned to his fate, that dark, unworldly spirits had been released by his actions. From beyond the grave Edouard Santhonax laughed; a great hollow laugh that brought him bolt upright from sleep and his old enemy melted into the gentle, uncomprehending pity of his own wife's face.

How would Elizabeth feel when she heard? What would Lord Dungarth conclude? What would John Barrow think of him?

'What will they say in England?' he whispered to himself. They had become too used to victory . . .

But that was no good. That was merely another excuse. Discontent had caused the leak and for that he alone was responsible. For several days his mind revolved along this morbid orbit. He sought consolation in the writing of his journal, but after the harrowing experience of recording the events in the log, he could put nothing in his private papers that did not reek of self-pity. He began to dismiss in his mind all mitigating factors. His own culpability began to assume its own stature and grow in his thoughts so that it threatened to unhinge him. But in the end long experience of a solitary existence saved him. The learnt disciplines of combating the blue-devils came to his rescue. At first he stood upon the table and scanned the anchorage, avoiding the sad sight of *Patrician*. He watched the merchant ships, half a dozen of which he could just see. The comings and goings of their boats, the laboriously swept lighters that crabbed out to them like giant water-beetles with the hides and tallow and

167

assorted exports of the colony. He could see among them, the *Abigail Starbuck*, a tall-sparred, handsome vessel, as were all the latest American ships. Once he thought he saw Jackson Grant, and once, quite ridiculously, the figure of the Quaker Derrick upon her deck.

It was that sighting that brought him to the recognition of his self-deception. It was clearly a ridiculous fancy! He would have to take hold of himself. Although he had not mitigated his self-blame, from that moment it ceased to be a passive response to his predicament and began to spur his resolution to transcend his plight. He began to write in his journal and in doing so called up incidents of the previous days that were not directly connected with the loss of the *Patrician*.

. . . *I realised the place of my imprisonment when I heard the laugh of Doña Ana Maria* . . .

He stopped writing as a thought struck him. If Grant had betrayed him to the Spanish, why had not Grant told Don José of the death of Rezanov? And if he had, why had the news not been communicated to the Russian's betrothed?

That laughter had been full of unalloyed joy, the expectant, irrepressible joy of someone expecting the arrival of a lover. Drinkwater recalled how her eyes had glowed as she had spoken of the Russian. He shook his head. The time for such abstruse preoccupations was over. He wrote on, dismissing the matter, for it made no sense to him and had no bearing on his fate.

He was woken next morning by the concussion of guns. For an instant hope leapt into his heart but the noise, answered somewhere to seaward, resolved itself into an exchange of salutes. He clambered up onto his table. For a long time he could see nothing and then, into his field of view and bringing up to an anchor slightly to seaward of the *Patrician*, was the heavy black hull of a Russian line-of-battle-ship.

James Quilhampton had seen her the previous day from the rocks of a small and insignificant headland a few miles north of the entrance to San Francisco. In the little cove behind him the cutter lay drawn up on the beach, while from the wooded slope that rose behind the strip of sand, came the dull sound of an axe.

Occasionally the snap of a musket betrayed Blixoe's hunting party.

They had crept into the cove to hide and recruit their strength while Quilhampton decided what to do. Sweet water streamed out of the dense woods and they slaked their thirst and rinsed the salt from their clothes and bodies. That night they bivouacked in the fragrant undergrowth and loafed the following morning away, waiting for the night. In the late afternoon they had sighted the big ship coming down from the northward. From the little promontory, Quilhampton saw she was a two-decked man-of-war, black-hulled and flying the dark, diagonal ensign of Russia.

It seemed the final bar on the stronghold of the enemy, setting awry his carefully made plan. Ordering the men to spend another day in idleness he languished in indecision. But game and water was plentiful, and the fresh meat emboldened him. When the next evening Blixoe came to him for orders, he had decided to throw everything to hazard.

'Very well,' he said as they lay back round the fire, licking their fingers clean of the juice of venison, 'this is what I intend that we do, and if any man will not gamble on the outcome he is free to take his chance . . .'

Quilhampton wanted none but willing spirits with him.

His fears were vindicated; he had no doubt this was the ship they had seen off Cape Horn and now she arrived like Nemesis. Through his glass he saw the twinkle of gold braid upon her quarter-deck, saw her entry manned and the Spanish officer board her. He could hear the faint piping shriek of the calls, given in the British style by officers who had trained with the Royal Navy. Drinkwater remembered Admiral Hanikov's fleet in the North Sea in the summer of 1797 and wondered whether this ship had come direct from Kronstadt or had been detached from Seniavin's Adriatic squadron.

He saw, too, the procession of boats leave the side of the Russian ship and, half an hour later, heard the sound of voices speaking French pass below his window, Russian officers ascending the path that wound upwards to the Residence from

169

the boat jetty and the battery below. Surely now the news of the death of Rezanov would be made known to Doña Ana Maria? To his recovering mind the preoccupation offered a point of focus beyond his own unhappiness.

'*Capitán*, I have the honour to present Prince Vladimir Rakitin, of His Imperial Majesty's ship *Suvorov*.'

Drinkwater gave a short and deliberately frigid bow. Although he was curious about the Russian his incarceration had made him angry and he fixed his eyes on Don José.

'Don José, I protest at the dishonour you have done to me. Where are my officers? Why have you not permitted a surgeon to visit me, or allowed me to exercise? What have you done with my people? I had always thought the Spanish a civilised nation. I am mortified to find myself, so recently a guest at your table, treated with every courtesy due an honourable enemy employed on a mission of humanity, suddenly deprived of the courteous formalities of war. You are, sir, guilty of having condoned the breaking of the terms of exchange by Captain Rubalcava and his men.'

Drinkwater felt invigorated by the cathartic effects of this outburst. He felt washed clean of the self-pity that had nearly drowned him in his confinement. Now there were other causes to fight, exposures to make before this newly arrived ally of the Spanish authorities. He turned towards the Russian officer: 'I am sure that His Imperial Majesty's Navy would not have treated the courtesies of war with such disdain . . .'

He bowed with an exaggerated politeness to the Russian officer. Both Don José and his brother were angry. They understood the gist of his wordy accusation although they wore smiles and made gestures of incomprehension. For a moment Drinkwater expected to be conducted peremptorily back to his cell, but it seemed that he had been brought here for other reasons.

'*Capitán*,' said Don Alejo, 'Don Jorge Rubalcava is a zealous officer . . . you see, I know the word from reading your newspapers . . . it is perhaps that he has been,' again the ritual of shrugging, 'much revenge to you . . . but, well, you are our enemy. England is . . .' Don Alejo waved towards the doorway and across the terrace upon which Drinkwater had waited the summons to meet the *Commandante* all those days ago. The gesture was redolent of vast, insurpassable distances.

'And you tell us you come to make war for Russia . . .' Don Alejo smiled and looked in the direction of Rakitin.

'Yes, Captain, you are come to make war on our posts in North America, eh?'

Drinkwater turned. The Russian was a man of middle height, with a powerful physique, deep-set eyes overhung by shaggy brows and a coarse sabre-wound upon his chin. His tight-buttoned blue tunic with its double row of gilt buttons was closed to his chin and heavy bullion epaulettes fringed his shoulders. He wore white breeches and heavy top-boots. His plumed hat was tucked beneath his arm and he was attended by a tall lieutenant and a pair of midshipmen who lounged languidly with the air of bored courtiers, their eyes only casually registering Drinkwater's presence, as though at some minor entertainment offered by a country cousin to visiting townsfolk.

'I have my orders, Captain . . .'

'Yes.' Rakitin turned and with a formally white-gloved hand, patted a small pile of documents on the table beside him. Drinkwater flushed scarlet. He had failed to secure his secret instructions, now they had fallen into the enemy's hands. Suddenly it did not seem relevant that they were imprecise and vague. He had let his orders and instructions, his code and signal books fall into the hands of the enemy! A void opened in his stomach and he made an effort to control himself. Don Alejo was smiling at him; Drinkwater drew himself up and affected to ignore the supercilious Spaniard.

'You speak excellent English, Captain Rakitin. Perhaps I can say that I have found no defence on earth effective against dishonourable men . . .'

The barb went home; Don Alejo's smile vanished, but Drinkwater found little comfort in Rakitin's reply.

'I learnt to speak English in your navy, Captain Drinkwater,' the Russian answered in a chilling bass, 'where I also learned that British officers do not do these things.' Rakitin paused to let the meaning of his words sink in, watching with satisfaction, the

171

colour drain from the Englishman's face. 'But you have no further use for them now you are a prisoner. You have failed . . .' Rakitin turned away dismissively. Drinkwater felt as though he had been struck. Shaking violently from a hopeless anger, he was led out of the room. He scarcely saw his suroundings as he stumbled beside his escort across a courtyard to the steps which led to his cell below the stables. A dark shape swam mistily into his vision and then the virago-face of Doña Helena was thrust into his. She wore an expression of triumph, her tiny eyes blue chips of vindictiveness.

'So God has delivered his enemies into our hands . . .'

Her vulturine swoop had halted Drinkwater. He pulled himself upright, suddenly recovering himself before this haggard crone. He mustered all the dignity of which he was capable and, remembering the old woman's office, said, 'Please convey to Doña Ana Maria my sincere condolences upon her tragic loss.'

And as he swept her aside he felt a small satisfaction that the words had come as a surprise and caught her at a disadvantage.

Drinkwater had been imprisoned before. In the hectic days before the great battle off Cape Trafalgar, on his way in a small coasting vessel to command one of Nelson's battle-ships, he had been captured and thrown into a filthy gaol in the Spanish town of Tarifa. From there he had been taken to Cadiz, transferred to the custody of the French and interrogated by Admiral Villeneuve, Commander-in-Chief of the Combined Fleets of France and Spain.* During this period there had been a suffocating sense of frustration at the ill-luck of falling captive, an angry railing against fate in which self-recrimination was absent. But he had been within the orbit of great events, events which were gathering a momentum in which his circumstances might be rapidly altered. Now, however, the hopelessness of his situation was absolute. There was no likelihood of sudden advantage, he could expect no support, no intervention, no miraculous rescue. His ship was taken, his mission exposed, his people scattered beyond recall. He was utterly ruined, having so conspicuously

* See *1805*

failed in his duty. In his heart he knew that providence had deserted him and that there was only one course of action open to an honourable man. For hours after his humiliating interview with the *Commandante*, Don Alejo and Prince Rakitin, he paced his cell; from time to time his fingers sought the pocketed shape of his pen-knife.

Resolved at last, he tore a page from his journal and began to write. His report to the Admiralty was a model of brevity, recording the essential facts without mentioning the disloyalty of his men, the cause of the leak or the overwhelming numbers of the enemy. Neither did he mention the breaking of their parole by Rubalcava and his men, nor the inhuman treatment he had been subjected to, for fear of Don José's destroying the despatch when it was discovered afterwards. As he wrote the superscription he knew it only necessary to record the end of *Patrician* and his own career. He sealed the folded paper with a blob of candle-wax, tore out another sheet and, dipping his pen, wrote *My Dearest Elizabeth* . . .

Then his nerve failed him and he sat staring into the empty air, fighting back the waves of sick despair that threatened to engulf him. He found he could not conjure the image of his wife's face in his imagination; it seemed their enforced estrangement lay like a great barrier between them. Perhaps, he thought, his death would be the easier to bear. As for his children . . . he threw aside the thought and drew the pen-knife from his pocket, opening the blade and staring at the dull shine of it. He had no idea how long he sat in this cataleptic state. Daylight faded and the cell was in darkness when he heard the lock grind in a cautious tripping of its levers. He was instantly alert to the possibility of treachery. To take his own life as the only recourse open to him was one thing, to be foully murdered by his captors was another, not to be submitted to without a struggle. He gripped the tiny knife and rose to his feet. Beyond the door he heard a whisper. To his astonishment it was a woman's voice.

'*Capitán* . . . please you give your word of honour you will not make to run away . . . I *must* speak with you.'

He knew the voice instantly, recalled her spectacular beauty and felt his heart hammer painfully in his breast. Her tone was insistent, foolhardy.

'*Sí, Señorita*. I understand . . . you have my word.'

How had she obtained the keys? Was she being used and was he about to die in circumstances that had been contrived to compromise not only his professional, but his personal honour? His fist crumpled the unwritten letter to his wife, then the bolts drew and the door swung suddenly inwards. She came inside, a wild perfumed swirl of dark brocade, to lean on the door, swiftly closed behind her.

'*Capitán* . . . ?' her voice was uncertain in the darkness of the cell. He could see the paleness of her skin and the heaving of her breast as he crossed to the table to strike a flint and steel, slipping the pen-knife into his pocket.

'Pardon, *Señorita*, I was not expecting a guest.'

The sarcasm did him good, driving the gloom from his mind. The tinder caught and he lit the candle stump. The flame rose brilliant and he turned towards her holding it in front of him. She drew in her breath sharply and he realised his appearance was unprepossessing. He rubbed his bearded cheek.

'A razor is not permitted . . .' The incongruity of the remark almost made him laugh, considering what he was about to attempt with his pen-knife blade, and then he saw the state she was in. The candlelight danced in eyes that were full of tears and the heaving of her breast was not due to the excitement of her strange tryst with an enemy officer or the animal stench of his quarters.

'*Señorita*, what is it? What is the matter?'

'*Capitán* . . . what is it that you mean by your words to Doña Helena? It is not true . . . tell me it is not true.'

He frowned, then drew out the chair for her. She shook her head. The candle caught the tears flung from her eyes, the dark shadow of a wave of hair fell across her forehead, too hurriedly put up.

'*Señorita* . . .'

'Prince Vladimir arrived today, but Nicolai is not with him. I ask where is Nicolai and Rakitin says nothing.' She spat the Russian's name as though flinging it from her with contempt.

174

'But I know his ship has come from the north, he must know about Nicolai.'

She was weeping now. He wanted to comfort her but dare not move. He knew now that he had seen Rakitin's ship off the Horn and that in the interval the Russian had been north to the Tsar's settlements on the coast of Alaska.

'What does your father tell you?' he asked gently. She shook her head, trying to speak through her grief.

'Nothing. Don Alejo promises Nicolai will come on the *Juno* as before,' she threw up her head, 'but I do not believe Don Alejo,' she said in a voice which conveyed the impression that she did not trust her uncle. 'And then you say that thing to Doña Helena,' there was a pause and then she added in a lower voice, a voice that spoke of confidentiality and trust, 'she would not believe you.'

Drinkwater sighed. The honour was one he could have done without at such a moment. '*Señorita*, I do not know that I can tell you the truth, I can only tell you what I have myself been told.' He paused and motioned her again to the chair. This time she moved slowly from the door and sank onto it. There was the faintest breath of air through the cell, reminding Drinkwater that the door was open. For a moment he was a prey to emotions as savage as those which tore at the young woman.

'I was told that Nicolai Rezanov was dead,' he said flatly.

The finality of the word seemed to staunch the flow of tears. Truth was, Drinkwater thought as he held her gaze, always easier to face than uncertainty. 'I may have been misinformed . . . told wrong. I hope, *Señorita*, that I have been . . .'

A ghost of a smile crossed her face and her fingers rested lightly upon his hand. 'Who told you, *Capitán*?'

'An American. Captain Jackson Grant.'

He saw her pupils contract and her nostrils flare with anger and he sensed her resolution. A sudden hope sprang into his mind. 'I know he is not to be trusted. Did he not come here to see your father and betray me?'

'Perhaps,' she frowned, 'yes . . . yes he was here. I heard he knew where your ship was.'

'Then he is *not* to be trusted,' Drinkwater said hopefully. 'He is a man who seeks for himself . . . one perhaps who would be in Nicolai Rezanov's place,' he added in a lower voice.

She flashed him a look of imperious suspicion, then her expression softened. 'And you, *Capitán*?' she asked raising her fingers from his hand, 'where do you wish to be? Are *you* to be trusted?'

'I can only tell you what I have been told, *Señorita*. I would not cause you distress. I have nothing. All I know is that you expected Rezanov and he has not come. Rakitin is silent, but Jackson told me he died in Krasnoiarsk . . . yes, that was the place.'

'He was a good man, *Capitán* . . . can you comprehend that?'

'Yes. Grant said that.'

But she seemed not to hear him. '. . . A good man, perhaps a saint . . . not like Rakitin.' Again the utterance of the Russian's name disgusted her. It appeared that Rakitin had joined the list of Doña Ana Maria's would-be and unwanted suitors. She let out a long, shuddering sigh. 'And in my heart I know he is dead.'

She crossed herself and Drinkwater put his hand gently upon her shoulder. The warmth of her flesh seemed to sear him. She looked up at him for a long moment so that the temptation to bend and kiss her flared across his brain and then she rose and the moment was gone.

'*Gracias, Capitán*, you have been . . . you have your own misfortune. I shall pray for you.'

Drinkwater recalled the papal attitudes to suicide. 'You do me too much honour, *Señorita* . . . pray for my wife and children.'

She paused in the act of turning for the door. In the gloom of the cell her dark dress and the black pile of her hair merged into the shadows, so that the single light of the candle threw her face into a spectral detachment which seemed to diminish from his vision as in a dream and he stood, long after her departure, with its lovely image imprinted on his retina, unaware of the grind of the bolts or the tumbling of the lock.

'"Whom the gods wish to destroy",' he quoted softly to himself, '"they first make mad."'

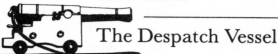

The Despatch Vessel

He did not go mad. The appearance, or perhaps the disappearance, of Doña Ana Maria saved him from himself. He no longer
paced like a lion confined in the Tower menagerie but stood
stock-still, held in that cataleptic state familiar to commanders of
ships whose duty requires their presence on deck long after the
exhausted body is capable of sustaining it. They stand, as Drinkwater stood now, immobilised, faculties reduced to the barely
necessary, like a submerged whale, eyes open yet in a strange
detachment, all but lost to exterior circumstances so that they
endure cold and sleeplessness unaware of cramps or the passage
of time, though instantly ready to respond to sudden
emergency.

In this condition the mind behaves oddly, ranging over vast
plains of consideration, soaring above mountains of fantasy and
pausing beside dark lakes of doubt, dispensing with the formality of language and encompassing thoughts and images beyond
the powers of expression. Drinkwater's thoughts came and went,
slipped in and out of rationality, leapt deep chasms of pure
reason and became part of an infinite consciousness beyond
himself. In this enchantment Drinkwater slipped the bonds of
honour and reaffirmed his faith in providence. All thoughts of
suicide left him and it seemed he felt, as he had once before felt
when lost in a small boat in the fog of the Greenland Sea, a
haunting intimacy with Elizabeth and his family.

He remained in this state for many hours. Even when the
candle stump expired with an upward and pungent twist of
smoke, he did no more than acknowledge the onset of total
blackness without it moving him. In this trance the night passed

and grey dawn filtered in through the barred window of his cell before he came to himself, shuddering with the cold and the pain of movement as he returned to full consciousness. But it was more than dawn that had woken him; his seaman's instincts had been stirred by distant noises in the fading night: the splash of an anchor, a few shouts and later the noise of impatient boots upon the steps that ran up from the boat landing somewhere below his cell-window. They echoed in the corridor beyond his barred door and he heard the guard accosted, and then the sounds faded. He dragged the chair to the window and strained to peer below. The harbour was still, the gentle ruffling of the slight breeze had kept the usual morning fog away, enabling the new-comer to work into the anchorage, close under the Residence. She was a schooner, an *aviso*, a Spanish despatch-vessel with tall, raked masts and the look of speed about her. From where had she come? Monterey? San Diego? Panama? And what news did she bring that was so urgent that her commander must bring her in so early and wake the *Commandante's* household? Did it concern him? Was he perhaps to be taken south, or disposed of in some Spanish oubliette? Inexplicably he felt his long-stilled pulse begin to race.

The noises died away and there followed a silence so full of suspense that it set him to a frustrated and angry pacing in which his mind now boiled with possibilities. For an hour he was a prey to such mental toil that the soothing effects of his catalepsy had evaporated by the time the sun had risen and the blood noise rushed through his ears so that he almost missed the sounds of departure, feet running hastily upon the path below. He re-occupied his spy-post and saw the *aviso's* boat pull out from the jetty and watched it go, not to the schooner but to the *Suvorov*. Later it returned and he heard the low sinister bass of Rakitin, grumbling at the *Commandante's* summons and the ungodly hour. Then, a little later still, the hasty retreat of the Russian's boots . . . and silence.

The turning of the lock and shooting of bolts startled him when it came. He half-expected release, so strung were his nerves, but it was only the grimy, sleep-sodden orderly who brought him bread, thin wine and an empty slop pail as he had done on so many, many previous mornings. The familiarity of the ritual, backed by the drawn sword of an officer outside cast Drinkwater's spirit into depression. But he could not eat and jumped upon the chair yet again when the thin, reedy piping of the bosun's calls preceded the stamp-and-go of a hundred feet in the heart-wrenching procedure of departure. Rakitin had learned much from the Royal Navy. Watching from a distance, Drinkwater might have been looking at a British man-of-war getting under weigh and in his mind he could hear the orders passed as the topmen went aloft and the topsails were cast loose in the buntlines, their clews hauled out. On the high steeved bowsprit of the *Suvorov* men scrambled, casting loose the robands that secured the jibs. On the fo'c's'le men leaned outboard, fishing with the cat-tackle for the anchor ring as it broke surface under the round, black bow of the Russian seventy-four. And then he suddenly realised with a pang that sent an actual stab of pain through his guts, his own *Patrician* was also getting under weigh. There were fewer men and it was clumsily done, but within the hour she was slipping out of his view, following in the wake of the *Suvorov*. The last he saw of her as she swung to round Point Lobos was her white St George's ensign: only it was no longer subordinate to the red and gold of Spain. Now above it flaunted the diagonal cross of Russia.

Lieutenant James Quilhampton had intended making the entrance to San Francisco Bay in the last hours of the night. The appearance of a light northerly breeze augured well and they had begun from their refuge in good time to be within the harbour by dawn, intending to hole-up on one of the islands and reconnoitre the shipping during the coming day. But they were turned back by the arrival of a fast schooner, whose commander beat up under the headland of Bonita Point before wearing for the anchorage below the battery near Point Lobos. This obstacle had cost them time, but caution dictated a retreat, and the *Patrician's* boat was put reluctantly about for the sanctuary of the hidden bay.

Quilhampton fumed at the delay. He had made his preparations with great care. Although his resources were limited he

179

knew that much depended on success. Everything, in fact, not least his very life and his future. He wished he had not sent that final letter to Catriona. To have someone, however distant, to whose image a man might cling in such desperate moments in his life, seemed to him a most desirable thing. But it would not have been fair to Catriona and, God alone knew, she had been ill-treated by neglect for too long already.

'I am stripped to the most indigent circumstances,' he muttered to himself as he cooled his heels on the little curve of sand withing the cove, 'stripped to the very last resort of the naked . . .'

The phrase pleased him; oddly it comforted him to come face-to-face with absolute desperation. He held his life cheap now, and that meant he could undertake any enterprise. Smiling grimly to himself he looked up, swinging his eyes to rake the small arc of the horizon visible between the two rocky headlands that concealed their hideaway. What he saw destroyed his resolution. Two ships stood out to sea, heading north, their crews making sail as they lay over on the starboard tack. The leading vessel was the big, black Russian two-decker. The other, he was certain, was the *Patrician*.

Quilhampton frowned. What the devil did it mean? Should he go on into San Francisco or follow the two ships? He swore venomously. If Drinkwater and his people were aboard the *Patrician*, it was out of the question for Quilhampton with a handful of men in an open boat to give chase. He was utterly without resources, the mood of his men was not encouraging, in short the mere consideration of such an enterprise was as foolhardy as it was impractical. But was the alternative any better? The plentiful game and easy living of the last few days had prompted muttering from the men. If they had the opportunity of spirits and access to women his control over them would be broken utterly, and any approach to San Francisco, however made, risked that.

And what could he do if he got there? With Captain Drinkwater and some of *Patrician*'s men they might have attempted something, but with the ship and, presumably, Drinkwater himself, carried off under Russian escort, what was the point of running his head into a noose? Sighing, he looked up. Beyond the headlands of the cove the sea-horizon was empty. A sudden, panicky fluttering formed in the pit of his gut and he felt a desperate surge of self-pity. For a moment the horizon misted and then he forced a wave of anger to over-lay the hideous sensation. Reluctantly he turned away from the sea and made his way up the tiny valley behind the cove. There really was no alternative open to him. He would have to give himself up to the Spanish authorities; that way he might survive the mutinous knives of his men.

Some time after the departure of *Patrician* Drinkwater fell into a profound sleep, his exhausted body seeking its revenge upon his shattered spirit. He woke ten hours later, cramped and wracked with pain in the mangled muscles of his mauled shoulder, but oddly alert and with his mind calmer than it had been for many days. There was no reason for this feeling beyond a half-remembered fragment of chill philosophy. He could not recall its source; Epictetus, perhaps, or Marcus Aurelius, the only classical reading he had ever found aboard a man-of-war, but the text soothed him. Nothing, the ancient averred, happens to any man which he is not formed by nature to bear.

The pegs upon which men hang their reason are oddly illogical, but Drinkwater put behind him all thoughts of suicide from that moment and sat quietly in the gathering darkness of the approaching night. In such a mood a man might escape, or be shot.

He heard the footfalls on the stone flags of the corridor. There were several of them and they approached purposefully. There was nothing furtive about the way the lock was sprung or the bolts withdrawn. By the time the door was flung open and de Soto entered the cell with a lantern, Drinkwater's heart was pounding. De Soto jerked his head imperiously and Drinkwater rose.

'*Adelante!*' De Soto stood aside and indicated Drinkwater should step outside. Apprehensively he did as he was bidden, the cool, night-fresh air wafting along the corridor sweet in his nostrils. The officer was accompanied by two soldiers bearing

181

muskets with bayonets fixed. They began to walk, Drinkwater with them, to where the corridor turned and joined the entrance gate through which the men from the boats had passed.

But he was not taken to be shot. They crossed the courtyard and entered the *Commandante*'s quarters where once (it seemed so long ago) he had dined in honour and now was brought in ignominy.

He had hoped for an interview with Don José, but it was before Don Alejo that he found himself. From various shreds of evidence, from their first encounter on the *Santa Monica*, to the innuendoes of Don Alejo's niece, Drinkwater had conceived a dislike of the Spaniard. He was as slippery as an eel, interested solely in his own intrigues, whatever they were. If Drinkwater had been hoping for some relaxation in his regimen he was to be disappointed. Don Alejo's remarks were obscure and not reassuring.

'Ah, *Capitán* Drinkwater, I see you are in good health, *buenas* . . .' Don Alejo smiled like a cat, ignoring the stink of his prisoner, the unshaven face, the filthy neck linen. 'We have been waiting for instructions from Panama . . .'

'What the hell have you done with my ship?'

'*Capitán*, please. She is not *your* ship. She fell a prize to the valour of Spain.'

'Where the hell has she gone?'

'Under escort . . . to a place of safety,' Don Alejo's eyes narrowed. 'How do you know about your ship?'

Drinkwater evaded the question. He did not want his tiny window stopped up. 'I am not a fool. You have also received news, Don Alejo, this I know, that an *aviso* arrived this morning . . .'

'Ah, but no news about you, *Capitán*. I regret . . .'

'Don Alejo, I demand that, at the very least, you accommodate me in quarters befitting my rank, that you oblige me by placing me under parole, that you allow me to shave, to see my officers and men . . .'

'*Capitán*, you are not in your quarterdeck, please.' The Spaniard's voice was harsh, cruel. 'It is not possible . . .'

182

'If I ever have the opportunity to lay even with you Don Alejo . . .'

The Spaniard had been sitting on the corner of a heavy oak table, one booted leg swinging, his manner disinterested. Now he came to his feet, face to face with his prisoner.

'Do not threaten me, *Capitán*. You have nothing to make me fear. You have no men, no guns, nothing.' He jerked his head at the guards and snarled something incomprehensible. Drinkwater was marched out, still wondering why he had been summoned.

They were crossing the courtyard when they met Doña Ana Maria and her duenna. Seeing him, she smiled sadly. 'A happy day, *Capitán*, for you . . .'

He frowned. Was she mocking him? 'For me *Señorita*? How so?'

De Soto's forbearance snapped and he disregarded the speaker's rank and connections, shouting the girl to silence and propelling Drinkwater suddenly forward with a blow on his shoulder that sent a wave of agony through him. He stumbled and all but fell, the pain blotting out all sensibility until he found himself once more in his cell and heard the heavy, final thud of bolts driving home. It was only then that he tried to make some sense out of the interview and its inexplicable sequel.

'Easy, lads, easy . . .'

The boat ghosted along, only a whisper of water under her bow accompanied by the drip of water from the motionless oar-blades. The dark hull of an anchored ship loomed over them; it was one of the anchored merchantmen and the noise of a squeeze-box and some languidly drunken singing came to them. Lights shone from her stern cabin and a gale of laughter told where her master entertained. The germ of an idea formed in Lieutenant Quilhampton's brain, but this vessel was too big by far, perhaps they would find something smaller, more suitable further into the anchorage. He did not have to surrender; at least not yet.

The need for caution receded now they were in the anchorage. There were other boats about, ferrying liberty-men to and from their ships. It was a contrast to the naval anchorages he was familiar with, where the fear of desertion made every ship row a guard and the passage of boats at night was strictly controlled. He began to relax, to cast about for a likely target, a small ship, like a schooner, easily manageable by a handful of desperate men. If he could strike quickly, divert his men's minds away from the thought of stews and whores he might, he just might . . .

'Sir . . .' the man at bow oar hissed in the darkness.

'What?'

'Listen, sir . . .'

He heard the voice immediately. 'Hold water!' he commanded, and when the boat lay stopped he cocked his ear again, getting his bearings.

The querulous voice was indisputably Yankee.

'Well, Friend, he was here but a minute ago . . . perhaps he pisseth against a wall . . .'

'Jesus, I thought you mother-fuckers were supposed to be seamen! I ain't a whit surprised the British are losing ships if they're driven to manning 'em with canting Quakers . . . you tell him to lay aft when he's finished for Chrissakes . . .'

'Thou takest too much in vain the Lord's name, Friend . . .'

A snigger of recognition came from the oarsmen, half amused, half admired at the Quaker's undaunted attitude. If Derrick was aboard the ship under whose stern they had stopped, who else might there be? Or had Derrick deserted alone, prompted by those ridiculous pacifistic views of his? The questions tumbled through Quilhampton's mind and he leaned forward.

'Give way, easy, lads, and keep deathly quiet,' he whispered, and the oars dipped into the water again. In the stern, Quilhampton pulled the tiller hard against his chest and swung the boat's bow towards the *Abigail Starbuck*.

'Oars . . .'

The men ceased rowing and the boat glided on. A tinkling sound could be heard and, peering ahead, Quilhampton caught the faint silver arc of urine falling from the height of a ship's forechains. As the boat slid under the bulk of the ship's hull he saw, against the slightly lighter darkness of the sky, the shape of a

184

man buttoning the flap of his trousers. As the boat got closer and the man turned inboard his face was suddenly illuminated. Caught with one foot on the rail as he swung round he paused.

'I heard him,' said a deep-burred and familiar voice, 'a right bloody bucko bastard of a Yankee Dandy . . .'

Quilhampton drew a breath. If the man holding the lantern was not Derrick, or there were others within earshot they might be ruined, but the moment was not to be lost and the occupants of the boat were all registering recognition and surprise so that their own silence could not be relied upon.

'Tregembo!' Quilhampton hissed.

Looking up, Quilhampton saw the man turn and peer down, saw a second head and a lantern.

'Put the fucking light out!' said one of the oarsmen.

'Tregembo, it's me, Mr Quilhampton . . .'

'By Gar . . . quick, Derrick, ower we go, afore that Yankee sees us . . .'

'Wait! Are there more of you?'

'Aye, but don't wait, zur . . .'

Tregembo was already clambering over the side, though Derrick appeared to hesitate. The Cornishman, his legs dangling from the chains, seeking a foot-hold in the boat looked up.

'Come on, damn 'ee, you can pull an oar if you can't fight!'

Someone stood and reached up. Tregembo fell heavily among grunts from his shipmates and the boat rocked dangerously and then Derrick was following and, a minute later, the long-boat was pulling cautiously off into the darkness.

When sufficient distance had been put between them and the *Abigail Starbuck* Quilhampton ordered them to cease rowing.

'Lay aft, Tregembo and report.'

'Willingly, zur.' Tregembo struggled down the boat as the men pulled aside for him until his scarred, grizzled and dependable features peered into Quilhampton's face.

'Thank God you came, zur . . . I'd been meditating on swimming ashore once I knowed where they'd got the Cap'n . . .'

'Where *is* he, Tregembo, d' you know?'

'Aye, zur, Mister Derrick, 'e found out. That was the Yankee hell-ship *Abigail Sommat-or-other* and if her mate hadn't had a

whore in his bunk we'd not have had the liberty for a piss to remind us we were free men . . .'

'The captain, Tregembo . . .'

'He's a prisoner in the Governor's Residence,' put in Derrick.
'I overheard the mate and Captain Grant discussing the matter
when the *Patrician* left harbour this morning.'

'I saw that,' Quilhampton cut the Quaker short. 'Do you know
the way to this Residence?'

'It's above the boat jetty, zur, where we was anchored before.'

'Very well . . . stand-by . . . give way together . . .'

As the boat once more gathered way, James Quilhampton
turned her in for the shore, conjuring up from his memory, the
lie of the land above the landing-jetty.

Drinkwater shut the log and doused the candle as he heard the
key turn cautiously in the lock. It seemed an age before the bolts
were drawn back, by which time her appearance did not surprise
him.

'*Capitán* . . . ?'

'Here, *Señorita* . . .'

'You do not know the news? They did not tell you? Not even
my father?'

'I have not seen your father, *Señorita* . . .'

'Ahhh . . .' she seemed relieved.

'But what news is this . . . ?'

'Ana Maria?' The voice of Doña Helena rasped anxiously
through the night and the hurried tap of her questing feet
approached.

'Please, *Capitán*, you go now . . . for our honour, you must go,
it is not right . . .'

'But I do not understand . . . you will be in trouble . . . there
is no need . . .'

'Please *Capitán*,' she beseeched him and he heard the prattle of
the duenna's voice suddenly louder, rattling something to someone else in quick, urgent Spanish. He heard the lugubrious tone
of the Franciscan father and then their shadows leapt large along
the wall of the corridor.

'*Vamos!* . . . go quick . . .' She stood aside and the priest loomed

186

in the doorway as Doña Helena screeched something. For the briefest fraction of a second indecision held the four of them in a trance and then Drinkwater acted. The priest held up an imperious hand, but Drinkwater brushed him aside and made for the end of the corridor. The guard was nowhere to be seen. Perhaps too long acquaintance with the English captain had made them careless, perhaps Doña Ana Maria had bribed them, he neither knew nor troubled to think of it, only an iron gate separated him from the terraced garden of oleanders and orange trees through which the path to the boat-jetty led downwards.

It was unlocked. Flinging it open he began to run, his muscles cracking under the unaccustomed strain of rapid descent.

Quilhampton remembered the battery that lay between the boat-jetty and the Residence above. It was not on the direct path, but lay off to the right, occupying a natural bastion, an outcrop of rock behind which earth-falls had filled in a roughly level area which the hand of man had improved with stone flags so that it supported heavy cannon mounted behind embrasures of stone.

He knew it would be guarded and his approach to the jetty was conducted with caution. He was astonished, therefore, when the noises of pursuit, of shouting and brief glimpses of lights came from above and, as the bowman jumped ashore with the boat-painter, he considered immediate withdrawal. But the knowledge that Drinkwater himself was up there somewhere made him stay his hand. He had quizzed both Derrick and Tregembo concerning the disappearance of the ship. They both agreed she had been carried off under Russian colours in full view of all the merchantmen anchored in the harbour; but he was unable to shake them from their conviction that Drinkwater had remained in San Francisco, a prisoner of the Spanish authorities. It occurred to Quilhampton that both men had a personal interest in the fate of the captain, and both were comparatively indifferent to that of the ship herself. If their information was correct and he had judged their motives correctly, then perhaps fortune might be persuaded to turn in their favour.

The noises coming from above certainly indicated that she

was not running in the favour of their enemies. A shot rang out, perhaps from the battery and the string of lights and the noise of pursuit came lower down the hillside. Whoever was running was important enough to warrant a full scale attempt at recapture.

'Sergeant Blixoe, your best shot to try and hit the leading lantern as soon as he can.'

'Very good sir.'

There was a stir of excitement in the boat and Quilhampton said, 'Sing, lads, sing loud and clear . . . sing *Spanish Ladies* . . . sing, damn you!'

It was a faltering start and they had no clue as to Quilhampton's crazy idea but something infectiously insane about his own cracked and tuneless voice made them join him.

"Farewell and adieu to you Spanish Ladies,
Farewell and Adieu to you ladies of Spain . . ."

They could afford to sing in English and indicate their presence to whoever was crashing through the bushes above them with musket balls singing into the night after him. There were enough Americans in port to justify a drunken outburst and no one on a clandestine mission would betray their presence with such impunity. What would happen if they had to suddenly conceal themselves again did not occur to Quilhampton. He had staked all on a single throw, arguing that only one man could be important enough to chase with such energy. It simply never occurred to him otherwise.

Beside him the kneeling marine fired. The snap and flash of the musket punctuated the old sea-song causing a missed beat, but they picked it up again.

". . . orders to sail for Old England
and we hope in a short-time to see you again."

Drinkwater heard the singing, taking comfort from the sound of drunken seamen that indicated the probable presence of a boat below. If there had been no boat he would have made for the town where the merchantmen's boats lay, but the sound of so ancient a sea-song beckoned him, and he tripped and stumbled as the first bullet whined past him. It is difficult to hit a target downhill, easier to fire upwards, but the shot that he saw from below made him check his flight. For a moment he was confused, then he heard an anguished roar from above and his heart leapt with hope. It was impossible, but surely whoever fired that lone shot had been aiming at his pursuers. He did not consider the matter an instant longer, but plunged headlong downwards.

Quilhampton saw the figure the second it broke cover from the undergrowth and challenged them.

'Who the hell are you?'

The voice was recognisable, the raw rasp of it familiar to men whom it had commanded for five years and more.

'Friends, Captain, hurry . . . !'

'Mr Q?'

'The same, sir.'

'Well met, by heaven, into the boat, quick . . . why this is *Patrician*'s cutter!'

They tumbled into the boat, Blixoe firing another shot at the Spaniards who were but a few yards behind Drinkwater. The oarsmen needed no special bidding to effort. They had swung the boat round and bent to their task with back-breaking energy that made the oar-looms bend and crack under the strain.

'There's a long-waisted Spanish *aviso*-schooner hard-by, Mr Q,' Drinkwater pointed into the night where two raked masts were just perceptible against the sky, 'and I judge most of her people to be ashore.'

'Aye, aye, sir . . . knives and foot-stretchers, lads, we're almost up to her . . . are you reloaded, Mr Blixoe?'

'We've two cartridges that ain't spoiled, sir . . .'

'Cold steel then . . .' Quilhampton turned to Drinkwater. 'I've no sword, sir . . .'

'Nor me, James . . .'

And then they bumped alongside the low hull of the schooner and were scrambling up her side, finding toe-holds on her gun-sills and swinging their legs over the rail.

The anchor watch had been alerted by the shots ashore, no more than two hundred yards away. But they had made the error of going and reporting the matter. The *aviso* had been left in the hands of a young midshipman, newly out from Spain, and

189

her crew were largely *mestizos*, unused to real action on a great ocean that their employers were apt to consider their own exclusive preserve. Only the midshipman put up a fight, to be skewered by Blixoe's bayonet for his gallantry. Within minutes the schooner had changed hands.

There were no boats at the jetty beyond a small dinghy with insufficient capacity for immediate pursuit. But the precise circumstances of Captain Drinkwater's disappearance were somewhat confusing to the pursuers, mixed as they were with treachery within the Residence. Neither did the Spanish immediately appreciate the danger their *aviso* lay in, so that Drinkwater and his companions were able to slip the cable of the schooner and make sail unmolested.

They felt the bow rise to the onshore swell from the mighty Pacific as soon as they rounded Point Lobos. The *aviso* heeled over as they belayed the halliards and Drinkwater came aft to Quilhampton at the helm.

'How does she steer, James?'

'Like a witch!' answered Quilhampton, his eyes dancing in the light from the binnacle.

'Like a witch, eh?' repeated Drinkwater in a lower voice, recalling another face lit from below by a poor glim. How would she fare now, he wondered? And what *was* the fateful news that had caused her to liberate him?

It was then that it occurred to him that had they not killed the midshipman they might have discovered it. 'Too late now,' he muttered sadly.

'Yes,' Quilhampton's voice agreed enthusiastically, 'they're much too late now to catch us.'

Drinkwater opened his mouth to explain, thought better of it and grunted agreement. 'D'you think we can find anything to eat aboard this hooker, Mr Q?'

190

The Virgin of Fair Weather

If the vicissitudes of the sea-service had thrown Nathaniel Drinkwater ignominiously out of one of the most powerful frigates in the Royal Navy, then the inexplicable actions of a beautiful woman had restored him to a position of some influence. He had hardly dared hope for such a sudden and apparently fortuitous reversal in his situation as had been precipitated by Doña Ana Maria's actions and consolidated by the appearance of James Quilhampton and his forlorn hope.

The sudden, easy taking of the schooner still struck him as an equally lucky link in the chain of events which had led him to liberty; he had yet to learn that there was more of cause and effect, and less of coincidence in these events than he then supposed. But, for the moment, little could dull the relief and joy that filled him as he watched the dawn over the distant coast and shivered in the fresh westerly breeze that blew onshore and under the influence of which the narrow gutted schooner laid her seething course northwards.

Drinkwater had to acknowledge that she was a smart, fast and rakish craft. Her long, low hull mounted twelve 6-pounder carriage guns, mere pop-guns that could serve to over-awe native craft or a merchantman, but amidships, where traditionally she might have carried her boats, she mounted a heavy carronade, the Spanish equivalent of a 32-pounder, he judged, curiously rigged on a rotating slide somewhat in the manner of the mortars in the old bomb-vessel *Virago*, so that the gun might be brought to bear on a target on either side if due care were taken of the intervening rigging. This powerful weapon gave Drinkwater fresh cause for hope, for with it he might yet achieve something worthwhile and there was only one task that demanded his relentless attention until it was accomplished, the recapture of the *Patrician*.

He looked aloft. The two raked masts carried huge gaff-rigged sails, the after one was capable of bearing a maintopsail which he could set at full daylight when the watch changed. For the time being he was content to act as officer of the watch as well as commander of his pathetically small crew. Still, they seemed happy enough, basking in their change of fortune and making free with the personal effects they had discovered on board. Properly, Drinkwater should have secured these, but he was not kindly disposed towards the Spanish of San Francisco after the breaking of their parole, the shameful way he had been held captive and the mature suspicion that Don Alejo and Rubalcava, at least, were involved in some action which, to them, justified their dishonourable treatment of their prisoners. Besides, the poor devils who had arrived with Quilhampton had only the rags they stood up in, and Drinkwater was far too considerate of his men's welfare to let the conventions of protecting private property stand in the way of their well-being.

'Forward there!'

A man named Lacey stood up from where he had been huddling under the weather rail dodging spray. 'Sir?'

'Ease the foresheets a little . . .'

'Aye, aye, sir.'

Drinkwater eased the helm and the schooner's head fell off the wind a point or two, her long bowsprit pointing at a shallower angle to the line of the coast.

'Ease the mainsheet,' he said to the seaman who stood at the helm beside him.

He felt the pressure on the rudder ease as the sheaves squealed slightly with the strain on the heavy mainsheet.

'She'm a flyer, sir,' said the man conversationally, resuming his post at Drinkwater's side and Drinkwater agreed, reflecting upon the alteration in their circumstances. Aboard the *Patrician* the man would not have dared address his commander in such familiar tones; here, doing duty beside him, it was the most natural thing in the world.

'She certainly is, Potter, and off the wind, on a reach, she'll fly faster than the wind.'

Potter digested this intelligence with a frown, but Drinkwater did not expand upon this curiosity of natural law. Instead he sowed the seeds of his intentions.

'Now we're well out of sight of the Dons, we'll close the coast again. That'll be Point Reyes, where we were crusing when we discovered that leak,' he pointed at the blue line of the Californian shore.

'Ahhh . . .' Potter nodded, pleased to be taken into the captain's confidence.

'Now what I think we should do, Potter, is chase north and find out what those damned Russians have done with our ship and shipmates.' Drinkwater paused and looked sideways at the man, an able-seaman and once rated captain of the foretop. 'What d'you think of that, eh?'

'Few more men'd be handy, sir, begging your pardon for saying so.'

'Yes, they would, but we've got a fair wind, a fast ship and at least one heavy cannon to play with . . . and we've got something else, Potter . . . surprise!'

They fell silent again and then Potter said, 'Sir . . . that leak, sir . . . it were done a'purpose.'

Drinkwater did not take his eyes off the horizon, though he knew Potter was eyeing him sidelong. 'I know,' he said shortly, then turned and smiled disarmingly at the seaman, 'and I'd hang the scum that did it if I had proof, Potter; but that's of no avail now. Do you cut along and call out the watch below. It's time you and I got some rest.' He took the helm and watched Potter scuttle forward.

James Quilhampton came on deck a few minutes later. He was smiling broadly, for it was a beautiful morning with clear visibility and a fresh breeze that made the blue seas turn white as they broke and from which a school of dolphins leapt and gambolled and ran in and out under the cutwater of the racing schooner.

'Morning sir.'

'Morning, James. We'll set proper watches now. You and

Tregembo, Marsden, Blixoe and one marine, together with the four seamen I've just called to form the larboard watch. I'll head the starboard with the rest . . . seventeen of us in all. I'm going to locate the *Patrician* if I can, James, and retake her . . .'

'We could do with a few more men for that sir,' remarked Quilhampton.

Drinkwater nodded. 'Yes, Potter's just told me that, but what we lack in men we might make up for with stealth and surprise.'

'Not to mention that confounded great "smasher" amidships . . .'

Drinkwater grinned. 'We are of one mind, James . . . here you are, head in for the coast. Keep a sharp lookout for sails or masts. I've no idea what those damned Russians intend to do with the ship, but I don't want to miss her for want of a pair of eyes.'

'Very well, sir.'

'I'm going below to get some sleep.'

They coasted northwards for over a week without the sight of a single sail. The year was well advanced and Drinkwater supposed that merchant ships were either finishing their lading in Alaskan waters and not yet ready to sail southwards, or that Russian ships loading provisions for the hardships of the northern winter had not yet departed from the Spanish settlements of California. Then, as they stood out to sea to round what the English navigators called Cape Disappointment but which, on Drinkwater's Spanish chart bore no name at all, they saw the masts of some ships hidden behind a low spit of land to the southward of the Cape.

'The mouth of the Columbia River, James . . . hoist Spanish colours and stand inshore. We'll take a closer look.'

It took them four hours to work their way up into the estuary of the river against a considerable current which, fuelled by the melting snows of distant mountains to the eastward, streamed out into the ocean with an impressive velocity. But the schooner stood inshore and the low point to the southward opened slowly to starboard, to reveal a shallow lagoon and a secondary headland from which the first grew in a long sandy spit. This

194

headland was covered with woods in which a clearing had been made and the stockade of a primitive fort erected. Above the fort flew the colours of Tsar Alexander I, though neither of the two vessels at anchor were larger than brigs.

'A Russian settlement, by Heaven,' muttered Drinkwater, staring through his looted glass at the group of curious men drawn up by a pair of boats on the beach.

'Fetch us an anchor James, close alongside the outer of those two brigs.'

'Aye, aye, sir.'

Drinkwater watched Quilhampton go forward, his wooden arm hanging incongruously below the Spanish uniform coat that was far too short for his long, lean frame. He grinned at the young man, and caught the mood of high excitement that infected his men. There were only a handful of them, but they had had time to settle well and, with the single exception of Derrick, were spoiling for a fight.

'Brail all . . .'

Quilhampton passed the agreed order quietly. The jibs fell, fluttering along the bowsprit with a rasp of their hanks on the stays, and a man clambered leisurely out along the spar to restrain them with a roband or two, while the main and foresails were brailed to the masts, their gaffs, standing spars. Against the current the schooner lost way and was brought to an anchor and a short scope of cable. Then they hauled the cutter alongside from its position towing astern. With some show it was manned and a Spanish boat ensign found and its staff stuck in the verdi-grised brass ferrule in the cutter's rudder-stock. Wearing an oddly cockaded Spanish bicorne Drinkwater took his place in the stern, a large light-cavalry sabre, that he had found hanging on the schooner's cabin bulkhead, held between his knees. A brace of primed, cocked and loaded pistols lay on the stern sheets beside him, while the oarsmen each had a cutlass from the schooner's capacious arms-chest concealed beneath their thwarts.

They cleared the stern of the schooner and Drinkwater looked up. 'God bless my soul!'

In a beautifully carved scroll worked beneath the cabin

windows he read her name for the first time: *Virgen de la Bonanza*. Several men caught the direction of his eye, grinning at the first word which was comprehensible to them. What the rest meant none of them knew. Drinkwater's face stiffened. They were supposed to be masquerading as Spaniards!

The group on the beach had grown by the time they reached it. About a score of villainously bearded and greasily apparelled men stood idly watching them. He took them all to be Russians, except perhaps one, a late arrival wearing the buckskins and moccasins of a mountain-man, the likes of which he had once seen, long ago in the Loyalist militia in New York. He was clearly something of a wonder to the others, for they looked at him curiously, drawing aside for him as he joined them. Drinkwater was close enough to observe these details, for the next instant the boat grazed the sand and he rose to his feet.

Drinkwater never had any Thespian pretentions, but his lack of familiarity with the Spanish tongue had driven him to an almost risible extreme in an attempt to head off the slightest suspicion that he was anything other than Spanish. 'Needs must when the devil drives,' he said to Quilhampton when explaining his intentions and the men's laughter had been muted by the order that one of them was going to have to carry him, piggyback, ashore. But it was at Derrick's suggestion that he bore the handkerchief, a large, ostentatious square of flowered silk that they guessed was a gift for the *Virgen*'s captain's paramour in Panama. The prominent manipulation of the kerchief alone ensured his disembarkation appeared alien enough and, ironically, he was glad of it himself, when he caught the stench of the Russians.

Potter put him down with a relieved grunt and Drinkwater, the heave sabre knocking his hip, strode amongst the group of grim watchers and swept his hat from his head.

'*Buenos días, Señors.*' He bowed, placed his hand on his breast and plunged on. '*El Capitán Rubalcava, del barco La Virgen de la Bonanza.*' The name of his assumed identity and that of his ship sounded marvellously authentic and the latter allowed a spate of eloquence that, he guessed, disarmed any suspicions amid the dull-eyed Russians. Of the effect upon the frontiersman he was less sure. He tried to recall the first-person singular and managed only a squeal. '*Eee, er, dos San Francisco* . . .' He allowed himself to peter-out and stare round at the men. Their eyes were blank with incomprehension.

'*No comprendez?*' They stared back. He turned to the mountain-man. He had blue eyes like the others, but there was a narrowing of them, a shred of suspicion in their cold appraisal. Drinkwater leaned forward with exaggerated Latin effusiveness.

'*Señor?*' he asked, directly.

'*No comprendez* . . .' the man said slowly. A spark of understanding formed in Drinkwater's mind and he said quickly, before the other revealed a perfect knowledge of Spanish,' Ahh, *Señor, muy amigo*, you spik English, *sí?*'

The man nodded.

Drinkwater straightened, took a step towards him and waved his handkerchief airily, approaching the mountain-man, appearing to dismiss the assembled Russians whose dull, peasant wits watched this show as though it was a visitation by a dancing bear and they would presently be requested to reach for *kopecks*, at which point they would scatter.

'Eet is good, hey?' Drinkwater plunged on, narrowing his eyes and leaning forward again in a mannerism he had copied subconsciously from Don Alejo. 'I come to find Eenglish ship . . . Eenglishmen . . . *comprendez?*' He bastardised the English words by elongation, relapsing into the odd Spanish word for punctuation with a speed he hoped continued to deceive.

The mountain-man regarded him for some time, a ruminative air about him, as though he spoke little, and when he did the words had to be dragged from him.

'Yeah. *Comprendez*. I ain't see'd no ship, but . . .'

Drinkwater drew back in disappointment. With no news of *Patrician* there was little point in risking his neck further; but something about the mountain-man held his attention. He played the charade a step further, aware that beyond the group and walking down from the direction of the stockade a uniformed officer and an escort of armed men were approaching.

'Eenglishmen, *Señor* . . . you see, *qué*?'

'Yeah . . . I see . . .'

''Ow many?'

'Twenty-two . . .' The man became aware of the approach of the officer and he jerked his head. 'Ask him.'

The Russians were falling back; some of them removed their fur hats in the presence of the officer. Drinkwater turned to the newcomer. He wore a uniform of brown cloth with red-facings, dark breeches tucked into high boots. His tie-wig was ill-kempt and old fashioned and the hat he bore in his hands had seen better days.

Drinkwater drew himself up and essayed a low bow, flourishing his handkerchief and never taking his eyes off the face of the Russian officer. It was a cruel face, pock-marked and thin with long deprivation, yet with an imperious pair of eyes deep set on either side of a beak of a nose. The voice, when he spoke, was thin and reedy. The officer was clearly at the opposite end of the social class at whose other extremity Captain Prince Vladimir Rakitin occupied a place.

Taking a deep breath and noticing that his boat's crew had turned the boat round and were standing knee deep in the water holding it ready for escape, Drinkwater began again.

'*Buenas días, Señor, Ee, er La Capitán . . .*'

''E says he's lookin' for Englishmen, Lootenant . . .'

A look of understanding passed between the two of them and the unpleasant Russian officer fixed his eyes upon Drinkwater. His glance was truly intimidating and, masquerading as he was, Drinkwater felt unequal to the task of staring him down. Instead he bowed again.

'*Niet!* No English. Here, Russia. You go!'

The officer turned on his heel, leaving Drinkwater half-recovered from his bow.

'Now you go, *amigo*,' said the mountain-man, his drawl lingering mockingly upon the Spanish word so that a worm of alarm writhed in Drinkwater's gut. '*Vamos!*'

Drinkwater turned and walked towards the boat. Potter bent his back and Drinkwater waved him aside, splashing through the shallows.

'*Vaya con Dios, Capitán Rubalcava,*' called the mountain-man and then added something which made the Russians around him laugh.

'They were lying, of that I'm certain,' Drinkwater said, accepting the glass of wine that Derrick handed him.

'About the ship, sir?' asked Quilhampton.

'No, about men, Englishmen.'

'Our men, sir?' Quilhampton frowned. 'I don't quite follow . . .'

'There's the rub, James, neither do I.' He felt the wine uncoil its warmth in his belly, relaxing him. 'But I mean to find out. That Yankee knew something, for he mentioned twenty-odd men and I've already been played false by one American. We'll reconnoitre that fort tonight. Any movement from it?'

'Nothing new. That cove is still spying on us from the platform over the gate.'

'And the brigs?'

'Nothing. They don't appear to be working cargo, though they've tackles rigged.'

'Perhaps we interrupted them.'

'It's possible. What would they be loading?'

'Furs perhaps, jerked meat, other staples, Indian corn, say, purchased with iron trinkets. It's a safe enough haven for refitting ships too. They need labour for that, skilled labour . . .'

Comprehension kindled in Quilhampton's eyes. 'You mean English seamen, sir?'

'Yes.'

'You mean men from the *Patrician*, sir?'

'Yes.'

'But we're miles away from Drake's Bay, sir . . .'

'We got here, James, and those brigs looked handy enough craft.'

'Good God!' Quilhampton paused.

'It looks as though the Russians took not only our ship but might be holding our men. Let's get under weigh now and beat a retreat with our tails between our legs. We can return in the cutter after dark.'

The Raid in the Rain

It began to rain as they left the schooner. Their last glimpse of her pitching in the swell, hove-to in the darkness, was swiftly eclipsed by a hissing curtain of drizzle which seemed to seal them in a hermetic world of sodden misery. It was not cold until those sitting still felt the rain penetrate to their skin and envied the steady labours of the oarsmen. The interminable night passage was accompanied by the steady splash of oars and the occasional staccato chatter of teeth.

But the rain killed the wind and flattened the sea to a greasy swell that, at last, thundered on the low sand-spit ahead of them and signalled their proximity to the estuary. Drinkwater swung the tiller and skirted the breakers, edging round the northern extremity of the spit until they knew by the feel of the boat that they were in the mouth of the river and could feel the bite of the seaward current.

'Oars.'

The men ceased rowing and bent over their looms. Drink-water ordered a tot passed to each man. It was *aguardiente*, Spanish fire-water, but none the worse for that. They would need all the courage it put into their bellies, for their powder was soaked and whatever they might achieve would be by cold steel.

'Stand-by . . . give way together . . .'

They pressed on until they could see the dull leap of orange flames from behind the Russian stockade. They paused again and Drinkwater gave his final instructions. A few moments later the cutter's stem grounded on the shore of the Columbia River for the second time, only on this occasion there was to be no masquerading. Leaving the boat keepers, Drinkwater led

Quilhampton and Blixoe, Tregembo and a handful of seamen inland. The rain still fell and they felt their feet sticking in the ooze which sucked tenaciously on the well-trodden path up from the landing place. After a few yards they reached the tideline where low scrub, grass and trees began.

Drinkwater led them off to the left, keeping between the river and the fort, but working round behind it, guided by the red glow of the fire within the stockade. The seething hiss of the rain on the sea and mud became a low roar as they moved beneath the trees, dripping in huge droplets upon them. Despite the discomfort it covered their approach and they were close enough to make out the dancing of flames through the interstices of the pine-log rampart. Motioning them to stop, Drinkwater edged forward alone to peer through one of these slender gaps.

By now his night-vision was acute. He could see the upper outline of the stockade against the sky and, except by the gate, it appeared to be unpierced by guns, although there was doubtless a walk-way behind it to allow defenders to fire over the top. For some yards clear of the fort, the trees and brushwood had been cleared, but the nature of the night allowed him to slip across this glacis undetected. Pressed against the resinous pine trunks he peered into the fort.

The interior of the post was roughly circular, a number of buildings within it provided quarters and stores. Outside what he supposed to be the main barrack block a large fire was crackling, the flames and sparks leaping skywards despite the efforts of the heavens to extinguish them. He could see a few men lounging under the overhanging roof of this block, and the blackening carcass of a deer being roasted on spits, but from his vantage point he could see little else. The garrison, however, seemed a small one and the governor doubtless lived in one of the log cabins, for Drinkwater could just make out a square of yellow light close to the gate, as though a lamp burned behind a crude window. Cautiously he returned to the others, whispering to Quilhampton: 'Damned if I can see what we're looking for.'

'Oh. What now, sir?'

'We'll edge round the place.'

They began to move forward again, a pall of dejection falling on the miserable little column. They became careless, snapping twigs and letting branches fly back into the faces of the men behind them. They lost touch with the stockade on their right, moving into dense brushwood that tore at them, aggravating their tempers and unsettling them. Drinkwater began to question the wisdom of proceeding further. Then he stopped, so abruptly that Quilhampton bumped into him. Not five yards ahead of them a tall figure had risen from the bracken, hurriedly knotting the cords of his breeches. Drinkwater knew instantly it was the mountain-man.

To what degree the man's preoccupation had prevented his hearing the approach of the party, Drinkwater could only guess. Such a *voyageur*, at once a hunter, tracker, trapper and forest dweller, must have possessed instincts keen as any stag, but at that moment they had been somnolent, intent on more fundamental physical needs. Their surprise was mutual and as they stared at each other in silence, Drinkwater could just see the gleam of the foreshortened rifle barrel.

'Another step and you're dead, Mister. I thought you bastards might be back . . .'

So, the mountain-man had not been taken in by the disguise of the morning, and with that realisation Drinkwater sought to temporise, capitalising on that brief confidence of the forenoon.

'I've come for those Englishmen you spoke of.'

The mountain-man gave a short, dry laugh. 'You won't find 'em here.'

'Where then?'

'Why the hell should I tell you?'

'You told the Russians . . . said they knew about the matter.' The mountain-man seemed to hesitate and Drinkwater added, 'I'm surprised you want the Russians on your doorstep.'

'I sure as hell don't want you British. We got rid of you back a-while and I aim to keep it that way . . .'

'And the Russians?' Drinkwater persisted.

'Ain't no trouble at all . . .'

'Bring you vodka for furs and whatever Indian women you can sell 'em I daresay,' said Drinkwater.

'What's that to you, Mister? I've been expecting you ever since

I found your damned men wanderin' about the back-country behind Bodega Bay.'

'So you knew we weren't Spanish?'

'I've been expecting the British a-lookin' for their deserters, Mister. You didn't even come close to convincin' me. You see I know Rubalcava, Mister.'

'And you're on friendly terms with the Russians too, eh? Do I take it you've sold my deserters to that cold-eyed bastard that commands here?'

'What makes you think I'm hugger-mugger with the damned Russkie, eh? I ain't particularly friendly with anybody, especially the bloody British.'

'But . . .'

'But . . . I can't shoot the lot of you so just turn about and walk back to your boat . . .'

'I doubt you can shoot anyone in this damned rain . . .'

'You ain't heard of a Chaumette breech, Mister, or a God-damned Ferguson rifle? I could blow the shit out of you right now and pick off another of you before you got into those trees . . .'

The click of the gun-lock sounded ominously above the drip and patter of the rain.

'If you don't want the British here, why don't you tell me where those men are?'

'Ain't answering any more questions. You get goin'. *Vamos, Capitán* . . .'

Drinkwater turned and the men parted for him. He looked back once. The rain had eased a little and the cloud thinned. The mountain-man stood watching their retreat, his long gun slung across his arm, the noise of laughter muffled by his huge beard. At the same instant the man threw back his head and loosed an Iroquois war-whoop into the night. The alarm stirred noises from the direction of the stockade and the crack of the man's rifle was swiftly followed by a cry and the crash of a man falling behind him, sprawling full length.

'Back to the boat!' Drinkwater hissed, waving them all past him and stopping only Mr Quilhampton as the two of them bent over the felled seaman. It was Lacey and he was past help; the mountain-man had been as good as his word. The ball had made a gaping hole in Lacey's neck, missing the larynx, but severing the carotid artery. The wound was mortal and Lacy was close to death, his blood streaming over Drinkwater's probing hands.

'Come James, there's nothing to be done . . .'

There was no sign of the mountain-man but from the fort came the shouts of men answering an alarm. Somewhere to their right they could hear their own party crashing through the undergrowth accompanied by a stream of oaths and curses.

'Go *on* James!'

'Not without you, sir.'

'Don't be a bloody fool . . .'

Between them Lacey rattled out his life and fell limp. Drinkwater wiped his hands on Lacey's gory jacket.

'Poor devil,' he said, wondering if the ball had been intended for himself.

'Come on then.'

They both began to run.

In the rain and confusion they reached the boat unmolested, but the Russians were already pouring out of the fort towards the landing place. By the time Drinkwater reached the cutter with Quilhampton most of his party had mustered, but two were missing, stumbling about near the fort.

'Where's Hughes?' called Quilhampton.

'Fuck knows, he was behind Tregembo . . .'

'Tregembo?' Drinkwater spun round. 'Is he missing?'

'Seems so, sir . . .'

'God's bones!' Drinkwater swore. 'Get that boat off into the water, hold off the beach. You take command, James.' He raised his voice, 'Tregembo!' He roared, 'Tregembo!'

He began to run back the way he had come. Somewhere to the right he could see the shapes of men running and then the flash and crack of a musket, soon followed by a fusillade of shot as the approaching Russians fired wildly into the night. There was a harsh order screeched out and it stopped. Drinkwater recognised the voice of the governor and then, clearly above the hiss of the rain, he could hear the awful slither and snick of bayonets

204

being fixed. He caught up the sabre he had looted from the schooner and hefted it for balance.

'Tregembo!'

He spat the rain from his mouth and almost retched on the sudden, overpowering stench of pigs. Somewhere close by was a sty and he heard the ruminant grunts of its occupants change to a squealing. Two men and the dull gleam of steel were approaching and must have disturbed the swine.

'Tregembo!'

How many shots had the mountain-man fired? Was Tregembo lying out there dying like Lacey, while he had run for his life?

The two men were nearer and he swung round to defend himself.

'Tregembo!' he roared in one last desperate attempt to locate his servant. Suddenly a third man was upon him, risen, it appeared, from the very ground itself.

'Clap a stopper on the noise, zur . . .'

'God damn you, Tregembo . . .'

Drinkwater slashed wildly at the first assailant and felt his sabre knock aside the bayonet thrust. Whirling the blade he caught the second man as he tried to work round Drinkwater's rear, driving both off for a second. He began to fall back, waving Tregembo behind, him, '. . . why the devil didn't you answer me?'

'I fell among swine,' Tregembo called as he moved towards the boat behind his commander.

'Then run, man, *run*!'

Drinkwater saw an opportunity and slashed again, slicing in above the thrusting bayonet as the Russian infantryman lunged forward. The man's face was a pale blur and Drinkwater saw the dark splotch of blood against his cheek as the point of the sabre caught it, and then he turned and began to run, leaping the tussocks of grass and then slithering through soft sand and mud. He tripped and fell full length in the shallows, hard on Tregembo's heels. The Cornishman turned and helped him to his feet.

'God! What a damned farce!'

205

They scrambled into the boat amid a confusion of limbs and bodies, dominated by Quilhampton's voice calling above the rain and the tumult, 'Where's the captain? Has anyone seen Captain Drinkwater?'

'Here . . . I'm here, Mr Q . . . now get this festerin' boat under way!'

'Thank God! Aye, aye, sir . . . out oars! Come on there . . . for Christ's sake! Give way!'

As the boat pulled out into the estuary, a storm of small shot whined over their heads and all they could see were a few shapes splashing about in the shallow water in almost as much confusion as themselves.

'Let's sort this boat out.' Drinkwater's own sense of dignity and his innate hatred of disorder surfaced in the rout. 'Be silent there,' he ordered for the noise of swearing continued unabated and it suddenly dawned on him that it was no longer his own men who were responsible.

'What the deuce?'

Drinkwater looked round, thinking for an instant he was going out of his mind for the noise came out of the night ahead of them and the oaths were unmistakably English. Then he saw the looming bulk of one of the anchored brigs athwart whose hawse the current was sweeping them.

It's the English prisoners, sir,' shouted Quilhampton in a moment of comprehension, 'they must have heard us . . .'

Drinkwater considered the odds. How many Russians were aboard the brig? But the current had committed him.

'Catch a-hold then . . . come lads quickly . . . up and board her! Come on there, lads, those are your festerin' shipmates aboard there, prisoners of the Russians . . .'

A groundswell of anger stirred the occupants of the boat and she rocked dangerously as men reached out at the passing hull. Then the cutter jarred against the brig with a crash and they found themselves jammed under her forechains and were swarming up over her ample tumblehome. Driven by their recent defeat and now finding themselves among the familiar surroundings of a ship, they swept the length of her deck within a minute. At her stern, the watch of a dozen men, confused by

206

the noises ashore, suddenly attacked by desperate assailants and mindful that below decks a score of rebellious prisoners only awaited liberty before cutting their gaolers to pieces, soon capitulated. Most jumped over the taffrail to save their lives by swimming ashore, though three were taken prisoner. Drinkwater realised he was in possession of a Russian brig at the same moment that he caught a glimpse of the unsecured cutter drifting away downstream.

'What is it Mr Derrick?'

There was an odd formality about those left aboard the *Virgen de la Bonanza*. Mr Marsden, the *Patrician*'s carpenter but the most experienced seaman on board, hurried to answer Derrick's summons. The Quaker's innate dignity, his literacy and his position as the captain's secretary, almost gave him the status of a gentleman, while his tenacious hold on his faith had elevated him from a mere curiosity to something of a sage among the hands.

'I believe it to be the cutter, Friend Marsden, and it appears to be empty.'

Marsden took up the offered glass and levelled it. The dawn was heavy with the night's rain, the sea a sluggish undulating plain of uniform grey. No wind above the whisper of a breeze ruffled its surface, as though the sea was suppressed beneath the sheer weight of the sky's bequest. Every rope and spar, every sail and block was sodden with water. Rain had run below through cracks and companion-ways, scuttles and ports and, though it was not actually falling at that moment, more was threatened and the coming of day was only a lightening of the tone of the gloom. Their visible horizon was bounded by mist, a murky perimeter into which the grey, unoccupied shell of the cutter rocked, not above six cables away, borne seawards by the inexorable current of the Columbia River.

Fifteen minutes later the thing lay not thirty yards off and they could clearly see it was empty. There were disorderly signs of hurried evacuation. Several of the oars were missing, one stuck up, its blade jammed in the thole pins. Another was broken, the jagged loom indicating it had struck hard against something.

207

The remnants of rags hung down from the rowlocks, where, the night before, they had muffled them. Oddly the painter lay neatly coiled in the bow.

'Damned if I understand the meaning o' this,' muttered Marsden.

'I think we are alone, Friend, left to our own resources,' said Derrick, his sonorous tone carrying the dreadful implication to Marsden.

'Streuth! What's to be done? And the cap'n gone, an' all . . .'

'Could we fetch San Francisco?'

Marsden shrugged. 'God knows . . . I suppose we could . . . ain't my trade, nor yours neither . . . hell and damnation take it!'

'Come Friend, such language availeth nothing.' Derrick turned away from the rail and looked along the schooner's deck. Their handful of a crew would be hard-pressed to bring the schooner back to San Francisco.

'Oh, my fuckin' oath,' moaned Marsden and Derrick turned. The carpenter was staring to starboard where, out of the mist, the grey shape of a ship was emerging. 'We be sunk good an' proper now, Mister Derrick, that's one o' them Russian brigs we saw yesterday. Reckon they know all about us an' what's happened to the Cap'n.'

'Shall we run then?' Derrick suggested querulously.

'Is that a Russkie?' asked one of the seamen, coming up to the two men while behind him the remainder stood and stared despairingly to leeward. Marsden looked at first Blixoe and then Derrick. He was not given to quick thinking.

'Run? Where to?'

'Anywhere . . . we're faster than a brig, can sail closer to the wind . . .'

Marsden looked at the Quaker with something akin to respect. 'I suppose running ain't fighting,' he said, rubbing his chin and considering the matter.

'Of course we'll run,' snapped the seaman shouting for them to start the headsail sheets and cast loose the lashings on the helm.

'Wait!' Derrick was staring through the telescope. 'I'd swear that was Mr Quilhampton on the knightheads . . .'

*　*　*

208

'Seems a shame, zur, to burn a prize like that,' Tregembo muttered watching Quilhampton's firing party at work and the flames take hold of the brig.

'She stank near as bad as you when you emerged out of that swine-midden,' remarked Drinkwater. 'I have never seen so slovenly maintained a ship.'

'You damned near had me finished with all that shouting,' said Tregembo.

'That's as maybe, Tregembo. Would you have had me abandon you? By God, Susan would never have let me forget it . . .'

They smiled at each other relieved, both aware that they had enjoyed a lucky escape. They withdrew from the stern window of the schooner, Drinkwater to pour himself a glass of the Spanish commander's excellent *oloroso*, Tregembo to fuss the elegant little cabin into something more befitting a British naval captain. The stink of smoke came in and Drinkwater waited for Quilhampton's party to get aboard. A moment or two later Quilhampton knocked on the door. He entered, grimy but smiling. He held out a rolled chart.

'A glass, James, you've earned it . . . what d' you have there?'

'The answer to the riddle, sir . . . yes, thank you.' Quilhampton took the glass from Tregembo, who gave him an old-fashioned, sideways look.

'How did they behave?' asked Drinkwater unrolling the chart and staring at it.

'The men, sir?'

'Yes.'

'Like lambs, all eagerness to please. Never seen a firing party so eager to destroy a prize, couldn't do enough for me . . . would have burnt the damn thing twice over if it'd been a fit plea for mitigation . . .'

Drinkwater looked up from the chart and eyed the lieutenant speculatively. 'You think it should be, James?'

'We've little choice, sir. In any case, they outnumber us and I'm not sure about the men that were with me. It was only circumstances and self-preservation that kept us together . . . Marsden's all right, Derrick's a canting neutral and I suppose we can rely on old Tregembo . . .'

209

'Less of the "old", Mr Quilhampton, zur, if you please,' growled the Cornishman.

Quilhampton grinned and downed his glass, winking at Drinkwater.

'Let's hope they all appreciate which side their bread's buttered on now,' said Drinkwater, finishing his own glass, 'even so, I'll have to read 'em the riot act.'

'I'll muster them, then, sir.'

'Yes, if you please, and try not to look so damned pleased with yourself.'

'I think you'll find something to smile about sir, if you study that chart.'

'Why?'

'I think it shows us where we may find *Patrician*.'

Drinkwater looked down at the chart with its unfamiliar script and mixture of incomprehensible Russian characters and French names favoured by more aristocratic hydrographers. 'Anyway,' went on Quilhampton, pausing by the cabin door, 'I'm uncommon pleased to be given a fighting chance again.'

'Yes,' agreed Drinkwater, 'it was quite a turn up for the books, eh?'

'Well, "fortune favours the brave", sir,' Quilhampton remarked sententiously.

'I think,' replied Drinkwater drily, 'that last night, fortune was merely inclined to favour the least incompetent.'

Quilhampton left with a chuckle, but Drinkwater exchanged a glance with Tregembo.

'I'll let 'ee know if I hear anything, zur, have no fear o' that.'

'Very well Tregembo,' Drinkwater nodded, 'only I've a notion to set eyes on my family again.'

'You ain't the only one, zur.'

Drinkwater poured himself a second glass of the *oloroso* and, while he waited for the men to be mustered on deck, he studied the chart. The brig's Russian master was an untidy navigator; the erasure of her track was imperfectly carried out. It was quite obvious that Captain Rakitin had a nearer rendezvous than Sitka and, studying the features of the inlet, it was the very place he himself would have chosen to hide a prize. Delighted, he tossed off the glass and composed his features. He was going to have to scold the men, but, by all accounts they had quite a tale to tell.

Quilhampton gathered the details, noting them down on a page torn from the schooner's log-book. The men who had absconded from Drake's Bay had found the same village that Quilhampton had been driven from and met the same reception from its inhabitants. Although a body of opinion sought revenge on the local *peons*, wiser councils prevailed and the deserters moved further inland, reducing the chances of being retaken by any parties sent out by Drinkwater. For a day or two they remained together until they reached the great sequoia woods where game, water and freedom had split them into groups and they had lost their discipline. For a few days they wandered happily about and then one party found an Indian village. Their attempt to establish friendly relations with the native women met a hostile rebuttal. Another party roamed into a Franciscan mission and were driven off by angry *mestizos* who had been told they were devils. Within a week the country was raised against them and several were killed or left to the mercies of the natives as the manhunt spread. Eventually twenty-two of them found themselves rounded up and turned over to a strange, English-speaking man in fringed buckskins whom the local people held in some awe.

To the British deserters he promised, with complicit winks and other indications of racial superiority, that if they played along, he would accomplish their rescue. There were prolonged parleys, exchanges of some form of gifts or money and then they were led off on the promise of good behaviour, by the mountain-man whom they knew by the obvious alias of 'Captain Mack'. Since the alternative was inevitable death at the hands of either Indians, half-caste Spanish or the tender ministrations of what they thought was the Inquisition, they shambled off in the wake of their rescuer.

After a march of three days, Captain Mack led them down to the sea, on the shores of Bodega Bay where, to their astonishment, they found soldiers who spoke a language they could not

211

understand, but was clearly not Spanish. It did not take them long to find out that they had unwittingly become the serfs of the Russian-American Company, and that they were to be shipped in one of the filthy brigs that lay in the bay, to the Company's more secure post on the Columbia River. Captain Mack had gone with them to strike his bargain with the commandant there, and had been waiting to return to the mountain forests of California when Drinkwater had arrived in the schooner. As for the men, they were to be employed refitting or serving in Russian ships in the Pacific.

'The hands are mustered, Captain.'

Drinkwater came out of his reverie to find Derrick confronting him. 'Eh? Oh, thank you, Derrick. I shall be up directly.'

There was something piratical about the assembly amidships. Whether it was the lean, dishevelled and indisciplined appearance of the men, or whether the character of the schooner under its false colours, or simply the crawling uncertainty that nagged at Drinkwater that contributed to this impression, he was not sure as they stared back at him. Despite his titular right to lead them, his tenure of command had never rested on such insubstantial foundations. Among the men confronting him were almost certainly those who had attempted to sabotage the *Patrician*.

'Very well,' he began, silencing them and studying their faces for traces of guilt, defiance, insolence or contrition. 'Fate has literally cast us in the same boat . . .' he slapped the rail beside him, 'and I intend to discover the whereabouts of the *Patrician* and free our shipmates from the kind of bestial treatment some of you have just subjected yourselves to. Make no mistake about it, there are worse forms of existence than service in the King's Navy.' He paused, to let the point sink in.

'I can offer you little beyond hardship and the possibility of retaking our ship from the Russians, clearing our name as a company and destroying our enemies.'

He paused again, clambering up on the carriage of a 6-pounder. 'Well, what d'you say? Are you for or against? Do we keep that rag aloft,' he pointed up at the red and gold ensign of Spain still at the main peak, 'or are we going to take this little hooker into Plymouth to be condemned as a prize to *Patrician*?'

There was a second's hesitation and then they were yelling stupidly and throwing their arms in the air in acclamation. Drinkwater got down from the gun carriage.

'Very well, Mr Q. Lay me a course of nor'-nor'-west. Happily their experiences as subjects of the Tsar have taught them that there are degrees even of injustice.'

The Trojan Horse

Drinkwater tapped the dividers on the chart and looked up, gauging his prisoner.

Vasili Zhdanov, one of the three men captured with the Russian brig, spoke English of a kind, having been in attendance upon his one-time master when that worthy had served as an officer with the Anglophile Seniavin. However, Zhdanov had been caught stealing and after a sound whipping had been sold to the Russian-American Company, so that he had found a kind of life as seaman in one of the company's trading brigs. Now the reek of him, and particularly of his Makhorka tobacco, filled the cabin.

'How do you know that the British ship *Patrician* is here?' Drinkwater pointed to the bay which lay far to the northward, on the south coast of distant Alaska. There were a thousand anchorages amid the archipelagoes of islands that extended northwards from the Strait of Juan de Fuca, not least that of Nootka Sound, but this remote spot . . .

'I see . . . she come . . . *Suvorov* come . . .' replied Zhdanov, haltingly.

'Who is captain of *Suvorov*?'

'*Barin* Vladimir Rakitin . . .'

'How many guns?'

Zhdanov shrugged; he was clearly not numerate. 'Do you wish to serve King George of Great Britain?'

'I fight with Royal Navy,' Zhdanov said with some dignity, but whether he referred to Drinkwater's proposed change of allegiance or to his own past history he was unable to make clear. Drinkwater looked up at Quilhampton.

'Split the three of them up, try and make them understand they can join us and swear 'em in. If they protest, you'll have to put 'em back in the bilboes . . .'

'Aye, aye, sir,' Quilhampton led the Russian out. Drinkwater opened a stern window to clear the air. The man reminded him of a strange cross between a feral animal like a bear, and a child. Yet there was something impressive about him, reminding Drinkwater of those vast numbers of such men he had seen encamped about the Lithuanian town of Tilsit a year earlier. Like patient beasts they had awaited their fates with an equanimity that struck him as stoic. Zhdanov had responded to his own autocratic proposal with the simple obedience that made the Tsar's armies almost invincible.

He looked again at the chart. There was logic in secreting a ship in such a place. It was well-surveyed, compared with the adjacent coast, a strange opening into the surrounding mountains, like a fiord except that its entrance, instead of being open, was almost closed off by rocky promontories. Between them, Drinkwater guessed, the tide would rip with considerable ferocity.

Inside, the fiord was deep, a single steep islet rising in its middle, beyond which there was a sudden, abrupt bifurcation, the bay's arms swinging north and south and terminating in glaciers. If Vasili Zhdanov was right, somewhere within those enclosing pincers of promontories, lay *Patrician*.

Drinkwater opened the dividers and stepped off the distance, laying the steel points of the instrument against the latitude scale; more than a thousand miles lay between their present position and the lone bay which nestled under the massive shoulder of Mount Elias and the great Alaskan Range. He stared unseeing from the stern windows. So much depended upon their success. Where were Fraser, and Frey, the punctilious Mount or Midshipman Wickham? Were they prisoners aboard their own ship, or had they been held at San Francisco?

If providence granted success to this venture, he would return thither and force those corrupt time-servers, the Arguello brothers, to release his men. And force some measure of expiation out of that dishonourable dog, Rubalcava!

215

He felt his pulse beat with the mere thought of revenge and a wave of anger swept over him as he recalled the humiliation he had suffered at the hands of Prince Vladimir Rakitin.

If, if only providence had turned her face upon him again, he might yet do something to retrieve the ragged flag of honour.

No matter how assiduously one studied a chart, the reality never quite conformed to the imagination. Assessment of the present landscape had not been helped by the unfamiliar topographical terms *Zaliv*, *Mys* or *Bukhta* rendered incomprehensible by the Cyrillic script. Neither was Drinkwater's familiarity with French sufficiently proficient to determine whether it was La Perouse or the Russian Kruzenstern who had named the places on the chart. What impressed him was the quality of the thing, manufactured as it had been, half a world away in the Russan hydrographic office in St Petersburg.

He raised the glass again and raked the shore, seeking the narrow, half-hidden entrance and avoiding the scenic seductions of the mountain range that seemed to beetle down upon the littoral. It was stunningly magnificent, this chain of mighty peaks, shining with the sunlit glitter of permanent ice, like the *nunataks* of Greenland. And then he saw her, the black tracery sharp in the crisp, cool air which sharpened every image with more intensity than the most cunningly wrought lens. He knew instantly that the ship anchored beyond the low headland was indeed *Patrician*.

He shut his glass with a snap. 'Hoist Spanish colours, if you please, and call all hands to their stations.'

He had assumed the worst and formed his ruse accordingly. *Patrician*, he theorised, would be well manned by the enemy, despite his inclination to believe the contrary due to her remote location. Her own people would have been removed in San Francisco, so there would be no spontaneous rising to assist; art and cunning must, therefore, be his chief weapons. He sent below for the Spanish uniforms and saw to his side-arms long before the approach to the entrance. When he was ready he turned the *Virgen de la Bonanza* to the north-east and, ascending to the foretop, spied out the narrow strait between the guardian headlands. From that elevation he saw at once why the entrance was so difficult to locate from the deck. The island which he knew lay within the bay, lay directly upon the line of sight when peering through the gap, so appearing to form one continuous coastline. Turning, he called down to Quilhampton by the helm, the course was altered and the bowsprit below him swung towards the narrows.

The schooner heeled, turning to larboard and bringing the wind fine on that bow and Drinkwater, surveying the entrance from his perch, felt the fine thrum of wind through the stays and the halliards that ran past him. The water ran suspiciously smooth in the gut, with darker corrugations rippling out from either side, corrugations which tore off into whorls and rips of gyrating turbulence, where unseen rocks or sudden treacherous shifts of current, manipulated the violent motion of an ebbing tide.

'Deck there!'

'Sir?' Quilhampton looked aloft.

'I want a steady hand on the helm . . . there's a deal of broken water ahead . . .'

'Aye, aye, zur.'

Drinkwater smiled as Tregembo took the helm and then turned his attention to the narrows again. Their progress was becoming slower, as they felt the increasing opposition of the tide. The schooner crabbed sideways under its influence, unable to point closer to the wind. Drinkwater bestowed a quick glance at the anchored ship.

She was alone, alone beneath those great slabs of mountains which lifted into the heavens behind her, their snow caps sliding into scree and talus, tussocked grass and low, stunted trees which, on the lower ground that fringed the fiord, changed to a dark, impenetrable mantle of firs. And she was most certainly the *Patrician*.

'Steady there . . .'

He felt the schooner lurch and looked below to see Tregembo anticipate the tide-rip's attempt to throw the vessel's head into the wind. The sea was slick with the speed of the tide, almost uninfluenced by the effect of the breeze as it rushed out into the ocean beyond the confines of the bay. Those dark corrugations resolved themselves into standing waves, foaming with energy as the mass of water forced itself out of the bay so that the schooner slowed, stood still and began to slip astern.

The heads of curious seals, impervious to the viciously running ebb, popped out of the grey water to stare like curious, ear-less dogs, their pinched nostrils flaring and closing in exaggerated expressions of outrage at the intrusion.

For an hour they hung, suspended in this fashion until almost suddenly, the tide slacked, relented and the power of the wind in their sails drove them forwards again. The low roar of the rush of water eased, the corrugations, the rips and eddies diminished and slowly disappeared. For a while the strait was one continuous glossy surface of still water, and then they were through, brought by this curious diminishing climax into sudden proximity with their quarry.

'And now,' said Drinkwater regaining the deck, 'we must play at a Trojan Horse.'

'After Scylla and Charybdis 'twill be little enough, sir,' remarked Quilhampton with unbecoming cheerfulness.

'Belay the classical allusions, Mr Q,' snapped Drinkwater, suddenly irritated, 'belay the loud-mouthed English and lower the boat, then you may carry out your instructions and fire that salute . . .'

The bunting of the Spanish ensign tickled Drinkwater's ear as he was rowed across the dark waters of the inlet towards the *Patrician*. The schooner's boat, hoisted normally under her stern, was smaller than the cutter they had lost in the Columbia River. But he hoped his approach was impressive enough and he was aware, from a flash of reflected light, that he was being scrutinised through a glass by one of the half-dozen men he could see on his own quarterdeck.

Behind him came the dull thud of the 6-pounder, echoing back after a delay to mix its repetition with the sound of the next signal-gun so that the air seemed to reverberate with the concussion of hundreds of guns as the echoes chased one

218

another into the distance in prolonged diminuendo.

No answering salute came from the fo'c's'le of the *Patrician*, no answering dip of her diagonally crossed ensign. He stood up, showing off the Spanish uniform with its plethora of lace, and holding out the bundle of papers that purported to be despatches.

He noted a flurry of activity at the entry with a sigh of mixed relief and satisfaction.

'How far is the schooner, Potter?' he asked the man pulling stroke-oar.

'She's just tacked, sir,' replied Potter, staring astern past Drinkwater, 'an' coming up nicely . . . they're tricing up the foot of the fores'l now, sir and the outer jib's just a-shivering . . . 'bout long pistol shot an' closing, sir.'

'Very well.' Drinkwater could smell the rum on the man's breath as he made his oar bite the water. Off to starboard an unconcerned tern hovered briefly, then plunged into the water and emerged a second later with a glistening fish in its dagger-like beak.

'We're closing fast, lads, be ready . . .' He paused, judged his moment and, in a low voice, ordered the oars tossed and stowed. Beside him Tregembo put the tiller over. Amid a clatter of oars coming inboard the bowman stood up and hooked onto *Patrician*'s chains.

Drinkwater looked up. A face stared down at him and then he began to climb, not daring to look around and ascertain the whereabouts of Quilhampton and the schooner. At the last moment he remembered to speak bastard-French, considering that it was not unreasonable for a Spanish officer to use that language when addressing a French-speaking ally. The fact that he spoke it barbarously was some comfort.

Stepping onto the deck he swept off his hat and bowed.

'*Bonjour, Señores*,' he managed, looking up with relief into the face of an officer he had never seen before, '*ou est votre capitaine, s'il vous plait?*'

'*Tiens! C'est le capitaine anglais!*'

Drinkwater jerked round. To his left stood one of the midshipmen he had last seen in Don José's Residence at San

219

Francisco. Hands flew to swords and he knew that his ruse had failed utterly. He flung the paper bundle at the young man's face and drew the cavalry sabre before either of the Russian officers had reacted fully. Letting out a bull-roar of alarm he swiped the heavy, curved blade upwards in a vicious cut that sent the senior officer, a lieutenant by his epaulettes, reeling backwards, his hands to his face, his dropped sword clattering on the deck.

'Come on you bastards!' Drinkwater bellowed into the split second's hiatus his quick reaction had brought him. 'Board!'

Would they come, those disloyal quondam deserters, or would they leave him to die like a dog, hacked down by the ring of steel that was forming about him? What would Quilhampton do? Carry out the plan of getting foul of the *Patrician*'s stern in a histrionic display of incompetence which was to have cut Drinkwater's inept French explanation and turned it into a farce of invective levelled by him at Quilhampton under whose cover the *Virgen de la Bonanza* was to have been run alongside the frigate. During this ludicrous performance his men were supposed to have come aboard . . .

Armed seamen with pikes from the arms' racks around the masts and marines with bayonets, men with spikes and rammers and gun-worms were closing, keeping their distance until they might all rush in and kill him.

'Board, you bastards!' he shouted again, his voice cracking with tension, his eyes moving from one to another of his enemies, seeking which was the natural leader, whose muscles would first tense for the kill and bring down Nemesis upon his reckless head . . .

It seemed he waited an age and then a shuffling of the midshipman's feet told him what he wanted to know. He thrust left, pronating his wrist and driving his arm forward so that the mangled muscles cracked with the speed of his lunge. The *pointe* of his sabre struck the young man on the breast-bone, cracked it and sent him backwards, gasping for breath in an agony of surprise. As he half-turned he sensed reaction to his right, a movement forward to threaten his unprotected back. He cut savagely, reversing the swing of his body, the heavy weapon singing through the air and cutting with a sickening crunch into the

220

upper arm of a bold seaman whose cannon-worm dropped from nerveless hands and who let out a howl of pain and surprise. And then he lost the initiative and was fighting a dozen assailants for his very life.

'Frey, I think you are an infatuated fool. That must be the twentieth portrait of La Belladonna you have done,' quipped Wickham, looking down at the watercolour, 'and they do not improve. Besides they are a waste of the dip . . .' he reached out with dampened fingers to pinch out the miserable flame that lit the thick air of the cold gunroom and received a sharp tap on the knuckles from Frey's brush.

'Go to the devil, Wickham! I purchased that dip out of my own funds . . .'

Wickham sat and put his head in his hands, staring across the grubby table at Frey. 'What d'you suppose they intend to do with us?'

'I don't know,' replied Frey without looking up, 'that's why I paint, so that I do not have to think about such things . . .' He put the brush in the pot of water and stared down at the face of Doña Ana Maria. Then, in a sudden savage movement, his hand screwed up the piece of paper and crumpled it up.

Wickham sat back with a start. 'Shame! It wasn't that bad!'

'No, perhaps not, but . . .'

'Was she really handsome?'

'Quite the most beautiful woman I have ever seen,' Frey waxed suddenly lyrical.

'How many women *have* you seen, Frey? You've been aboard here since . . .'

'What was that?' asked Frey sharply, sitting upright.

'One of the men cursing those bastard Russians for being too free with their knouts, I expect,' said Wickham in a bored tone.

'No! Listen!'

It came again, an agonised bellow of command and there was something vaguely familiar about the voice. Frey's eyes opened wide.

'It can't be . . .'

'Can't be what . . . ?'

The shout came again and then there were the screams and bellows of a fight somewhere above them. Both midshipmen stood. Their sentry, a slovenly Russian marine, stirred uneasily, hefting his neglected musket, his thumb poised on its hammer.

There was a sudden buzz throughout the ship as other men, confined in irons or about their imposed duties realised something momentous was happening on deck. For too many days now they had rotted in a regime of inactivity, required only occasionally to turn out and pump the bilges, or tend the cable. For the most part they had languished in almost total darkness, separated from their officers, uncertain of their future, toying with rumours that, when the *Suvorov* returned, many of them would be drafted into her, or into other Russian ships or settlements. For Prince Rakitin such a draft of healthy labour seemed like a blessing from heaven, sufficient to restore the fortunes of the Russian-America Company after the loss of Rezanov.

Frey stood cautiously, not wishing to alarm the sentry. He had learned enough about their gaolers to realise that the man would display no initiative, did not dare to, and would remain at his post until someone came down and relieved or shot him.

'What the devil is going on?' Frey asked in an agony of uncertainty.

'Damned if I know . . .'

Then there was an outburst of the most horrible noise, a howling ululation that reminded the two youths of stories of Iroquois massacres they had heard old men tell from the Seven Years War. It was much closer than the upper deck, and provoking responses even nearer as the captive British seamen joined in with whoops and shouts of their own. The two midshipmen could hear shouts of joyful recognition, of the clank of chains and the thud-thud of axes, the sharp clink as they struck iron links, more shouts and then, to compound the confusion, *Patrician* lurched as something large and heavy struck her.

'Come on, Wickham!' Frey's hand scooped the water-pot from the table and hurled it in the face of their sentry. Momentarily blind the man squeezed the trigger of his musket and the confined space reverberated with the crack of the shot. The ball buried itself in the deck-head and the Russian stabbed out with his bayonet but the thing was unwieldy in the small space, and the two midshipmen dodged nimbly past him.

Out on the gun-deck the scene was like a painting of the Last Judgement. Russians lay dead or writhing in agony, like the damned on their way to hell-fire. A handful of piratical British seamen led by Captain Drinkwater's coxswain Tregembo were turning up the hatchways like avenging angels and out of the hold poured a starveling rabble of pale and ragged bodies, corpses new-released from their tombs, some dragging irons, some half-free of them so that they held the loose links and went howling after their captors, swinging the deadly knuckle-dusters in a whirl-wind of vengeful pursuit.

'Tregembo, by all that's holy!' Frey stood for an instant, taking in the scene, then ran to a still-writhing Russian, tore the cutlass from his dying grasp and hurried on deck.

Lieutenant Quilhampton lost his cheerfulness the instant Captain Drinkwater left in the schooner's boat. All his attention had to be paid to split-second timing, to bring the *Virgen de la Bonanza* up under *Patrician*'s stern, to fail in an attempt to tack and fall alongside the frigate in a display of Hispanic incompetence that, if he was a yard or two short, would condemn Captain Drinkwater to an untimely death.

His throat was dry and his heart thudded painfully as he sought to concentrate, gauging the relative angle of approach, his speed, and the set of a tide that was already flooding in through the narrows behind him.

'A point to larboard, if you please,' he forced himself to say, feigning complete mastery of himself and seeing Drinkwater ascend the *Patrician*'s side by the manropes.

What would happen if Quilhampton failed and Drinkwater died? For himself he knew that he could never return and press his suit for the hand of Catriona MacEwan. Somehow such a course of action would be altogether dishonourable, knowing that he had failed the one man who had ever shown him kindness. And what of Drinkwater? Quilhampton knew of his distant devotion to his family, for all the estrangement imposed by the

223

naval service, and this particular commission. Did Drinkwater expect him to fail? Would Drinkwater rather die in this remote and staggeringly beautiful corner of the world, attempting to recapture his own ship, rather than live with the knowledge of having lost her? If so the responsibility he bore was even heavier, the bonds of true friendship imposing a greater burden than he felt he had skill to meet.

And then he felt the tide, flooding in with increasing strength. *Patrician* was already lying head to it, his own course crabbed across; another point to larboard perhaps . . .

'Larboard a point.'

'Larboard a point more, sir.' There was warning in the helmsman's voice. Quilhampton looked up; the luff of the mainsail was just lifting.

'She's a-shiver, sir,' Marsden said from amidships.

Quilhampton did not answer, he was watching the schooner's bowsprit, watching it cross the empty sky until . . .

'Down helm!'

The *Virgen de la Bonanza* turned slowly into the wind.

'Midships!'

He stole a quick look along the deck. Apart from the half-a-dozen men at the sheets, the remainder, armed to the teeth, lay in the shadow of the starboard rail or crouched under the carelessly thrown down tarpaulin amidships.

The *Virgen de la Bonanza* lost way. The quarter of the *Patrician* loomed over them. They could see marks of neglect about the frigate, odds and ends of rope, scuffed paintwork . . .

A terrible bellow of range came from the deck above. With mounting anxiety Quilhampton suddenly knew he had now to concentrate more than ever before. Such a howl had not been planned, something was wrong, very wrong. He could abandon all pretence.

'Up helm! Shift the heads'l sheets!'

He checked the swing. 'Steady there, lads, not yet, not yet . . .'

The schooner began to swing backwards. He looked over the side. The boat, bobbing under the main chains of the *Patrician*, was already empty. He saw the last pair of heels disappear in through an open gun-port with relief. Drinkwater had at least the support of Tregembo and his boat's crew. A moment later the boat was crushed between the schooner and the frigate as the two hulls jarred together.

'Now!'

There was an ear-splitting roar from amidships. The big carronade, trained forward at maximum elevation and stuffed with langridge, ripped through the rigging of the forechains and, in the wake of that iron storm, Quilhampton loosed his boarders.

Drinkwater parried the first wave of the attack. There was a curious life in the cavalry sabre; centrifugal force kept it swinging in a wide and dangerous swathe though it tore mercilessly at the wrecked muscles of his wounded right shoulder. How long he could keep such a defence going he did not know, but he knew that he would have been a dead man already had he been armed only with his old hanger. He had fired two of the three pistols he had carried and foolishly thrown them down, intending to draw the third, but he could not free it from his belt, and it ground into his belly as he twisted and dodged his assailants.

He did not escape unscathed. He was cut twice about the face and received a deep wound upon his extended forearm. A ball galled his left shoulder and a pike thrust from the rear took him ignominiously in the fleshy part of the right buttock. He began to feel his strength ebb, aware that one last rally from his opponents would result in his death-wound, for he could fight no more.

His vision was blurring, though his mind retained that coolness that had saved him before and fought off the weakness of his reactions for as long as possible. A man loomed in front of him, he swung the sabre . . . and missed. Tensing his exposed stomach he waited for the searing pain of the pike thrust.

'Fuck me! It's the Cap'n!'

The pike-head whistled past his face as the wielder put it up. Suddenly all opposition melted away, there were friendly faces round him, men he had known once, long ago, long ago when he had commanded the *Patrician* . . .

*   *   *

225

But it was not Valhalla he woke to, nor had it been the faces of the dead he had seen. Some intelligence beyond mere consciousness had allowed him to faint at last, recognising his part in the fight need no longer be sustained. His men had followed him, wiping out the stain of their desertion.

Somewhere far above him voices were discussing him. Impertinent voices that spoke as though he was nothing more than a blood-horse whose health was uncertain.

'Will he pull through, Mr Lallo?'

'Of course, Mr Q, 'tis only a drop of blood he's lost. He'll save me the trouble of prescribing a remedy. There's nothing serious, though that cut in his *gluteus maximus* will embarrass him . . .'

'His *what*?'

'Arse, Mr Q. He'll not sit for a week without it reminding him of its presence.'

Quilhampton laughed. 'I'll go and see about some food . . .'

'Go and find him a bottle of port. Nothing reconstitutes the blood better than a fortified wine.'

'There's some excellent *oloroso* aboard the *Virgen* . . .'

'What a damnably blasphemous name . . . go and get some then . . .'

'You're a pair of impertinent dogs,' Drinkwater muttered, fully conscious.

'There, Mr Q, I told you recovery would be complete . . . welcome aboard, sir.'

'Thank you Mr Lallo, how many men do we muster?'

Dos de Mayo

'I believe they call you "Captain Mack",' Drinkwater said. His wounded buttock still troubled him and he preferred to stand, his back to the stern-windows, a grim imperturbable silhouette regarding his prisoner. Mack's eyes were defiant, truculent. He nodded, but held his tongue.

'I understood you did your hunting further south, amid the barrens of California.'

'They ain't barrens,' said Mack shortly, with a half-smile that was at once menacing and secretive.

'Perhaps not,' replied Drinkwater dismissively; he had learned the term in the American War and its precise meaning was unimportant now.

'You are a citizen of the United States of America, are you not?'

'I suppose I am . . .'

'You *suppose*?'

'In so far as I'm under any man's jurisdiction. I reckon to be born free, Mister, I respect it in others, I expect it from them.'

'Meaning you could have shot to kill me when we disturbed you at your office?'

'Sure. I can hit a running moose . . .'

'You didn't respect the freedom of my men, you turned them over to the Russians.'

'Hell, Cap'n, that's bull-shit. You didn't respect their freedom either, an' that's supposing they was free in the first place, instead of run from this here ship.'

Drinkwater smiled. 'But you didn't turn 'em over to the Russkies for love of Old England . . .'

'Sure as hell I didn't.'

'Then why?'

'They was trespassin', Cap'n.'

'So were you, on Spanish territory. Did you sell 'em?'

'What the hell would I want with roubles, Cap'n?' the mountain-man answered contemptuously.

'I presume you require powder and shot,' Drinkwater replied coolly, 'and gold is always gold . . .'

A spark of something flared in the mountain-man's eyes, hostility, malice perhaps, Drinkwater could not be sure beyond knowing he had touched a nerve.

'You are a solitary, Captain Mack. A man apart. I do not pretend to understand your motives and my men would have you hang for your treachery.'

'I promised them nothing!'

'Maybe not. Would you have me hand you over to the Spanish authorities at San Francisco . . . ?'

Patrician lifted to the swell and leaned gently over to the increasing breeze as, on deck, Lieutenant Fraser crowded on sail. Drinkwater smiled with grim satisfaction, for a wave of nausea passed visibly over Mack's features.

'You will do as you please, I reckon,' he said with some difficulty. Drinkwater jerked his head at Sergeant Blixoe.

'Take him below, Sergeant.'

He could afford clemency. It was good to have them all back together. Fraser, Lallo, Mount, Quilhampton, even the lugubrious chaplain, Jonathan Henderson. He looked astern through the cabin windows where, under Hill and Frey, the *Virgen de la Bonanza* danced in their wake. Perhaps best of all was to see little Mr Belchambers's cheerful smile, for Drinkwater did not think he could have brought himself to have written to explain the boy's loss to his trusting parents. It was true that there were still men missing, men who had been pressed by the Spaniards to labour on the wharves of San Francisco, but for the great majority the raid on the outpost on the Columbia River had reunited them in spirit, wiping out memories of discontent, disloyalty and desertion. It was less easy for Drinkwater to forget the depths to which he had sunk, of how near he had been to suicide; less easy to forget the risks he had run in his desperation, but the raid had had its effect, paltry enough though it had been in terms of military glory. They had landed by boat in the mist of early morning in a brief and bloody affair in whch all the advantage had been with the assailants. They had carried off all that they had not destroyed, even Tregembo's swine, setting fire to the fort with the same enthusiasm they had burnt the first brig.

Drinkwater turned from the stern windows and glanced down at the chart on his table. They would do the same to the Russian outpost at Bodega Bay, where the mysterious mountain-man had first enslaved his own deserters. His men would enjoy that and he could set free Captain Mack, leave him to his damnable wilderness. Then he would return to San Francisco. His heart-beat quickened at the thought of confronting the Arguello brothers. How unexpected were the twists of fortune and how close he had come to ending his own life in the cell below the *Commandante's* residence. If it had not been for Doña Ana Maria . . .

He forced his mind into safer channels. His first consideration was the destruction of the second Russian post at Bodega Bay.

Lieutenant Quilhampton jumped into the water of Bodega Bay and led the men ashore. They splashed behind him, Mount leading the marines, Frey with his incendiary party. They met only token resistance. A couple of shots were fired at them out of bravado, but the two grubby wretches immediately flung down their muskets and surrendered. Surprise had been total and the British party entered the now familiar stockade with its stink of urine, grease and unwashed humanity, to set about its destruction.

Only when he saw the flicker of flames did Drinkwater leave the ship in the boat. In the stern-sheets, escorted by two of Mount's marines, sat Captain Mack. Wading ashore with the mountain-man's long rifle, Drinkwater indicated that the marines were to follow him with their prisoner. As they walked towards the blazing pine logs that exploded and split in great upwellings of sparks as the resin within them expanded and took

229

fire, they met Quilhampton's party escorting a pathetic collection of bearded *moujiks* back to the boats.

'Where's the commandant?'

'No one seems to be in command, sir, just this handful of peasants.'

'He's a-fucking Indian women, Cap'n, or lying dead-drunk under a redwood tree,' drawled Captain Mack.

'Very well. Let him go.' Drinkwater motioned to the marines and they stood back. He jerked his head at the mountain-man. '*Vamos!*'

Mack half-smiled at the irony, but held out his hand. 'My gun, Cap'n.'

'You get out of my sight now. When my boat pulls off the beach I'll leave your rifle on that boulder. You can get it then.'

'You don't trust me?'

'Somebody once told me the Cherokees called you people Yankees because they didn't trust you.'

'Ah, but others called us English then . . .'

Mack grinned, reluctantly acknowledging an equal and stalked away. He did not look back and his buckskins were soon as one with the alternate light and shade that lay beneath the trees. Drinkwater turned back to the incendiary roar and crackle of the burning fort when there came a shout, the snap of branches and a roar of anger. Drinkwater spun round.

Mack was running back towards them, pursued by a dark figure in an odd, old-fashioned full-length waistcoat. The man had lost his wig and hat but he held out a pistol and, as he took in the sight of the burning fort, he fired it screaming some frightful accusation after Mack. The mountain-man fell full length, his spine broken by the ball and Drinkwater ran up to him as he breathed his last. Behind Drinkwater the marines brought down the wigless Russian.

Drinkwater bent over the dying Mack. '. . . Thought . . . I'd betrayed . . .' he got out through clenched teeth, and Drinkwater looked at the Russian, rolling beneath the bayonets of the marines. It must have been the returning commandant, misinterpreting the mayhem before him as his post blazed and Mack walked insouciantly away from the scene.

230

Drinkwater watched as life ebbed from the tumbled goliath, shot so ignominiously by a debauched ne'er-do-well, and felt that sharp pang of regret, that sense of universal loss that accompanied certain of the deaths he had witnessed. He was about to stand when his eye fell upon something bright.

Half a dozen huge nuggets of the purest gold had rolled out of the mountain-man's leather pouch.

'Bury 'em both,' he called to the marines, and scooping up the treasure he swept them into his pocket.

Gold.

It threw off the reflections of the candle flames leaping and guttering as *Patrician* worked her way off shore in the first hours of the night. Tomorrow she would appear off Point Lobos, but tonight she would hide herself and her prize in the vastness of the Pacific.

Gold.

A king's ransom lay before him. No wonder Mack had scorned the idea of payment for passing *Patrician*'s deserters to the Russians, and no wonder he had not wanted those same men wandering over wherever it was he found the stuff, for that was the only implication that fitted his deed and his character. He would not encourage the Spaniards, for their tentacles would spread inexorably northwards, while the Russians could supply him with those necessities he was compelled to get from civilisation. Powder, shot, steel needles, flints . . . Drinkwater had no idea how many natural resoures the wilderness contained.

But it contained gold.

And what the devil would such an unworldly man as 'Captain Mack' do with such a treasure? That was a mystery past his divining.

'Cleared for action, sir!'

'Very well, Mr Fraser.'

Above their heads the white ensign snapped in the breeze from the north that had blown fresh throughout the night and was only now losing its strength as they came under the lee of the land. From his post on the gun-deck, Quilhampton tried to locate the little cove where he and the cutter's crew had holed up and from where he had seen the *Patrician* carried off into captivity. Suppose the *Suvorov* was waiting for them under the protection of the Spanish battery on Point Lobos? What would be the outcome of the action they were about to fight?

He found he dare not contemplate defeat, and felt the atmosphere aboard the ship imbued with such a feeling of renewal that defeat must be impossible, no matter what the odds. Those two raids, little enough in themselves, had patched up morale, made of them all a ship's company again, a ship's company that had endured much. There was talk of going home after the job was done, after the Spanish and the Russians had been made to eat their own shit, and the gun-captains kneeled with their lanyards taut in their fists in anticipation of this event.

'Thou art my battle-axe and weapons of war,' the Reverend Jonathan Henderson had declaimed at Divine Service that morning, 'for with Thee I will break in pieces the nations, and with Thee I will destroy kingdoms,' he had railed, and if no one understood the finer theological points of his subsequent deductions, all made the blasphemous connection between Jeremiah's imputed words and themselves.

'Stand ready, sir,' Mr Belchambers squeaked at the companionway, 'maximum elevation,' he went on repeating Drinkwater's orders from the quarterdeck, 'no sign of the Russian ships. Target to be the battery, starboard broadside.'

Quilhampton grinned. The boy had the phrases arse-about-face, but he was cool enough. He stooped and peered through the adjacent gun-port. He saw the smoke suddenly mushroom from the end cannon, wafting outwards in a great smoke-ring, but no fall of shot followed.

'Make ready!' Belchambers's squeak came again.

'Make ready there, starbowlines!' Quilhampton roared with mounting excitement.

A second smoke-ring mushroomed from the embrasures of Point Lobos.

'They're bloody well saluting us,' muttered Quilhampton, frowning.

'Hold your fire, sir! There's a flag of truce putting off from the shore.'

A groan of disappointment ran along the gun-deck.

'*Capitán*, my brother, Don José Arguello de Salas, *Commandante* of His Most Catholic Majesty's city of San Francisco extends his most profound apologies for this most unfortunate mistake.'

'Damn you Don Alejo. Where *is* your brother? I demand to know more of this affair, this so-called *mistake* which I know to be nothing short of a towering fabrication, a . . . a . . .' words failed to express Drinkwater's angry sense of outrage.

So many half-guessed-at truths had found their answers in the hour since the flag-of-truce had first been seen. But Don Alejo was not a man to concede a thing. As Drinkwater faltered, the wily Spaniard rammed home his counter-stroke.

'We are both guilty, *Capitán*. You, please, you steal our schooner, *La Virgen de la Bonanza*.'

'That is an outrageous allegation . . .'

'*Capitán*, please, it is one of the confusions of this war.'

'If you had informed me, as you were duty bound to do, that she brought news of our new alliance, I should not have been forced to capture her. You, Don Alejo, acted outside all international law by selling, yes sir, *selling* His Britannic Majesty's ship *Patrician* to the Russian power in the person of Prince Rakitin *after* you had heard that your country was once again an ally of mine. Such an action is the basest and most dishonourable that I have ever heard of.'

'A little mistake, *Capitán* Drinkwater,' snapped Don Alejo,' a little . . . what did your English papers say, eh? Ah, *sí*, a quibble, like when your ships come under your Admirality orders and attack Bustamente's frigates and blow up the *Mercedes* and send *women* to God before you have a declaration of war! It is nothing! Nothing!' Don Alejo made a gesture contemptuous dismissal.

'But you traded, Don Alejo, *sold* my ship. You have been trading with the Russians ever since Rezanov came, eh? Your Most Catholic Master does not approve of his servants trading in his monopolies.'

'It was for my country that I remove your ship. You too-much

233

disturb trade. Now we are at peace and allies, you have your ship back.' Don Alejo spoke in a lower key. 'Perhaps, *Capitán* Drinkwater, you should be a little obliged to me . . .'

'Upon my soul, why?' asked Drinkwater aback.

'When you first take me prisoner, *Capitán*, Don Jorge Rubalcava, he want to tell you to go to Monterey. There you not escape. There you lose your ship. Here in San Francisco . . .' He shrugged, a gesture full of implications and Drinkwater understood that Don Alejo was beyond his comprehension in cunning. Whatever the venal sins of his brother, Don Alejo would emerge on the winning side. If he knew of the presence of gold in California, as that shrewd observation of Quilhampton's suggested, Don Alejo was not the man to make the knowledge public. Had he in some subtle way suggested to Doña Ana Maria that honour was at stake and so ensured Drinkwater's escape through her action? Looking at him, Drinkwater thought the thing at least a possibility. And Don Alejo had nothing to lose by it, for Drinkwater might have failed, lost in some obscure and savage *fracas* on the coast. He shuddered at the mere recollection of the night raid on the Columbia River.

'Now, *Capitán*, as to the matter of your men . . .' said the Spaniard smoothly.

Drinkwater frowned. 'I shall expect them returned instantly.'

'As soon as Don Jorge takes possession of the *aviso*, *Capitán*.' Don Alejo smiled victoriously. Drinkwater opened his mouth to protest the injustice of losing their prize. Then he remembered the gold and felt the weight of those nuggets dragging down the tails of his full-dress coat. When the time came, he thought, he could purchase comforts enough to compensate his men for the loss of their paltry share in the schooner. Perhaps they were better off, for the matter might lay before a prize-court for years, and only the attorneys would benefit. Besides, he had other matters to attend to. There were despatches, brought weeks earlier, carried overland to Panama with the news of the rising against the French, then up the coast in *La Virgen de la Bonanza*. Don Alejo swore he had intended to pass them to Drinkwater on his release, the very day Drinkwater had succeeded in escaping. And there was still the Russian power to destroy.

Don Alejo was holding out a glass.

'A toast to our new alliance, *Capitán* . . . to *Dos de Mayo* . . . the second day of May, the day Madrid rose against the French. It is a pity good news travels so slow, eh?'

He knew he was not supposed to see her, that she broke some imposition of her father's or her uncle's to contrive this clumsy meeting on the path. She was as lovely as ever and yet there was something infinitely sad about the cast of her features, despite her smile. She held two books out to him. They were his log and journal and he took them, thanking her and tucking them under his arm with the bundle of despatches Don Alejo had at last given him. He smiled back at her.

'*Señorita*, I am indebted to you for ever for my freedom, even,' he added, the smile passing from his face, 'for my very life.' He paused, recalling how close he had come to the ultimate act of despair and her face reflected her own grief. Then he brightened. 'And thank you for your kindness in retrieving my books.'

'It was nothing . . .'

'You knew about the changes in your country's circumstances?'
She nodded. '*Sí*.'

'And disobeyed your father?'

'My father is sometimes deceived by Don Alejo.' Drinkwater remembered her obvious dislike of Don Alejo.

'He was engaged in some illegal traffic with the Russians?'
She shrugged. 'All would have been well had Nicolai lived.'

'It was fated otherwise, Señorita.'

'*Sí. Qué será será*,' she murmured.

'Why did you release me?'

She looked him full in the face then. 'Because you told the truth about Nicolai.'

'It was a small thing.'

'For me it was not. It has changed my life. I am to go into a convent.'

He remembered the Franciscan. 'It is the world's loss, *Señorita*.'

'I prayed for your wife and family . . . *Adiós, Capitán*.'

'*Adiós, Señorita*.' He bowed as she turned away.

*　　*　　*

235

Drinkwater watched through his glass as Hill brought *La Virgen de la Bonanza* to her anchor under Point Lobos that evening. He watched Don Jorge Rubalcava board her and wished he could shoot the treacherous dog with Mack's long rifle that now lay below in his cabin. Then he swung his glass to see if the rest of the bargain was being kept. He watched the boat approach, returning the ragged remnants of his men from the chain gang of servitude. By the time Hill and Frey came back from the schooner, *Patrician*'s anchor was a-trip.

'I would not stay in this pestilential spot another moment,' he remarked to Hill as the sailing master made his report. The knot of officers within hearing nodded in general agreement. Only Mr Frey stood pensively staring astern.

'She intends to become a nun, Mr Frey,' he snapped, an unwonted harshness in his voice.

The Night Action

Drinkwater stared at the empty bulkhead. The paint was faintly discoloured where the portraits of Elizabeth and the children used to hang. Before him, on the table, were scattered the contents of the despatch brought weeks ago by the *aviso*. It had been a day of explanations, not least that of the most perplexing of his worries, one that had concerned him months earlier at the time of their departure from the Nore.

Some departmental inefficiency had delayed it and now it had been sent out after him to the West Indies, overland to Panama by mule and shipped up the Isthmus, to be opened and scrutinised by Don Alejo Arguello, no doubt, before finding its way to him. It was months old, so old, in fact, that its contents were rendered meaningless by the train of events, except that they heartened him, gave him some insight into his apparent abandonment by the head of the Admiralty's Secret Department, Lord Dungarth. He read the relevant passage through again.

I write these notes for your better guidance, my dear Drinkwater, for I find, upon my return from Government business elsewhere, that Barrow has sent you out insufficiently prepared. Seniavin declined to serve against us after his Imperial master succumbed to the seductions of Bonaparte, having seen service with us at an earlier period in his career. Rakitin is a less honourable man, untroubled by such scruples and well-known to some of your fellow officers. I would have you know these things before you reach the Pacific, for it reaches me that he is to command a ship of some force, perhaps a seventy-four, and capitalise upon the work done by Rezanov . . .

Drinkwater folded the letter. So, Dungarth had been absent on Government business elsewhere. Drinkwater was intrigued as to where that business might have been. Had his Lordship been back to France? He had made some vague allusions to Hortense Santhonax having become the mistress of Talleyrand. She had turned her coat before, might she not do so again?

He thrust the ridiculous assumption aside. That was altogether too fanciful. What advantage could either Hortense Santhonax or the French Foreign Minister derive from betraying such an unassailably powerful man as the Emperor Napoleon? It was a preposterous daydream. He picked up another letter. The superscription was familiar, but he could not place it. Then he recollected the hand of his friend, Richard White. Drinkwater slit the seal, anticipating his old shipmate must be writing to inform him he had hoisted a rear-admiral's flag.

A deck below Captain Drinkwater, Lieutenant Quilhampton was also reading a letter.

I am sure you meant no unkindness, Catriona had written, *but I assure you that if the necessity to which you were put was painful to you, it was doubly so to me. You had the benefit of long consideration, I had only the most profound of shocks. I have burned those letters you returned but, sir, circumstanced as I am, I must risk all reputation and request you repent yourself of so rash an act.*

'God bless my soul,' he muttered, 'what a surprise! What a marvellous, bloody surprise!'

Drinkwater read White's letter with a profound sense of horror. Following so soon upon the last he could scarce believe its contents and compared the dates. But White's was written a full fortnight after Lord Dungarth's and he had no reason to doubt its accuracy.

My main purpose in writing, my dear Nathaniel, is to acquaint you of the event of Thursday last when, on a lonely stretch of the Canterbury road near Blackheath, an incendiary device exploded beneath the coach of Lord Dungarth and his lordship's life is feared for . . .

He ruffled through the remaining papers (some routine

238

communications from the Navy Office and an enquiry from the Sick and Hurt Board) for a later letter informing him of Dungarth's death, but could find nothing. A feeling of guilt stole over him; he had condemned a friend without cause and now Dungarth might be dead. And there was not even a letter from Elizabeth to console him. He looked up at the bare patches on the forward bulkhead and shook off the omen.

'Is she gaining on us, Mr Hill?' Drinkwater looked astern at the big, dark hull with the bow wave foaming under her forefoot and her pale patches of sails braced sharp up in pursuit of them. There was no doubt of her identity, she was the Russian seventy-four *Suvorov*.

'Gaining steadily, sir,' reported the sailing master.

'Good,' said Drinkwater, expressing satisfaction. He swung to the west where the day was leaching out of the sky and banks of inkily wet cumulus rolled menacingly against the fading light. The pale green pallor of the unclouded portion of the sky promised a full gale by morning. For the time being the wind was fresh and steady from the north-west. 'It'll be dark in an hour, that'll be our time. So you ease that weather foretack, Mr Hill, slow her down a little, I don't want him to lose sight of us, keep him thinking he has all the advantages.'

'Aye, aye sir.'

'Mr Fraser!'

'Sir?'

'Have you inspected all the preparations?'

'Aye, sir, and your permission to pipe the men below for something to eat, if you please.'

'Most certainly; and a tot for 'em, I want devils tonight.'

'Aye, aye, sir.' Fraser touched the fore-cock of his hat and turned. Drinkwater went below himself, leaving the deck to Hill. In his cabin Mullender poured him a glass of rum and mixed it with water.

'There's some cold pork, sir, sour cabbage and some figgy duff. Tregembo's put a keen edge on your sabre, sir, and your pistols are in the case.'

Mullender indicated the plates and weapons laid in readiness along the sill of the stern windows where the settee cushions had been removed. Drinkwater had lost the privacy of his cabin bulkheads, since *Patrician* was cleared for action and only a curtain separated him from the gun-deck beyond.

'And I found the portraits, sir, they're all right.'

'Good. Where were they?'

'Tossed in the hold.'

Drinkwater nodded and stared through the windows astern. 'Put out the candles, Mullender, I'll eat in the dark.'

He did not want to lose his night vision and the extinguishing of even so feeble a light would indicate some form of preparation was being made aboard *Patrician*. Drinkwater fervently hoped that Prince Vladimir Rakitin's opinion of him remained low. It had wounded him at the time it had been expressed, but Drinkwater sought now to fling it in the Russian's face.

But he must not tempt providence. She was a fickle deity, much given to casting down men in the throes of over-weening pride.

On deck again it was completely dark. They were near the autumnal equinox and already an approaching winter was casting its cold shadow over the water of the North Pacific. They pitched easily over the great swells, thumping into the occasional waves so that the spray streamed aft after every pale explosion on the weather bow.

'Very well, Mr Hill, pass word for all hands to stand to. Divisional officers to report when ready.'

When he received word that the ship was ready for action and every man at his station he gave his next order.

'Shorten sail!'

They were prepared for it. The lieutenants, midshipmen and mates took up the word and *Patrician* lost the driving force of her main and foresails. Men ran aloft to secure the flogging canvas. Neither sail had been set to much advantage, but not to have carried them would have alerted Rakitin. Now, with the onset of night, Drinkwater doubted the Russian officers would be able to see the reduction in sail. From the *Suvorov*, *Patrician* would be a grey blur in the night, and spanker and topsails would convey that impression just as well.

'Tack ship, Mr Hill.'

The master gave the routine orders with his usual quiet confidence. *Patrician* turned, passing her bow through the wind so that the wind and the spray came over the larboard bow and she stood back to the north-east, slightly across the *Suvorov*'s track, but in an attempt to elude her heavy pursuer's chase. It was precisely, Drinkwater argued, what Rakitin would assume he would do in an attempt to escape. It crossed Drinkwater's mind to wonder what exactly had passed between Rakitin and the Arguellos by way of a purchase price for his ship. He chuckled to himself in the darkness. This time there would be no humiliation, no *superior sailing* with which to reproach himself. This time, he felt in his bones, his ship's company had come through too much to let it go to the devil for want of a purpose.

'Ahhh . . .'

He could just see the *Suvorov*, swinging to starboard having seen the *Patrician* tack. He raised his speaking trumpet. 'Let fall!'

With a thunderous shudder bunt and clew-garnets were let go. Ropes whistled through the blocks and the great sails dropped from the yards, their clews drawn up to chess-tree and bumpkin as they were hauled taut. Drinkwater could almost feel *Patrician* accelerate, an illusion that was confirmed by the sudden change in relative bearing as the two ships closed in the darkness, *Patrician* rushing across the bow of the swinging Russian as she jibbed in stays, taking her wind as she sought to outwit her quarry.

'Hoist your lantern, Mr Belchambers! Mr Q! starboard battery as they bear!'

The noise of the wind and the tamed thunder of the sails gave way to something more urgent. The rushing of the sea between the two hulls, shouts of alarms from the Russian and, beneath their feet the sinister rumbling of the guns as they were run out through the ports.

They were on top of her now, the range was point-blank, and no sooner were they run out, than the gun captains jerked their lanyards. On the fo'c's'le the heavy calibre carronades fired first and the smoke and concussion rolled aft with an awful and impressive rolling broadside that lit the night with the flames of its lethal explosions, yellow tongues of fire that belched their iron vomit into the heart of the enemy.

Above and behind Drinkwater Mr Belchambers succeeded in hoisting the battle lantern that was to illuminate the ensign straining from the peak of the gaff. It reached its station just as Drinkwater looked up at the spanker.

'Brail up the spanker! Up helm! Shorten sail!'

Patrician turned again, cocking her stern up into the wind, shortening sail again to manoeuvre alongside her shattered victim. The *Suvorov* lay in irons, her head yards aback and gathering stern-way. Drinkwater had no time to assess the damage for they had yet to run the gauntlet of her starboard broadside where she mounted a greater weight of metal than her opponent.

'For what we are about to receive . . .' someone muttered the old blasphemy but Quilhampton's gunners were equal to the challenge. As a row of orange flashes lit the side of the *Suvorov* the bow guns of *Patrician*, reloaded and made swiftly ready by the furious exertions of their crews, returned fire. *Patrician* shook from the onslaught of shot. Beside him Hill reeled, spinning round and crashing into him with a violent shock, covering him with gore. Drinkwater grabbed him.

'My God, Hill!' he called, but the old man was already dead and Drinkwater laid him on the deck. Somewhere close-by someone was shrieking in agony. It was a marine whose head had been pierced by langridge.

'Silence there!' roared Lieutenant Mount, but the man was beyond the reach of discipline and Blixoe discharged his musket into the man's back. He too fell to the deck. Drinkwater recovered himself, spun round and looked at his enemy.

The *Suvorov* had broached. He could see much of her foremast had gone, and her fo'c's'le was a mass of shattered spars and canvas.

'Down helm! Braces there . . . !'

He brought *Patrician* back towards his enemy and raked her stern from long pistol shot. She was almost helpless, firing hardly a gun in retaliation. Nothing but her stern-chasers would bear now and their ports were too low to open in such a rising sea.

242

For two hours Drinkwater worked his frigate back and forth, ranging up under the *Suvorov*'s stern, hammering her great black hull with impunity from his position of undisputed advantage. A rising moon shone fitfully between curtains of scud and the vast ocean heaved beneath the two labouring ships. The Russians fought back with small arms and those quarter guns they could bring to bear, but it was only later that Drinkwater learned that their complement was much weakened by the length of their cruise and that Rakitin's eagerness to acquire pressed recruits from the British Navy was to make good these deficiencies. But Russian tenacity was to no avail, for *Suvorov* wallowed unmanageable, a supine victim of *Patrician*'s hot guns whose captains had the range too well and whose 24-pound balls crashed into her fabric with destructive precision. For those two hours they played their fire into their quondam pursuer, rescuing their reputation and the honour of their commander.

Towards four bells in the first watch the pace of *Patrician*'s fire slackened and Drinkwater drew off, heaving-to under easy sail until daylight. Men lay exhausted at their guns and Drinkwater dozed, jammed against the mizen rigging, wrapped in his cloak.

It was Belchambers's excited squeal that woke him. Dawn was upon them and the wallowing hull of the Russian lay less than a mile away. A shred of smoke was drifting away on the wind, for the predicted gale was upon them, the sea rolling down from the north-west, its surface streaked by spume and shredded to leeward in a mist of spray through which the dark shape of a frigate-bird slipped on swept-back wings. The *Suvorov* had rolled all her masts overboard, but a second defiant shot followed the first and the dark, diagonal cross of the Tsar still flew from the stump of her mainmast. In the rough sea she was incapable of further manoeuvre and awaited only the *coup-de-grace*.

Drinkwater roused his ship and the men stood to their guns again. There was a curiously intent look about them now as they stared over the heaving waste of the grey seas at the wallowing Russian.

'Larboard battery make ready!'

All along the deck the hands went up. 'Ready sir!'

'Fire!'

243

Fully half their shot hit the sea, sending up plumes of white which were instantly dissipated by the gale, but clouds of splinters erupted in little explosions along the line of the Russian's hull.

'Ready sir!'

'Fire!'

They timed it better that time. The concussion of the guns beat at Drinkwater's brain as his eyes registered the destruction their iron was causing to their enemy. He wondered if Rakitin was still alive and found he no longer cared.

'Ready sir!'

'Fire!'

He raised his glass. They were reducing the *Suvorov* to a shambles; as she rolled helplessly towards them he could see the havoc about her decks. Under the fallen wreckage of her masts and spars a fire had started, a faint growing flicker that sent a rapidly thickening pall of smoke over the sea towards them.

'She's struck sir!'

Belchambers pointed eagerly at the enemy ship. The boy was right. The Tsar's ensign was being hauled down. 'Cease fire, there! Cease fire!'

'Congratulations, sir,' said Fraser, coming aft.

Drinkwater shook his head. 'Pass my thanks to the ship's company,' he said tersely. Fraser drew back and left Drinkwater staring down at the body of Hill. He had executed the Admiralty's instructions, carried out his particular service to prevent a Russian incursion south of the coast of Alaska.

As he bent over the body of the old sailing master he felt the heavy nuggets in the tail pockets of his coat touch the deck. It came to him that he might be a wealthy man and he wondered if the presence of gold in California was known to anyone in London. He thought of Lord Dungarth and the infernal device. Reaching out his hand he touched Hill's face, then stood and stared to windward, mourning his friends.

Author's Note

Russian penetration of the Pacific coast of North America extended as far south as Fort Ross, on Bodega Bay. The posts of the Russian-American Company are assumed to have been founded in 1811, but Nicolai Rezanov attempted a lodgement in 1806 which apparently failed, perhaps for the reasons here revealed. Conditions under the Company were notoriously poor, even by contemporary Russian standards, and Indian raids were frequent. Had he lived, Rezanov would undoubtedly have achieved much needed reforms, but his tragic death in March 1807, in the obscure Siberian town of Krasnoiarsk, prevented this. He had been on his way to obtain the Tsar's ratification of a treaty to trade with the Spanish colonies which he had agreed in principle with Don José Arguello, *Commandante* at San Francisco. Prior to his landing at San Francisco, Rezanov had headed an embassy to the Japanese capital at Yedo as part of Kruzenstern's circumnavigation. This, too, ended in failure.

Don Alejo is my own invention, for Don José seems to have been a man of honour, unwilling to trade against the wishes of Madrid, although he had reached some form of accommodation with Rezanov. It seemed reasonable to assume his daughter had inherited her father's high-minded character and that she should be attracted to that of Rezanov, for she too existed, famed for her extraordinary beauty. She first met the Russian in April 1806, they fell in love and announced their betrothal. When she finally learnt of his untimely death, the Spanish beauty became a nun.

Descriptions of Russian merchant ships may be found in the pages of Dana, who met them in San Francisco in the 1840s, shortly before the abandonment of the posts at Bodega Bay (Fort

Ross) and the Columbia River, and some twenty-odd years before the sale of Alaska to the United States. Several countries laid a spurious claim to this wild and lovely coast in the early years of the last century and it is fascinating to speculate upon the turn of events had the presence of gold been known forty years earlier than it is generally thought to have been. It is not inconceivable that its presence was known to a few who, for reasons of their own, wished it to remain secret.